THE GOLD DOUBLOONS

Jerome Mysteries
Book 3

Suzanne J. Bratcher

Scrivenings
PRESS
Quench your thirst for story.
www.ScriveningsPress.com

Scrivenings Press LLC
15 Lucky Lane
Morrilton, Arkansas 72110
https://ScriveningsPress.com

Printed in the United States of America

Paperback ISBN 978-1-64917-252-5

eBook ISBN 978-1-64917-253-2

Editors: Erin R. Howard and Linda Fulkerson

Cover by Linda Fulkerson www.bookmarketinggraphics.com

All characters are fictional, and any resemblance to real people, either factual or historical, is purely coincidental.

For my daughter Jorie, a treasure more precious than gold.

"Now faith, hope, and love remain, these three, and the greatest of these is love."
~ *1 Corinthians 13:13*

PROLOGUE

1542
Spring

Aurélio looked over his shoulder. Something, or someone, was following him. Cactus. Orange dirt. Sparse gray-green vegetation. Nothing moved. Maybe it would be better if his tracker were human. The odds would be closer to even. Not as fast as a wolf. Not as strong as a bear. Not as stealthy as a mountain lion. But a man following him would mean another conquistador had missed the gold.

He scanned the mountainside for a place to hide the doubloons. Once he stashed them, he could return to camp where he would be safe. No one the wiser. Where to conceal the bag? Under one of the boulders, in a tree cavity? A cave would work. The hill was riddled with them.

Wherever he hid the coins had to be close. He was running out of time. Already the sun was too low. Soon a moonless night would close in on him.

Aurélio wasn't sure why he'd snatched up the bag except

that it was there, unguarded and tempting. It wasn't as if he could use the doubloons to get passage on a ship home. Home ... His mother would weep with happiness when he walked through the door. Aurélio sighed. He didn't even know where the coast was from where he stood. East. Northeast, Southeast, over Mingus Mountain, or back into the desert?

The soft noises that chased him came again, bringing him back across the ocean to the New World. The doubloons wouldn't have to be hidden long, just until the camp was searched. Coronado wouldn't suspect him. He was one of the quiet ones who never questioned orders, even when everyone but *Capitán* Coronado had given up on the seven cities of gold that didn't exist.

Aurélio moved stealthily, one booted foot after the other, straining his ears. Cicadas building to a crescendo, a desert frog out of tune, a mockingbird calling for a mate. He allowed himself a breath, then two. After a moment, he started out again. A rock collided with another rock. A third rock slid downhill.

Stopping, Aurélio held his breath and listened. The rocks on the hill behind him were silent. Something, or someone, must be following him. A mountain lion or a wolf would keep coming. Only a man would move when he moved, stop when he stopped. He had to find a hiding place, somewhere he could hide with the gold until his tracker gave up.

He moved again. Behind him a stone clattered. He moved faster. The footsteps came on, slow and steady. Maybe it wasn't a man. A bear might follow slow-moving prey, stopping when it found spring berries, moving again when the man moved.

Finally, Aurélio spotted a shadow darker than the other shadows. If it was a cave, he was saved. If not ... He pushed the thought away, kept moving. Ten feet from safety, his heart sank. A mesquite covered with purple blossoms cast a shadow that mingled with other shadows. The illusion of an entrance into a sheer rock face mocked him.

The footsteps were closer now. Desperate, he picked up his pace. He was so sure he'd seen an entrance to a cave. If he could disappear, even for a few minutes, whoever, whatever that followed him would turn back, believing it chased a shadow.

A small cave would do. Even a cavity, the beginning of a cave, would be enough to hide him. If not that, in the growing dark the mesquite might hide him well enough.

Giving up on the cave, he ducked behind the mesquite. His right foot slipped in mud, and he hit the ground. Instead of slamming into the side of the mountain, he rolled and kept rolling into the cave he had searched for. He breathed in the pungent odor of disturbed earth, wet dog, and rotting meat. Not just any cave—a bear's den. A bear, not a man, had followed him up the mountain. The last thing Aurélio heard was a baby bear whining for its mother.

1

Mid-July, about 500 years later
Monday

T he loudspeaker crackled. "Reed Harper to lumber."

Reed checked the clock over the door. Three-thirty. The interviews closed at five. He needed at least twenty minutes to get from the hardware store to Spook Hall, even if the road was clear and he pushed the speed limit. If he left now, he could stop at Bernie's, snag the journal, and sneak into the interviews under the wire. He might be the last one in, but the journal would get him the job.

New companies were uncommon in the Verde Valley. In Jerome, they were as rare as the dinosaur bone fossils Scott was always talking about. *Seven Cities Adventure Tours* offered a rare opportunity for people who wanted to get ahead. If he could get hired on as a trainee ...

"Reed Harper to lumber!" Denny. Reed's nemesis. A couple of years older, already finished with high school, the son of the owner, Denny was obviously on the fast-track to taking over the business from his old man.

Reed swallowed a groan and hurried toward the lumber counter at the back. Something to carry, no doubt. He hoped it was small enough to heft on his own, not a big order he'd have to load on the dolly, drag out to a pickup, and unload.

"Reed ..."

"Here, Den!"

Denny stepped back from the mic and pointed to a large stack of lumber. 2x4x8 studs. What was the guy building? Bigger than a doghouse. Smaller than an extra room. He'd estimate and take his best guess as he loaded the pickup. A stupid game, but it kept him thinking, and it seemed to entertain the customers. Whether he guessed right or wrong, they liked the personal interest in their projects. Except for the professional builders. He knew them by sight and kept his guesses to himself.

As he trundled the dolly out through the double doors to where the boards had been cut, he recognized Mr. Mitchell—one of the big guys. This job was something to do with a remodel. A bigger job than Bernie's, but not as big as a new addition.

He started stacking the boards. "How's it going, Mr. Mitchell?"

The man nodded in his direction, but kept his attention focused on Denny. "How's your dad? I expected to see him."

"Flat on his back with a strained muscle. The chiropractor told him to take it easy for a couple of days. But he'll be back by Monday."

"Glad to hear it. It's nice you're finally old enough to step in when he's indisposed. One of these days, I expect to hear you're the assistant manager."

Denny smirked at Reed. Reed ignored it. Or pretended to.

Every time the guy did that it made him feel like dirt. He knew what Denny was thinking. He'd heard it often enough. "Reed's a loser. A whole year behind in his school credits. He's going to graduate high school next spring with the juniors. And you know about his dad. A drunk who ran off and left his son behind. No wonder Reed's the way he is."

Reed balanced the last board on top of the load and pushed the cart toward the double doors that swung out into the parking lot. He knew Mr. Mitchell's truck without asking—the new red Silverado. No doubt with all the extras and a price tag higher than both the Russells' cars combined. Who cared?

One of these days he was going to make it out of this little town. He was going make it big—own his own business, like Denny's dad or Mr. Mitchell. Or maybe he would go the education route like Uncle Paul. Get a doctorate. Or a different degree. But after high school he had to get a four-year degree from a top-notch school—from the University of Virginia where Uncle Paul went. That was going to take a boatload of money. Which was why he needed a second job.

Reed loaded the last board into the bed of the pickup and flipped up the tailgate. Almost as soon as it snapped in place, the pickup roared into life and took off. Mr. Mitchell didn't even bother to look around. Most of the customers thanked him. A few tipped him, but not Mitchell. Plenty of time for Denny, but not even a wave for the help.

Reed trundled the cart as fast as it would go back into the store and checked the clock. 3:45. He had to leave now. The boss had understood, promised him he could leave in plenty of time. He spotted Denny up front talking to a customer at the cash register. Reed headed for his locker, pulling the orange apron over his head as he walked. Grabbing his backpack, helmet, and keys, he headed for the side entrance. He was in the parking lot, almost to his motorcycle when he heard

Denny's voice, "Your shift isn't over, Harper! Where do you think you're going?"

Reed kept walking. "Job interview. Your dad said it would be okay."

"I'm in charge today, and I say it's not okay!"

Following Mr. Mitchell's example, Reed got aboard his motorcycle without so much as a glance in Denny's direction. Skipping the warm-up, he flipped the kill switch, turned the key, and opened the throttle. Pulling onto Highway 260, he headed for the junction with 89A. The road carried its usual heavy load of afternoon traffic, but if he could get a break, 89A would be clear, and he could go full throttle up Mingus Mountain to Jerome.

Pushing away a stab of guilt about breaking his promise to Uncle Paul, Reed considered the idea of riding all the way bare-headed. At the current snail's pace, it would be easy to pull into a parking lot and jam his helmet on, but he could almost the feel the way the air would flow around his face and lift his hair once he could get up to speed. Besides, it was only ten miles to Jerome.

Eleven if he counted the mile to Bernie's. He had to stop and borrow that journal. It practically guaranteed him a job if he showed it to the guys from *Seven Cities*. If they thought they knew about Coronado and his men coming through the Verde Valley looking for the Seven Cities of Gold, Bernie's journal would be an eye-opener. Bernie had evidence of gold more real than the mythical cities.

The turn lane for 89A was just ahead. Two cars were in line to turn in front of him. Frustrated, Reed leaned out and considered passing them. One was a black and white sheriff's car. No way would he pass now. He knew he should put on his helmet in case the cop pulled off. He wasn't eighteen yet. But he'd lose his place in line. Maybe the cop was headed for

Clarkdale. Reed decided that as long as he kept a car between himself and the black and white, he'd be okay.

He made the turn. Just ahead a late model dark blue Ram hauling a silver Airstream pulled out of a parking lot onto the highway. Reed considered zipping around it, but that was the kind of driving that would get him noticed by the cop. The traffic crept. Reed alternated between wanting to pass the Airstream and being grateful to hide behind it.

At the concrete plant that sat at the base of Mingus Mountain, the cop turned right into Clarkdale, but the Airstream stayed with 89A as it climbed toward Jerome. Gritting his teeth, Reed stared at the weathered sign that labeled Jerome "the largest ghost town in America." Sometimes he couldn't believe he actually lived in a place with a population of four hundred. When his mom was still with his dad and they were a family, they'd lived in L.A., a real city with things to do.

He gave himself an inward shake. He should be grateful— he was grateful—to Scott for being willing to be his friend when no one else would and to Uncle Paul and Aunt Marty for taking him into their home. Still, he had to get a second job. He needed the money. He edged out, just enough to see around the Airstream to pass, but a solid stream of cars headed down the narrow two-lane road squelched any hope. Not enough room, not even for a small, fast-moving motorcycle. With a groan, he pulled back in. At each switchback, Reed tried again, every time with the same result.

As they topped the hill and headed across the hogback, he felt the first raindrops. If this afternoon monsoon lasted more than a few minutes, it would drop enough water to seep through the basalt and limestone hill to feed the springs in Mingus Mountain. Reed didn't mind getting wet. The monsoon would stop before he got to Bernie's.

Reed caught the first break in the traffic when the Airstream slowed at the *Jerome—Billion Dollar Copper Camp* sign and then turned into the narrow road that ended at the Jerome State Historic Park. They would be disappointed because the place closed at five p.m. Served them right. What were they thinking, dragging that monstrosity up the mountain into the narrow streets of Jerome?

Reed took advantage of the suddenly empty lane and poured on the gas. He didn't know how long it had taken to get here, but he knew he was running out of time. Bernie lived at the top of a steep hill on a one-lane road with enough cobblestones protruding from the dirt to make it rough enough that he had to work hard to keep the motorcycle from flipping. But he'd been up here so many times, he knew every bump.

The house had sat empty for so many years, it looked almost as bad as the shack Uncle Paul tried to rebuild until the forest fire took out the side of the Cleopatra Hill. Bernie's house still needed paint, but he'd put a new roof on it. Bernie had used composition tiles that would probably last longer than the old guy would. How Bernie had managed by himself, Reed couldn't imagine.

Reed expected Bernie to be on the front porch, waving the journal, and telling him to hurry. But the porch was empty. He stopped in front, expecting to see Bernie's bald head bent over the pitiful flower garden. He cut the engine and shouted. "Bernie! Where are you? I'm here!"

Nothing happened. The old guy didn't bang open the door and thump out onto the listing front porch. Dismounting, Reed raced to the porch. He took the steps two at a time and knocked loud enough to wake the dead. Had Bernie forgotten? "It's Reed! I need that journal for the interview."

No answer. Reed looked in the wavy glass of the front window, but the overstuffed chair was empty. Knowing his friend wouldn't care, Reed tried the door. Locked. He shouted again. "Bernie! You here?"

Still no answer. It wasn't like Bernie to forget, but Reed knew he was out of time. If he didn't leave now, he would miss the interviews completely. He'd have to tell whoever was in charge about the journal and promise to bring it in later. Bernie was sure to let him borrow it whenever he needed it. The old guy was going to feel terrible that he'd forgotten.

Jumping back on his motorcycle, Reed made a quick turn and headed back down the steep hill. The road was already dry, and even though it was almost five, he still had plenty of light to see. Near the bottom of the street, he checked the convex mirror mounted on an old telephone pole for oncoming traffic. In the middle of summer, the one-way stretch of the highway was bumper-to-bumper.

Reed wanted to curse the way his father had, but he hated everything about his father. Uncle Paul wouldn't curse. He would take a deep breath and wait for a break in the traffic. Reed swallowed the words he was thinking and took a breath. Three cars passed.

A little farther back, between a new green RAV4 and a well-used black Escalade, he spotted a small break. Not big enough for a car, but big enough for a motorcycle. Reed slid neatly into the gap. The driver of the Escalade honked, but Reed just raised a hand to say thanks and headed for Spook Hall.

The small strip parking lot in front of Jerome's gathering place was almost empty. Reed knew he was cutting it close, but he couldn't have missed the interview times. They must have closed early. He parked and locked his motorcycle. Slinging his pack over one shoulder, he ran to the door. A piece of white paper tacked to the door announced in black magic marker, "All Positions Filled."

"Paul Russell, is that you?"

Paul looked up from his computer. A familiar figure stood in his doorway, five feet nine, a perfect figure, sparkling blue eyes. But the golden hair that flowed around her shoulders in college was pulled back from her face and twisted into a knot. Her lips were fuller, her smile more confident. The lacy white top and high-heeled boots dressed up the jeans that fit her slender legs nicely. The pretty girl had matured into a stunning woman.

"Jessica Jensen!" Pushing back from his desk, he crossed his tiny office to pull her into a quick hug.

As he released her she said, "So it is you. You're still as tall, dark, and handsome as ever, but you have a beard! As many years as we've known each other, I've never seen you with a beard." She reached out and stroked his face. "I like it. It makes you look mysterious, maybe even a little dangerous. And you're a park ranger! Do park rangers deal with criminals?"

A memory of kissing Jessie came out of nowhere. Paul pushed it away and concentrated on the question she'd asked, inconsequential as it was. "Jerome had its share of criminals in the past, but today it's a busy tourist town. The worst thing that happens is the occasional drunken brawl, and that's the sheriff's job." He looked at his watch 4:15. Not quite time to quit. His plan had been to finish transcribing the latest oral history interview. But plans were meant to be changed. The transcription could wait.

"I'm sorry," she said. "I've come at a bad time. But I just heard you were here—what on earth happened to Flagstaff and the University of Northern Arizona?"

"It's a long story." He smiled to erase any hint of a brush-off.

She shrugged, somehow transforming the slight movement into an elegant gesture. "I'm going to be in the area for the rest of the summer. Let's make a date for coffee sometime next week."

"We don't have to wait that long! Give me ten minutes to finish a couple of emails"

Jessie looked around his tiny office, no doubt for a chair.

"Sorry. We need more space. My office used to be a janitor's closet. You can wait on the back veranda. I'll close up shop and meet you."

"Deal. But you have to promise to tell what happened to your university job and how you ended up as a park ranger."

"If you tell me what brings you here for the summer."

As she turned to go, she gave him the full-lipped smile he remembered so well.

Paul sat back down at his desk and woke up the computer. But his mind wasn't on the emails. The past seemed more real than his day's work.

How long since he'd seen Jessie? She had been Linda's Maid of Honor in their wedding, and she'd been at Linda's funeral. But in between? He was sure Jessie had seen Scott two or three times, but not in Arizona. That put it back at least five years, and he had the feeling it was longer ago than that.

Forcing himself to concentrate, he finished the email that was open on his desktop. The others could wait until tomorrow.

He found her in one of the wicker rockers on the back veranda, looking out over the Verde Valley. Pulling up another one, he settled in and stretched out his legs. "So, Jessie Jones— what brings you to Jerome, Arizona, on this clear June afternoon? It's not exactly a crossroads."

She laughed, the soft chuckle he remembered. "That's almost a professional secret. Can I trust you with it?"

Jessie had always been a tease, but he heard something

more in her voice. He bit back the joking comeback that had characterized their conversation in the past. "Of course."

"I'm looking for archaeological evidence to prove there's more to the Aztec names of the landmarks in this area than tradition based on a layman's misunderstanding."

"You mean Montezuma Castle."

"And Montezuma Well."

He studied her. She returned his gaze almost defiantly. "You've set yourself a tall order, Jessie. There's plenty of evidence to show Montezuma never traveled out of the area we call Mexico. And we know the Sinagua built the cliff-dwelling here that people call 'the castle.'"

"Yes. But we also have evidence that Coronado and his men came through this area in 1542, looking for the mythical Seven Cities of Gold."

"No one was living here then. The builders of the cliff dwellings decamped at least a hundred years before Coronado showed up."

"True. But Coronado's men knew about Montezuma. They were uneducated and wouldn't have known the difference between the Sinagua and the Aztecs. To them, all the people who lived in the new world were 'Indians.' What if Coronado's men named the sites?"

Paul stretched out his legs, leaned back, and linked his hands behind his head. "That's quite a stretch. We don't know the exact route Coronado took, only that he came through the Verde Valley. Who knows if they even saw the cliff-dwelling?"

"But what if they heard of the cliff-dwelling and thought it was one of the cities of gold? What if when they realized it was nothing more than a deserted stone apartment house, they dubbed it 'Montezuma Castle' out of contempt?" She leaned forward and tapped his knee. "What if the name stuck and was carried down from generation to generation the way nursery rhymes are?"

He sat up straight, moving his knee out from under her hand. "That's a lot of what-ifs, Jessie."

"I know. But if I can prove my theory, I can write a paper that will set the Southwest Symposium Archaeological Conference buzzing."

"You have funding for your project?"

"I've got a grant from the UNM Office of Contract Archaeology."

Paul whistled. "Beyond writing the paper, what's your goal —ready to leave the University of New Mexico?"

"Maybe. Ever heard of the Disney Chair of Archaeology at Cambridge?"

"Your paper would make that kind of waves?"

"Not by itself. But as part of my larger body of work, it might. Anyway, you promised to tell me why you left academia."

Paul shifted his gaze to the San Francisco Peaks that presided over the valley. "I got tired of playing the academic game."

"You got bored with teaching?"

"Not at all. I wanted to teach, but to keep my teaching job, I had to write a book. I could have written what they wanted, but I didn't really like being cooped up in an office all day."

Jessie raised her eyebrows in mock surprise. "I found you cooped up in an office just now, didn't I?"

"But just for a couple of hours. I spent this morning interviewing a source for an oral history of this area I'm working on."

"Oral history always was your focus. If I remember correctly, your dissertation was an oral history of the football program at some high school."

"Please! That high school was my alma mater, and the first high school in the state of Virginia to organize a football team."

"I take your point. It got you the Ph.D. But surely you don't need a doctorate for the job you're doing here."

"Nope."

"So, what's that expensive degree doing?"

"For the time being, it makes an impressive wall-hanging in my office. Later on, who knows? As I learn the rules of the park ranger game, I might find a use for it."

"Excuse me, Paul ..."

Paul looked over his shoulder. One of his co-workers stood in the doorway. "Jorge! What's up?"

"Sorry to interrupt, but it's past closing time. I'm going to have to run you and this pretty lady off the premises."

Paul glanced at his watch—5:10. The park closed at 5:00. He was usually more aware of time. As he stood, he noticed the frank curiosity on the other ranger's face. Holding out a hand to Jessie, he said, "Jorge, let me introduce you to Jessie Jensen. She's a friend from college days. Jessie, this is Jorge Freeman."

"Hello, Jorge." Jessie rose and offered him her hand. "I'm going to be working in the area this summer, and you may have some useful resources in your archives. So, I may see you again."

"That'll me mighty nice, ma'am. I'll look forward to it."

The wide grin on the other man's face surprised Paul. But Jorge was single, and Jessie's ring finger was bare. Paul swallowed a chuckle. He had two teen-aged boys at home. He hadn't realized he was working with another one.

Jorge seemed rooted to the spot, so Paul decided to rescue him. "Come on, Jessie," he said, "We don't have to go back through the house. Steps at the end of the veranda lead down to the parking lot." As Jessie turned away, Paul couldn't resist winking at Jorge. The other man winked back. It was all Paul could do to keep from laughing.

At the bottom of the concrete steps, Jessie took his arm and tilted her head slightly to look him in the eyes, a little taller than Linda, so much taller than Marty.

"We've skimmed the work surface of our lives, Paul, but we haven't touched the core. How are you, really? The last time I saw you was at the funeral." She nodded at his left hand. "I see you're still wearing your wedding ring."

"It's not the same ring. There's no reason for you to remember, but my first ring was yellow gold. Marty and I chose white gold." For some reason he felt almost guilty as he explained, as if he'd somehow betrayed Linda.

Jessie's eyebrows rose. "Marty? You've remarried! I hadn't heard. Congratulations! When do I get to meet the lucky lady?"

"How about right now? Come home with me for supper. You can see Scott and meet Marty and our foster son, Reed. Unless, of course, you have other plans."

Jessie smiled. "No plans. It sounds like you've acquired an entire family. I'd love to meet them. If you think Marty won't mind. I don't want her to have to go to any trouble."

"No trouble. It's pizza night. Scott's picking up two large, loaded pizzas. Reed will join us when he gets off work. We always have some left over." He chuckled. "Reed loves cold pizza for breakfast. Trust me, he'll be the only who might mind."

2

Marty ran her hand along the now smooth surface of the antique oak library table. The table would have fetched a much higher price if she'd been able to save the finish, but forty years in Mrs. Johnson's garage covered with only a plastic tarp had taken a heavy toll. Still, the wood was good, and the carved women's heads on the legs fascinated her. Each one was a different face—famous women from history? Maybe Paul would recognize them or tell her how to research their identity. Unless they were women in the craftsman's family.

Finding an unusual piece and restoring it to an approximation of its original condition was the part of her business she loved. Sales and the maintenance of a showroom, not so much. One of these days her tiny business would grow into a small business, and she could afford to hire Carly full-time. Carly was learning the ropes quickly. An outgoing young woman who never met a stranger, she was already a better salesperson than Marty.

She turned on the sander and went back to work. Who had owned this table? Who would buy it? What use might it be put to now? A light tap on her back made her jump. No one was supposed to be here. Paul was at the Park, Scott at the shop with Carly, and Reed at the hardware store.

She whirled, holding the spinning sander in front of her almost like a shield.

Paul jumped back, holding his hands up as if in surrender. Marty turned off the sander and put it on the table. "Paul! What are you doing home so early? You scared me."

Paul wrapped his arms around her and kissed her.

She melted against him. Sometimes she still couldn't believe it. She had actually married Paul. It had been almost a year now. Every single one of her misgivings had turned out to be baseless. She put her arms around his neck and pulled him down for another kiss.

He laughed and stepped back. "Marty, I want you to meet an old friend of mine." Putting his arm around her waist, he turned her toward the door.

A tall blonde woman dressed in designer jeans and an expensive top stood in the doorway. She looked like a model. Instinctively, Marty reached around to untie her work smock and take it off. Not that her khaki capris and green T-shirt were much better. At least they were clean. Taking a deep breath, Marty stepped forward and held out her hand. "I'm Marty Gr —Russell." Even after a year, she sometimes forgot her new name. Usually it didn't matter, but now it did. A lot.

"Jessie Jensen."

Paul dropped an arm around Jessie's shoulders. "We went to school together. Jessie was Linda's roommate. In fact, Jessie was the one who introduced me to Linda."

Jessie made a wry face. "The age-old story. I had a crush on Paul. I finally got him to ask me out, and then three dates later he met my roommate. That was the end of my great college romance."

They both laughed, but Marty wasn't sure that Jessie was as amused as Paul was. Had she come to Jerome to look up her old flame, assuming he was still single? Maybe she'd thought he would wait more than a year to get involved with someone else.

Marty shook off the suspicion. Absurd. Three years had passed since Linda's death. She and Paul met the year after Linda died. They'd spent a year getting to know each other. Now they'd been married almost a year. That added up to three years. Besides, how long she and Paul had spent getting to know each other shouldn't matter to Jessie. She heard herself say, "What brought you to Jerome, Jessie? It's not exactly on the way to anywhere."

Paul laughed. "That's almost exactly what I said to her."

Because it was true. The woman had to have some reason. She wasn't just stopping by.

"Let's go over to the house," he said. "I'll let her explain."

Jessie smiled, showing even white teeth. "No doubt boring to someone who isn't a historian. The short version is I'm an archaeologist working at Montezuma Well this summer."

Paul opened the door. "After you, ladies."

"You go on," Marty said. "I need to put my tools away."

Ignoring Paul and the open door, Jessie crossed to the table and ran her hand along the smooth surface. "What do you do, Marty? I can tell you're sanding, but did you build this table?"

Marty laughed. "Heavens, no! It's an old library table I found at an estate sale. I restore antique furniture."

Paul joined them. "She has a shop in Clarkdale, *Old and Treasured*, the finest antique furniture shop in northern Arizona."

"My shop is the only one that specializes in furniture."

"True. But you're building a reputation in Sedona and Flagstaff."

"Why don't the two of you go on," she said. "Paul, start a

pot of coffee. If the boys didn't get into them at breakfast, we have a few of Sofia's churros left to go with it. I'll be right there."

Jessie shook her head. "No need."

Reaching for Marty, Paul placed his hands on her shoulders and began to massage. She leaned against him, enjoying his touch. "I invited Jessie to have supper with us. She gets to know you, see Scott, and meet Reed."

Marty tried not to stiffen. Too late.

Paul turned her around to face him. "That's okay, isn't it?"

Marty managed a smile. To buy herself a moment to get used to the idea, she pulled his head down for a quick peck on the cheek. "Of course it is. I'm just surprised. I'm not exactly dressed for entertaining."

Paul laughed. "It's pizza night, and we're not entertaining Jessie, just spending the evening. The first of many, I hope. Jessie and I go way back. I want the two of you to be friends."

Marty hoped that was all Jessie wanted. Turning to face the other woman, she leaned back against Paul, feeling strangely possessive. Giving Jessie what she hoped was a warm smile, she said, "I need to warn you. Our house isn't finished. We're building it ourselves, and we're not quite as far along as we'd hoped to be by now."

Paul tipped up her head and looked affronted. "Please, darling. I think for amateurs with day jobs we've made amazing progress. Jessie, I'll have you know we have a solid foundation, straight walls, a watertight roof, and sturdy floors. The kitchen and bathrooms are all functional. The stairs even have railings."

Stepping away from him, Marty put her hands on her hips and picked up the teasing argument. "But dearest, the floors are bare, the walls need paint, and the furniture is a hodgepodge from your house, my apartment, and odds and ends from Carly's Treasure Trove."

Jessie clapped, somehow an elegant gesture. "I can't wait to see it! I've never known a family who lived in a house before it was finished, much less built it with their own hands."

Paul grinned. "Try eight hands. One of the requirements for living with the Russells is manual labor."

"How exciting! I can't wait to see it."

Marty shook her head. "There's not much to see. But if you insist, Paul can give you the tour while I put my tools away. I'll meet you in the kitchen in fifteen."

Marty watched them leave, two tall gorgeous late-thirties people who made a striking couple. No wonder Jessie had had a crush on Paul. When? Seventeen or eighteen years ago. Marty would have been in sixth or seventh grade. Telling herself the flutterings of jealousy were ridiculous, she picked up the sander and wound the cord around it. Still, Jessie wasn't wearing a wedding ring. No doubt it was true the other woman was working at Montezuma Well for the summer, but why had she contacted Paul in person, at closing time, dressed for a casual night out?

REED SLUMPED AGAINST THE WALL. This couldn't be happening! They couldn't have filled all the positions on the very first day of interviews. Maybe if Bernie had been on the porch with the journal, he could have made it. Or if he hadn't stopped at Bernie's. But he needed the family's record.

What was Bernie going to say? He was the one who'd found out about the company and told Reed about the hiring. Bernie was going to be almost as disappointed as Reed was. Should he even tell the old guy? Maybe he should just say he changed his mind and didn't go to the interviews. But Bernie wouldn't believe him. He would want the truth. Then he'd say,

"What are you, kid—a quitter? Why didn't you go in there and tell them if they were out of jobs they had to make one more for you? Because you've got something no one else has! You've got the real history behind the gold in Jerome. And it wasn't no ancient city of Cibola."

Reed straightened up and took a deep breath. He wasn't a quitter. He had to have this job. And Bernie was right. He had something these guys needed. He faced the door with its sign and took hold of the knob. It was probably locked, but maybe not.

His streak of bad luck changed. The knob turned, and the door opened. The long room was practically empty. At the far end, a dolly stacked with metal folding chairs announced that whatever had gone on in here was over a long time ago. In the middle of the room a scuffed wooden desk sat unattended.

The unfinished boards of the wood floor creaked under Reed's weight, and his footsteps echoed as he crossed to the desk. His breathing sounded loud. No wonder they called this place "Spook Hall." At least it wasn't dark yet. The top of the desk was empty except for two wire baskets. One held blank application forms. The other, a stack of the same forms filled out. Reed picked up the forms with the names on them and flipped through. He recognized a few of the names, but not many. The age blank seemed to be filled with numbers higher than his nineteen.

A door in the back of the room opened and a round bald man hurried out. "You, there! What do you think you're doing?"

Reed dropped the forms back into their basket and dragged out his best smile. "Just checking out my competition."

The man grabbed the forms out of both of the baskets as if he expected Reed to steal them. "Competition? Can't you read?"

"Yes, sir. I saw all your positions are filled, but I have something none of the other candidates have, something you need."

The man snorted. "Just what might that be?"

"The history of Coronado's gold in these hills."

"You're crazy! Coronado didn't find any gold—not here or anywhere. That seven cities of gold report turned out to be a myth. Or don't you know anything about your own local history?"

Reed's temper rose a notch. The man didn't have to be sarcastic. "What do you want to bet I know more than you do, mister?"

The man, probably three inches shorter than Reed, narrowed his eyes.

Another voice, deeper than the little round guy's, boomed, "That's not the best tone of voice to use if you're trying to get an interview."

Reed turned his attention to the source of the new voice. A tall, powerfully built man with an air of authority came through the same door, evidently from an office. Reed wanted to complain that the little round guy should change his tone of voice, but he knew that would make him sound like a squabbling child. Using his most formal voice, he said, "Yes, sir. I mean no, sir." He offered what he hoped was a confident smile.

"I heard part of what you told Mr. Lewis. Just exactly what do you have?"

The demand put Reed on his guard. His father's voice echoed in his head. "Never trust your quarry until you have what you want. That's the first rule of bargaining. The second rule is to hold your cards close to your chest. Don't let them guess too much."

If he told them about Bernie's journal, they could just go to

Bernie and buy it. He knew his friend wouldn't sell the original, but he might sell these two men a copy. He'd be out of a job before he even got an interview. That journal was the only card in his hand. "I have a source of some local history most people around here haven't heard of. It's been in my family for six generations." He hoped that was right. The journal had originated with Bernie's great-grandpa. It didn't matter. The point was it was really old.

The tall man quirked an eyebrow. "That long, huh? Just when was Jerome founded?"

Reed knew the answer to that one. Bernie had told him the story often enough. "The first prospectors came here in the late 1800s. My great-great uncle came in the first wave. He stayed. And he kept a journal."

Mr. Lewis snorted again. "Most of those prospectors couldn't read, much less write."

"Maybe so," Reed snapped. "But mine could. My grand uncle has the journal. It's filled with stories the old guy heard. I've read it." Oops. He'd stretched the truth there. He'd heard Bernie talk about it. But he trusted Bernie and his stories.

Mr. Lewis looked at the tall man, "Don, this kid is just wasting our time. He doesn't have anything like it."

Don, Mr. whatever his name, made a dismissive gesture. "What's your name, kid?"

"Reed. Reed Harper."

"I take it you grew up around here?"

"No. But my grand uncle's lived here all his life. When my family moved here, we looked him up." That was a spider's web of truth and lies, but Reed didn't care. He had to have this job, and Don acted interested.

"Okay, Reed. Tell me in one sentence what's in your family journal we need to know to run our business."

"One of Coronado's men hid a bag of gold doubloons in a cave on Mingus Mountain."

Don whistled. "Does your great-uncle's journal say where this cave is?"

The little round guy held up his hand in a signal to stop. "But Mr. Parnell—"

"Not now, Freddie."

Reed knew he had to be careful, give them enough to keep them interested but keep the details hazy enough they'd need him to come back and bring the journal with him. "I don't think so, but it records stories told by the Yavapai people about some gold circles they found and made into jewelry."

"Gold circles—like the doubloons in the legend?"

Reed shrugged. "I'll have to double check."

"I thought you said you'd read it."

"He's playing games with us boss. I bet that journal doesn't even exist."

Reed crossed his arms over his chest. "It exists, all right. But if I tell you everything I know, what do you need me for? I need a job. You need the information in Uncle Bernie's journal. Let's make a deal."

Mr. Parnell scowled. After a tense moment, he laughed. "I like your thinking, kid! I'll tell you what. You come back tomorrow and bring that journal with you. If it's like you describe it, it's given me an idea I have to think through. I just may have a job for you after all."

Reed hitched his pack on his shoulder. "I work at the hardware store in Cottonwood." At least he hoped he still did. But he could talk his way back into Mr. O'Riley's good graces. "I can't come till I get off work. Will five-thirty do?"

Mr. Lewis started to object, but Mr. Parnell nodded. "I'll meet you here."

Reed knew his luck had changed. He'd stop at Bernie's on

the way home and pick up the journal. Later this evening, he'd call Mr. O'Riley and explain. Everything was going to work out.

By the time he got to his motorcycle his elation had settled into a hopeful confidence. He knew Bernie would let him borrow the journal. Maybe Bernie would even come with him and talk to the Big Boss. When Bernie told those stories, you were as sure they happened as if you'd been there. While the motorcycle was warming up, he put on his helmet. He didn't know if either of his new bosses was watching, but just in case, he wanted to look reliable.

Instead of making his own opening in the constant stream of one-way traffic on this loop through town, he waited for a generous space before he pulled out. He longed to turn around and work his way against the flow. Bernie's street wasn't that far back. But he couldn't risk it. Not that anything would happen, he could handle his motorcycle fine.

Taking a deep breath, he kept his place in line until he could turn right. While he crept behind a ten-year-old Ford pulling a pop-up camper, he tried to decide what wage he would ask for. More than minimum wage, that was for sure. He'd ask Bernie. Maybe Scott. Scott would know better what entry-level wages were for a skilled job. Because whatever idea Mr. Parnell had for him, it had to have something to do with all that history in Bernie's journal. Maybe he would be assigned to put together the background information for a flier. He'd never done anything like that, but Uncle Paul would help him with the research, and Aunt Marty had a great eye for design.

He reached Bernie's street and downshifted to make the steep grade. He parked in his usual place, took off his helmet, and locked his motorcycle. Dumping his things in a lawn chair on Bernie's porch, he knocked for the second time that afternoon on the front door. Surely his friend was home now. "Bernie—it's Reed! I've got some news!"

No answer. He peered in the front window, but everything looked just like it had before. Maybe the old guy was around back in the shack he called his workshop.

The workshop door, like something that belonged on a barn, hung open. The light was on, but no Bernie inside. The back door was unlocked, so Reed went in. "Bernie? It's me—Reed. I've got some great news!" His voice echoed back to him like the house was empty. But Bernie would never have left his shop wide open like that. Maybe leave the back door unlocked, but not the shop. He had some nice tools.

"Bernie?"

Reed's stomach knotted. This wasn't like the old guy. Had something happened to him? Bernie wasn't in the kitchen. A few dirty dishes were stacked in the sink, but that was normal. The living room was as empty as it had looked through the window. Ditto for the bathroom and Bernie's bedroom.

Footsteps dragging, Reed went to check the spare room that Bernie was redoing to make into an office. The walls needed plaster, the ceiling should be lowered, and the floor was dangerously uneven. For all the time Bernie spent at his computer, he didn't do that much work. But he loved to play solitaire on the screen. Reed thought computer game room would be a better name than office, but it was the old guy's house. He could call the room whatever he wanted to.

"Bernie?" The name came out kind of soft. The house was too quiet. Silly to be nervous. Reed cleared his throat and tried again. "Bernie?"

No answer. Reed rounded the corner of the hall. Bernie lay on his back, half in the hall, half in the office. That uneven sill where the house had settled! Reed had told Bernie he needed to level it. He'd even tried to do it for him once, but Bernie kept saying that doorway was like him. Kind of crooked with age, but still working just fine.

"Bernie!" Reed knelt beside his friend, but even before he touched the old guy's face, he knew it was too late. His faded blue eyes stared up at the ceiling. And sure enough, his skin was cold to the touch. How long had he been there? If he'd taken the time to go around back instead of rushing off to the interview, could he have saved Bernie?

Reed sat back on his heels and tried to decide what to do. He should call someone, probably the sheriff. Or at least Uncle Paul. But once he made that call all sorts of things would happen in a hurry. The fire department and the sheriff's office were less than five minutes away. He needed more time. He had to find the journal to get the job, and he knew Bernie would want him to have it. No way could he explain to the sheriff. The guy hated his guts. He actually hated his dad's guts, but since Lloyd, Sr., had taken off and left him behind, the sheriff took his feelings out on Reed. If he called Uncle Paul, his foster father would have to call the sheriff.

Getting to his feet, he looked down at his friend's still face. He had to close Bernie's eyes the way he'd seen people do on TV shows, but he already knew Bernie's skin was cold. He couldn't just leave him like that for the sheriff to see. It left Bernie too vulnerable somehow. Taking a deep breath, he ran his hand over Bernie's eyes, bring the eyelids down. A lump formed in his throat, but he couldn't stop to feel anything now. He had to find that journal.

3

Marty locked the door to her workshop. Even though few people drove as far up the hill as their house, locking up was a habit she'd never given up from her days in the antiques district of Georgetown, Virginia. She started up the bare dirt incline that had once been Granny Lois's driveway but would one day be a breezeway connecting her workshop to the garage. Work on the house had gone slower than she and Paul had hoped, but they'd come a long way in the year since their wedding.

Stopping in front of the house, she studied it, doing her best to see it as a stranger, as Jessie, might see it. Even though they'd built on almost the same footprint as Granny's house, it didn't look much like its predecessor. It was two stories with a wraparound porch on the first floor, but that's where the similarities ended. Where Granny's house had been a lovely old Victorian, their house—the Russell home—looked like a vacation retreat with its blue metal roof, white siding, and windows galore.

The interior was as different as the exterior. Granny's

house had been laid out like so many houses of its generation, formal entryway, living room on the right, sitting room on the left. The formal dining room had been connected to the kitchen, which was where most of the life of the house took place.

Their open-concept house combined entry, living room, and sitting room into one airy space. The kitchen was tucked into one corner of the huge room, and the dining nook wasn't a room at all, just a long table with easy access to the kitchen area.

Shaking off her odd reluctance to enter, Marty went up the two steps to the porch and opened the front door. Laughter greeted her before she was even inside. Paul, Jessie, and Scott sat on the cream leather couch that had come from Paul's house. As they sat there, heads bent over something, the resemblance between Jessie and Linda struck her. Even more unsettling, Scott could have been Jessie's son. Marty moved restlessly. The three looked like a family. In a portrait, Jessie would look more like the wife and mother than she could ever hope to. Paul noticed Marty, then and motioned for her to join them.

Twisting around to see her, Scott held up a blue bobblehead. "Look what I found, M2! This CavMan toy Dr. J gave me when I was a kid. I forgot about it until she asked me where it was."

At least she was still Scott's *Mom Too*, now just M2.

Marty blinked. What was she thinking? Of course she was still Scott's M2. Jessie was a guest. Someone from Paul and Scott's past she hadn't met until today. She had plenty of friends from her past that Paul and Scott hadn't had a chance to meet. Crossing the shining faux wood vinyl floor they'd installed two weeks ago, Marty reached out and took the bobblehead from Scott. A stout little man wearing a navy-blue uniform bobbed his hat with its long feather. "Nice to meet you, CavMan. Tell me about yourself."

Jessie threw up in her hands in mock horror. "Paul Russell! Don't tell me you haven't introduced your new wife to CavMan."

Something about the way Jessie said "new wife" rubbed Marty the wrong way. She looked over Scott's head at Paul. Her *new* husband looked slightly guilty, as if he'd actually forgotten to do something important.

Scott rolled his eyes. "No worries, M2. CavMan is the mascot for the University of Virginia Cavaliers."

"Where your dad was on the football team." Marty handed CavMan back to Scott and went to perch on the arm of the sofa beside Paul.

"I brought CavMan to you when you were ten," Jessie said. "You were quite grown up for a fifth grader. Not as grown up as you are now, of course." Jessie patted Scott's knee. "I'm afraid I've lost track. How old are you now, honey?"

Scott looked insulted. "Sixteen. I'm going to be a junior next year."

"My goodness—your first prom. Can you believe it? Your mom and I double-dated to our first prom."

Marty turned to study Paul. If Jessie and Linda had known each other in high school, Jessie had been part of Paul's life since he met Linda. With a friendship that long-standing, why hadn't Jessie come to their wedding? Marty was about to ask when Jessie leaned around Paul to look at her. "That was a tiny bit over twenty years ago. Where were you twenty years ago, Marty?"

Twenty years ago, she'd been nine. Marty forced a smile. "I was living with my parents."

"You must have been in middle school."

Scott shook his head. "She's twenty-nine. That means she was in elementary school!"

"My goodness, Romeo. You robbed the cradle with this one."

Marty expected Paul to object. Instead, he looked uncomfortable, as if the accusation fit. Worse, Scott looked like he was trying not to laugh. She felt her face flush, but not with embarrassment.

"Romeo," Scott whispered. "Mom used to call you that, Dad."

Marty got to her feet. "I'll just slide the pizza in the oven to keep it warm and then go change clothes. Dinner in fifteen minutes."

Paul reached for her arm, but she was done with this conversation. Brushing a kiss on his cheek, she twisted away.

"Reed's late," Marty said. "Maybe you should call and check on him." She probably sounded cranky, but she couldn't help that. She needed a few minutes to regroup and figure out how to get through the rest of the evening.

For the first time since they'd moved in, she questioned the wisdom of the open living area. She longed for a swinging door to separate the kitchen from the living area—like the one in Granny's kitchen. Because of the open concept, she had to hold her irritation in check until she could escape downstairs.

It didn't take long. As soon as she closed the master bedroom door she felt better. Free to be annoyed. She did *not* like Jessie's attitude, acting as though she knew Paul and Scott better than she did. She stripped off her paint-stained jeans and well-worn T-shirt, tossed them into the hamper in the closet, and marched into the bathroom.

She wasn't Linda, and she had no intention of trying to be like Linda. She'd made that plain before she and Paul married. He'd agreed. He'd told her he loved her for who she was, not for how she might replace Linda. She'd addressed the age discrepancy head-on, told him ten years was a significant difference. He said it didn't matter. But if he was embarrassed about it around a woman his own age, evidently it did matter.

And Scott! He'd looked like he was enjoying her discomfort. At least Reed hadn't been in on the fun. He would be more of an outsider than she was.

Marty went into the bathroom and splashed cold water on her face. She wasn't an outsider. Paul was her husband. The fact that she didn't call him Romeo or know about the mascot of his college football team didn't mean a thing. She worked lotion into her face and then dusted it lightly with powder to take the shine off and make her freckles less noticeable. As she brushed out her long curls, she studied herself in the mirror. She was cute enough, but red hair, green eyes, and freckles would never come together in the stunning beauty of blonde hair, blue eyes, and ivory skin.

She turned away from the mirror. So what? The last time she checked, this wasn't a beauty contest. Feeling more confident, she went to her closet and slid the mirror door open. Without hesitation she reached for an emerald-green sleeveless jumpsuit she's only worn a couple of times. She slipped it on, then slid her feet into comfortable huaraches. For an instant she considered a pair of high-heeled sandals, but they belonged to another life. No longer career-woman Marty Greenlaw doing her best to make her way in the competitive world of antiques that revolved around Washington, D.C. Now she was homebuilder Marty Russell, happy with her workshop behind her house and her storefront in Clarkdale, Arizona.

The outer woman was ready. Now to make sure the inner one was just as ready. Crossing the room, she looked out the sliding glass door that opened onto the deck. It was almost six, still bright afternoon in the Verde Valley, but here near the top of Mingus Mountain, the early dusk of the mountains dusted the ground with darkness. As she watched the shadows join until they spread across the bare ground that hid an old mine tunnel, she wondered why people talked about night "falling." Here night seemed to rise, starting under the trees and stretching up until it swallowed the sunset.

Turning from the view, she whispered a prayer she'd used so many times before—breathe in, *God's strength*; breathe out, *God's peace*. This was her home. Jessie Jensen was her guest, and she refused to be on the defensive.

If Jessie had been part of this family from the beginning, she would continue to visit. Where she'd been the last two years was a bit of a mystery. But why Jessie had chosen this moment to show up interested Marty even more. She would find the answers to those questions eventually, but tonight her goal was simply to get to know Jessie.

Marty stopped at the bottom of the stairs. Closing her eyes she repeated their family motto. *Faith, hope, and love abide, these three. But the greatest of these is love.* She and Paul had chosen 1 Corinthians 13:13 as their motto before they moved into this house. They wanted it to be the foundation of the family they were creating on this tiny piece of Cleopatra Hill. She needed to remember it now, needed to know Paul hadn't forgotten it.

Faith, hope, and love—three times, and she was at the top of the stairs. Paul, Jessie, and Scott were sitting at the table playing a game of dominoes. Marty went to Paul, put her arms around his neck, and looked over his shoulder. "Who's ahead?"

Scott grinned. "I am! Reed and I have been playing Mexican Train since we started hanging out together. Isn't that right, Dad?"

"Don't forget who taught you to play this game, buddy. Everything you know, you learned from me."

"Not everything, Dad. The basics—yes. The finer points I figured out on my own."

Jessie winked at Marty. "Male competition! Are they always like this?"

Marty smiled. "Only when they're playing games. When we're working, Paul is the construction boss, and we all say, 'Yes, sir.'"

Paul nodded solemnly. "As it should be all the time."

Scott rolled his eyes.

Marty straightened and headed for the oven. "So, who's hungry?"

"All of us!" Scott shouted.

Marty turned off the oven and took out the pizza. "What's the word on Reed?"

Paul pushed back his chair and went to the cupboard where they kept the plates. "Running late—no surprise. On his way and will be here shortly."

"Should we wait for him?"

Paul shook his head. "No. Let's go ahead and eat. No sense everyone going hungry. He knew what time supper was. We'll save him some."

Scott picked up the dominoes and put them back in the box. "Maybe one piece. We have an extra mouth to feed."

Jessie put her hands on her hips. "Please, I hope I'm more than an extra mouth!"

Marty put the first pizza on the table, placing it squarely in front of Jessie. "Of course, you are. You're our guest. I'm so glad to have the opportunity to get to know you a little bit."

"What have you heard? I hope Romeo has only told you the good things."

Marty shot Paul a quick glance. He shrugged and looked away. "He's never said a negative thing about you." That was true. He hadn't said anything at all about Jessie, but that was a topic for another conversation—with Paul.

Marty handed Jessie the pizza cutter. "Guests go first. Tell me, Jessie, what brings you to Jerome? Are you sight-seeing?"

Jessie sliced a thin piece and slid it on to her plate. As she handed the pizza cutter to Scott and pushed the box toward him, she laughed. "Goodness, no! I'm working near here this summer—excavating a small pueblo ruin by Montezuma Well."

Paul raised his water glass in a salute. "Jessie is the archaeologist in charge of the dig."

"You mean *Dr.* Jessie," Scott corrected.

Jessie touched her glass to Paul's. "A job requirement. I like digging in the dirt, but no one would pay any attention to what I found if I didn't have the union card."

God's strength in, God's peace out ... "The one-room dwelling high up in the far wall of the Well?"

"You know the area?"

Marty nodded. "Paul introduced me to it one afternoon when we all needed a break from putting up drywall. Are you looking for anything in particular?"

"Only evidence that will demolish the prevailing theory about the names of both Montezuma Castle and Well," Paul said. "And thus earn Jessie quite a feather in her cap."

Marty chewed her suddenly tasteless pizza.

Scott reached for another piece of pizza. "How are you going to do it?"

"Not alone. I have a colleague working with me this summer—Dr. Ken Dexter, a geoarchaeologist."

Scott stared at Jessie. "An archaeologist who's also a geologist?"

Jessie nodded. "He's interested in what geology can tell us archaeologists."

"I'm going to be a geologist, but I've never heard of that specialty."

Paul looked at Jessie. "You don't have any way to know this, but Scott's headed for to the Colorado School of Mines after high school."

Jessie considered Scott. "So, you're serious."

"Yes, ma'am. I've wanted to be a geologist ever since I knew you could make a living from collecting rocks."

"Why don't you come out to the site tomorrow and talk to Dr. Dexter? He was complaining this morning about the fact his graduate assistant wasn't with him. He might be able to use you. I don't know what he could pay—if anything."

"That wouldn't matter. If I can learn something new, I don't need money to motivate me. What time should I be there?"

"We start about seven, but eight would be fine."

"I'll be there!" Scott swallowed and looked at Marty. "I mean I'll be there if M2 says I can skip work at Old and Treasured tomorrow."

Marty wanted to remind Scott he'd made a commitment to Carly, but she knew that would be an unpopular move. "Go ahead. But if Dr. Dexter wants your help, you'll have to juggle your work with Carly."

"Woo-hoo! I can do that."

The front door opened, and Reed came in, his backpack slung over one shoulder. Marty smiled and motioned him over. "Pizza's on! We saved you a couple of pieces."

Reed gave her a half smile. He looked a little gray, almost as if he were getting sick. "Thanks," he said. "Not hungry right now. Maybe later."

Something was definitely wrong. Reed was always hungry.

Paul appeared not to notice. "Come over and meet an old

friend of mine!" Paul stood and went to pull Jessie's chair out for her.

Jessie's beautifully tinted lips turned down at the corners. "Be careful how you throw the word *old* around." She got to her feet and punched Paul's arm playfully.

Reed crossed the room as requested but his smile looked pasted on. Now Marty was even more concerned. Reed was always appreciative of beautiful women, no matter their age. He tried to hide it from her, but she saw the furtive glances he gave pretty ladies.

"This is Dr. Jensen," Paul said. "She and I have known each other since college."

Scott made a long face. "Practically forever. She's been around since before I was born."

Jessie ruffled Scott's hair. "Watch it, kid."

Reed stuck out his hand, "Nice to meet you, Dr. Jensen." He shifted his gaze to Paul. "If you don't mind, sir, I'm really tired. I'd like to go up to my room."

Marty stared at Reed. Something was definitely wrong.

Paul clapped Reed on the back. "Surely you've got enough energy to visit for a few minutes. It's an occasion when Jessie comes calling."

Jessie put a hand on Paul's arm. "It's okay, Paul. I'm going to be around the rest of the summer, maybe even into the fall. I'm sure there will be another time when Reed and I can get to know each other."

Reed gave Jessie a grateful smile.

Paul looked surprised but didn't insist. "It must have been a really rough day if you're not even hungry. Sure, go on and get some rest."

"Thanks." Reed headed for the stairs. Marty looked at Scott and raised her eyebrows.

Scott got up from the table. "I think I'll take this pizza up to Reed, share what's left with him."

Jessie smiled at Marty. "I need to be going too. "This has been lovely. I hope we can do something simple like this again soon. Or maybe you and I can go out one evening—just the two of us. I really want to get to know Paul's new wife."

There it was again, the new wife crack. Marty hoped her smile looked more natural than it felt. Still, the woman was leaving, and she was staying. "We'll find a time to do just that."

Paul walked Jessie to the door, "Where are you staying?"

"I found a tiny house to rent in McGuireville. I've got one bedroom, Ken has the other, and we share the kitchen and living space. It's not ideal, but it's better than camping."

Not sure why she did, Marty followed the other two to the front door. Just before Jessie went out, she turned and put her arms loosely around Paul's neck, settling her hands on his shoulders. Marty noticed her hands were free of rings—because of the work she did or because she was single? Jessie kissed Paul lightly, nothing more than a friendly farewell, but with a pang Marty noticed they were the right height for each other. Jessie didn't need to pull Paul's head down like she did.

"See you soon, Romeo." The promise was quiet, but Marty heard it as well as if Jessie had announced it over a loudspeaker.

SCOTT BALANCED the soda can on the pizza box and knocked on Reed's door. When he didn't get an answer, he tried again. "Hey, bro! Can I come in?"

Still no answer. Maybe Reed had his headphones on. He was about to open the door just enough to look in when it swung opened.

Reed frowned down at him. His adopted brother was still a

couple of inches taller, but at the rate he was growing Scott expected to catch Reed before Christmas. Not that it mattered or like it was anything he was doing better than Reed. Mr. Harper wasn't nearly as tall as Dad.

Scott studied his foster brother. Had Reed been crying?

"What do you want, Scott? I'm busy."

Busy with what? Reed had taken the summer off from schoolwork after Marty promised to tutor him in the fall, and he didn't have homework from the hardware store. Scott thrust the pizza box at Reed, rescuing the soda just before it toppled to the floor. "You didn't eat."

Reed held the box out as if to give it back. "I'm not very hungry."

Scott ignored the dismissal. Pushing the box back against Reed's chest, he stepped around Reed and went into the room. Reed hadn't exactly invited him in, but he hadn't told him to leave. He plopped down on Reed's perfectly made bed and leaned against the reading pillow. The room looked like a motel room, everything neat and tidy. The only sign that anyone had come in was Reed's backpack leaning against the closet door. No pictures, no posters, nothing personal.

Reed's room always made Scott feel slightly guilty. He wasn't exactly a slob, but he liked to have his things out where he could reach them. His poster of the Colorado School of Mines kept him focused. He had to make top grades if he expected to get early acceptance. And silly things like CavMan helped him remember when he was a kid. He might leave the little guy out now that Jessie had showed back up. What was that about anyway? She hadn't even come to the wedding.

Scott shifted his attention to Reed. His brother was sitting at his desk, the pizza box open. He'd popped the soda can and was taking a swig.

"What's up, bro?"

Reed shrugged. "Nothing. I'm just tired. Not all that hungry."

"Something must've happened. You're not like you usually are when you're tired. Look at me, man. Whatever it is I'm on your side. Brothers until we die—remember?"

Reed finally met his eyes. "Denny was hassling me again. Mr. O'Riley was out with his back, and Denny always treats me like dirt when he's in charge. I'm sick of it!"

"What burr got under Denny's saddle this time?"

Reed huffed. "I had to leave a few minutes early. I had it all worked out with Mr. O, but then Denny didn't want to let me go. I left anyway. For all I know he'll talk his dad into firing me."

Scott whistled. "It must have been pretty important. What did you leave for?"

"It was important! Mr. O understood. I had an interview for a second job. Something I can work around my schedule at the hardware store."

"You don't need a second job. You work hard enough with the job you have and all the work we do around here."

"You don't understand, Scott. You don't need a second job, but I'm not you!"

"Explain."

"You've got your college all sewed up. As long as you keep your grades up, you get in wherever you want to go. You're bound to get a bunch of scholarships. But me—if I want to go to a good school, I'll have to pay my way. A little measly job hauling planks isn't going to get me where I need to go."

"Okay. What's the job?"

"There's this new company coming to town—Seven Cities Adventure Tours. They're mapping out the route Coronado took when he and his men marched through looking for the Seven Cities of Gold. They've decided Jerome is one of the stops—Montezuma Castle actually, but Jerome is where they're setting up business. They need extra help."

"Is it like a tour job?"

"I don't know yet. I have to go back tomorrow for a second interview."

Scott snagged the last piece of pizza. It was clear Reed wasn't going to eat it, so no use for it to go to waste. "That sounds promising. You made the first cut."

"All I have to do is bring them Bernie's great-grandpa's journal."

"Sounds pretty old. But it can't go back to Coronado."

"Course not. It goes back to the really early days of Jerome mining, though. It tells about a necklace the guy bought from one of the people who lived over by Tuzigoot. It was really old —a gold coin. These guys at the Seven Cities Tour Company want to know Coronado came through here—there's the proof!"

Scott groaned. "Oh, man. Don't tell me you fell for that!"

"Fell for what? I've seen the journal."

"There's a legend that's been floating around here for years about a lost treasure—a chest of gold doubloons."

Reed shook his head. "Not a chest, a bag. Bernie says—"

"Bernie's that old guy Dad talks to for his oral history projects, right?"

"Yes."

"You can't take most of what he says seriously. Even Dad admits that. There's a fine line between oral history and tall tales. Of course, the tall tales are part of—"

"It's not a tall tale! I can show ..." Reed stopped mid-sentence.

"You can show me what? The necklace? Don't tell me Bernie has a reproduction gold doubloon made up to look like an ancient Sinagua relic!"

"You don't understand, Scott."

The look on Reed's face pulled Scott up short. His friend looked defeated. "What don't I understand?"

"What Bernie had."

"Had? Did he lose it?"

Reed shut the pizza box and stood up. "What Bernie has. He didn't lose it. I just misspoke."

"I get that this job is important to you—for whatever reason. I hope you get it."

"Yeah. Thanks." Reed squeezed his empty soda can and tossed it in the trash. Then he handed the empty pizza box back to Scott. "Thanks for bringing this up. I'm just not hungry."

Scott suddenly felt like he'd made a mess of the conversation. He didn't want to leave his buddy in a funk. The whole idea had been to find out what was going on and help him feel better. Maybe a change of subject would help. "I think I've got a lead on a second job too."

"Yeah—What?"

"You met Dr. Jessie downstairs."

"Sure. She's nice-looking for an older lady. She looks a little like my mom. M2 didn't dress up as much as Dr. Jessie tonight, but M2 was just as pretty."

"Okay. We know Dr. Jessie is pretty. What's that got to do with a job?"

"She's here working a dig out a Montezuma Well, and she's got a geoarchaeologist working with her. She thinks maybe the guy might take me on as a sort of gofer."

"Good for you. I know what a gofer is, but what's a geoarchaeologist?"

"Just like it sounds—a geologist who works with archaeology. I never heard of it before tonight either, but I've been thinking about it, and it makes sense. Petroglyphs for one thing. They're a link between archeology and geology."

"I guess. I'm glad things are going your way, but I'm really tired, and I've got to go in early to try to talk Mr. O'Riley into not firing me and letting me go early again for my second interview. Tomorrow's going to be a tough day. I hate to boot you out, but ..."

Scott got up off of Reed's bed, feeling like he was missing something important. But he couldn't think of the right question. "Did something else happen today, bro?"

"Nothing I haven't already told you."

Scott studied Reed. His brother looked really sad. "Are you sure? You seem more upset than Denny razing you."

Reed opened his door. "You can't help, Scott. You wouldn't understand. Just leave me alone."

Scott hesitated. Something else was wrong. He knew his foster brother had trust issues. He didn't blame him. Family had never been a safe place for Reed. But sometimes, he wanted to shake his buddy. He thought about pushing now, but one look at Reed's set face told him it was no use. He just hoped whatever was going on Reed would trust someone before he got in over his head.

4

P aul strolled toward the house after seeing Jessie to her car. It had been an odd feeling, seeing her in completely new surroundings, first at the park and then here at home. In his office he'd realized, partly from his own reaction and partly from Jorge's reaction—what a beauty Jessie had matured into. She looked enough like Linda to have been her sister. Seeing Jessie with Scott had taken him straight back to his old life, the life before the accident. For a moment it was almost as if Linda was simply in another room and would join them at any second. Then Marty came in, and the bubble of memory burst. He was back in the house they were building atop Cleopatra Hill.

He hesitated by the front door, reluctant to go back inside. Shaking off the feeling, he opened the door. The house felt oddly empty. The boys were upstairs, probably both in Reed's room. "Marty?" He'd expected to see her cleaning up the kitchen, but that corner of the wide expanse was empty. He went to see what needed to be cleaned up, but the few dishes they'd used were already in the dishwasher, the table and counters were wiped clean, and the coffee was ready to be turned on in the morning. He didn't think he'd been outside with Jessie long enough for Marty to have finished everything, but maybe his sense of time was off. They had talked about Linda for a few minutes. It was such a relief to be able to talk about Linda. Of course he was happy with his current marriage, but Linda had been such a big part of his life for so long. He kept wanting to tell Linda about Marty, about Reed, about the new house project. Jessie had seemed interested, so since he couldn't tell Linda, he told her.

He headed for the stairs. Marty must have gone down to change into something a little less formal. It was only 8:00, not nearly time for bed, but he recognized the jumpsuit as a new purchase. Neither Linda nor Jessie would ever wear a jumpsuit, but it looked good on Marty. Maybe because she was so much shorter. The door to their bedroom stood open. "Marty?"

No answer. The bathroom door was ajar and the light out. He checked the utility room because it was right there. No Marty. He supposed she could have gone upstairs to check on the boys. Reed had seemed upset, but it might have just been the new face. He'd been terribly formal as well, calling him "sir," a habit they had put behind them long ago. Paul climbed the stairs that had been such a challenge to get right. He'd had no idea how hard it was to make sure each step was the same width and depth and the same distance apart.

The door to Reed's room was closed, but Scott's door stood open. His son was sitting cross-legged on the floor in front of the built-in floor-to-ceiling display case filled with his rock collection. His laptop was open in front of him, and he was reading intently. "Hey, buddy," Paul said. "What are you up to?"

Scott looked up and motioned his dad to come look.

Squatting, Paul read the computer screen: *What does a geoarchaeologist do?* "You're serious about following up on the lead Jessie gave you?"

"Yep. It sounds cool. I've always been interested in archaeology, but I never thought geology would intersect it."

"Montezuma Well would be the perfect place. The geology of the Well must be worth studying. It's a sinkhole fed by a spring."

"But what caused the sinkhole? And when did it happen?"

Paul got to his feet. "Very good questions to impress Dr. Dexter with. Have you talked to Carly about coming to work late?"

"I texted her. She's cool with it. As long as I put in my six hours, she doesn't care when. It's not like I'm dealing with customers or anything like that."

"What's up with Reed? Did you find out?"

"He told me Denny yelled at him today at work, and he left. He thinks Mr. O'Riley might fire him."

"I doubt it. I think Joe has a pretty good idea of how his son treats Reed, and I don't think he likes it. This might be the incident that jogs him into sitting down and having a heart-to-heart with Denny. Did Reed's temper get the better of him—is that why he left?"

"Nope. He went to a job interview."

"He's quitting the hardware store?"

Scott shook his head. "He thinks he needs a second job to save up for college. He's determined to go to UVA."

Paul shook his head. "I wish I could convince him Yavapai Community College would be a better choice. I'll talk with him again."

"Dad, something else is going on. He seems sad, but he won't tell me what's got him upset."

"It takes a long time to win trust. Give him time."

"I'm trying."

"That's all we can do." Time to get back to his original quest. "Have you seen M2?"

"She hasn't been up here. I thought she was cleaning up the kitchen."

"I thought so, too, but she's not there. Never mind, maybe she went to her workshop."

In the catwalk that connected the boy's rooms, Paul considered knocking on Reed's closed door. Could he succeed where Scott had failed? He decided to follow his own advice to give Reed some time. He'd let the young man to come to him.

That decision made, Paul headed for Marty's workshop. As he stepped out into the cool July night, he looked out over the lights of Jerome, past the white squat lighted building of the Douglas Mansion where he worked, down into the twinkling lights of the Verde Valley. He could see the twin sparks of headlights wending their way from Cottonwood to Sedona through the summer heat. At five thousand feet, the temperatures dropped into the low seventies. Overhead, a million stars showed in a clear black sky scrubbed clean by the afternoon monsoon.

He knew he was putting off facing Marty. She rarely went to her workshop after supper. Only when she had an order due in the next twenty-four hours, and he was pretty sure no such order existed right now. Something about Jessie's visit must have upset her, but for the life of him, he couldn't figure out what it might have been.

He took a deep breath. Only one way to find out. Following the gravel path that would one day be a breezeway, he went to the workshop that stood where the old carriage house/garage had been. Now a no-nonsense square building with a thousand square feet of workspace, it represented how he thought of

Marty. A practical woman with excellent skills. Of course, there was more to Marty than that.

At the door, he hesitated. Knock or go in?

He knocked and opened the door at the same time like he always did. Marty was bent over the table, focused on the close work of polishing a corner with fine sandpaper. She didn't look up, even though she must have heard the door open. Mystified, he went to put his hands on her shoulders. As he started to work out the tension, he said, "You have a deadline on this piece?"

She didn't look up. "I like to get ahead with my restoration. I never know what's going to happen at the shop."

He reached around her and gently took the sandpaper out of her hands. Turning her to face him, he said, "You're upset."

"Just busy."

"Did something happen this afternoon that I need to know about?"

She pulled away and started gathering up her tools in the closing-up-shop routine he recognized. "Nothing happened. I'm fine."

Paul studied her tense movements. If nothing had happened earlier in the day, whatever was wrong had to do with Jessie, but he couldn't for the life of him think of anything that had happened to upset her. "You're not fine. Are we having our first fight?"

"Don't be silly. I just needed to get some things done before bed."

Paul went to sit on her workbench. "Talk to me while you clean up."

With a sigh, she finally looked at him. "What do you want to talk about?"

"How about we start with Jessie? What did you think of her?"

Marty looked away, but not before he caught a glimpse of on her face—not dislike, maybe dismay.

"Come on," he coaxed. "Tell me what you thought."

"She looks a lot like the pictures I've seen of Linda."

Paul studied Marty. This indirect communication wasn't like her. He'd asked a direct question. Instead of answering, she had countered with a comment. Maybe a long response would give her time to decide to tell him what was bothering her. "Linda and Jessie met in middle school, and almost from the start people who saw them together and didn't know their families assumed they were sisters. Linda had three brothers, all considerably older, and Jessie was an only child. I guess over the years they filled the sister role in each other's lives." He paused, waiting for Marty to tell him what was bothering her. When she started to stack the sandpaper by size in her toolbox, he tried again. "Why does the fact that Jessie looks like Linda bother you?"

"It doesn't. You asked me what I think of Jessie."

"Okay. You think she looks like Linda. Tell me what else you thought."

Marty hung up her work smock and finally turned to look at him. "I think Jessie has been in your life since you met Linda. I didn't realize you were a threesome."

"We weren't a threesome, Marty. I was in love with Linda. Jessie was Linda's best friend."

"Like I said, Jessie's been in your life since you met Linda."

"Since we're digging up ancient history, I knew Jessie first. We were both history majors. We went on a couple of dates. Jessie introduced me to Linda. But from the first time we met, Linda and I knew were meant for each other."

Marty made a soft sound, not quite a sigh. "You and Linda fell in love at first sight?"

He smiled. "It happens. Not often. But once in a while."

"How did Jessie take it?"

"She was happy for us. I'm sure Jessie felt the same way I did."

"She remained friends with both of you?"

"Of course! She was Maid of Honor in our wedding. When Scott was born, we asked her to be his honorary aunt."

"Why on earth didn't you invite her to our wedding?"

"I did. She told me she couldn't come."

"Was she upset you were getting married again?"

"Not at all. She was happy for me. She sent her regrets and wished us every happiness. She had a conflict with the date—I honestly don't remember what it was."

Marty retrieved her cell phone from the pocket of her smock and went to the door. She acted like she thought the conversation was over, but he wasn't satisfied to leave it like this. She still hadn't told him what was bothering her.

Puzzled, he followed her out. After she locked the door, he turned her to face him. "Something about Jessie has you upset, hon. Something you haven't told me. You know I can't read your mind. We agreed we weren't going to expect that of each other."

For a moment he thought she wasn't going to answer. When she looked up at him, moonlight caught her face and he thought he saw fear in her eyes. But what was there to be afraid of?

"Jessie's just an old friend, sweetheart. Surely you have old friends I haven't met yet."

"No one like Jessie." She reached up and touched his face. "When I saw her with you and Scott ..."

Her voice trailed off. After a moment he prompted. "When you saw Jessie with me and Scott, what?"

"I thought how much the three of you looked like a family. Scott looks enough like Jessie that he could be her son. Jessie's the right age for you. I suppose I wondered why you didn't marry her. Did you think about it?"

He pulled her into his arms. "Of course not!"

She pushed back and looked up at him. "You must have thought about marrying her after Linda died. Were you in touch?"

"She was grieving as much as I was."

"Jessie already knew Scott. She was a professor like you were."

He tipped up her chin so she had to look at him. "I can honestly say the thought never crossed my mind."

"Why not?"

"Honey, Jessie was married!"

"But if she'd been single, would you have thought about it?"

"I don't know, sweetheart. What matters is I married you!" Even as he kissed her, he wondered.

REED STOOD by his bedroom window and looked out over the driveway. Uncle Paul and Aunt Marty were in a serious conversation. Were they running short on money? Before his life with the Russells when the bat tattoo on his back defined him, that was the number one topic of conversation with his dad. For some reason, they never had enough. Sometimes he wondered what his dad did with his paycheck. They had to pay rent, but he didn't spend much on food. His dad drank way too much.

Reed turned away from the window. He didn't need to be going back over his old life. He lived with the Russells now. What he needed was to figure out a way to get the journal from Bernie's before his interview in the morning. If he could show Mr. Parnell the stories Bernie had told him—especially the one about the necklace made from a gold doubloon—he could get the job. They would need him to provide them with real background stories to make their stop at Montezuma Castle by way of Jerome seem attractive to adventure seekers.

He'd meant to get it before he left Bernie's the first time. But Uncle Paul's call had interrupted his search. Actually, it had stopped it before he even started. He knew eventually he would have to trust someone enough to tell that Bernie was dead, but the longer he waited, the harder it got. As soon as he told Uncle Paul, or even Scott, he would have to think about his life from now on—without Bernie. Besides, he had to find the journal first. As soon as he told, cops would seal off the house. He'd never have a chance at that job then.

Reed heard the door into the side door into the garage open and close. Good, that meant Uncle Paul and Aunt Marty had come in. But he needed to wait until they were asleep. Scott too. Usually he could count on Scott to help him. But tonight he was on his own.

Turning out the light, Reed dropped on his bed. He was tired. His old friend's face filled his mind. "Oh, Bernie," he muttered. "Why did you have to go and trip on that uneven floor?"

If it hadn't been for the wood stove behind him, he would have had a bad headache. But that's all—he wouldn't be dead. Reed hoped Bernie hadn't lain there for hours hoping he would come by and find him. Reed closed his eyes and tried to find Bernie to say he was sorry for not coming in.

He must have dozed off because when he looked at, the clock by his bed, it said 3 a.m. Reed sat up. He hadn't meant to go to Bernie's this late. It felt a lot like not telling. The longer he waited, the harder it got. He didn't want to go in that room again. Right now, he didn't think he could bear to see his friend lying so still. Reed gritted his teeth and made himself get to his feet. He had to have the journal before his interview, and he had no idea how long it was going to take to find it.

He waited in the hall for a minute, listening, but everything was quiet. Scott's bedroom door was closed, and for a moment he considered asking Scott to come along. A bad idea. Scott would want to tell Uncle Paul that Bernie was dead. Reed tiptoed down the stairs, though he knew there weren't any loose boards to creak. Moving to the top of the stairs that led down to Uncle Paul and Aunt Marty's room, he listened again. Silence.

Taking a deep breath, he headed for the door from the kitchen into the garage. He started to move his motorcycle, and then he stopped. To get it outside, he would have to raise the garage door. Even if he did it manually, it would make a sound. That was one of the weird things about living up here on the top of the hill—how quiet it was. His motorcycle would make a lot of noise as he rode through the streets to Bernie's house. He could always walk, but now that he had his mind made up, he wanted to get it over with.

Moving as quietly as he could, he opened the side door of the garage and wheeled his motorcycle through. He stood for just a moment letting his eyes adjust to the light. The moon had already set, but it was a clear night. The town of Jerome lay below, mostly dark. Busy with tourists during the day, at night it looked like the ghost town it took so much pride in being. Mostly the tourists came for the day, going on to Phoenix or Flagstaff or Sedona at night. Farther below, a few lights showed along the highway in Clarkdale.

He was wasting time, putting it off. Taking a deep breath, Reed got on the motorcycle and let it roll down the gravel drive. Once he was past Marty's workshop, and on the road itself, he started to relax. He hated sneaking out like this—it was the first time he'd snuck out in a long time. Never at Uncle Paul's house. But he couldn't explain it to anyone, not until he had the journal. Then he would tell.

Just before the Holy Family Catholic Church, the blacktop started. Full of potholes, but easier to ride on than the gravel. At the bottom of the hill, he turned right, coasting against the one-way sign. But no one would be out, and even if a car came by, he could hop the motorcycle up onto the sidewalk. He passed the police station, glad it closed up at 5:00, leaving emergencies to the fire department.

At Bernie's street he turned right again. The hill was steep, but he downshifted and got off the motorcycle in front of Bernie's house and wheeled it around to the back door. Leaning it against the house, he switched on his flashlight and went up on the porch. As he put his hand on the door, he hesitated again. Maybe Bernie's body would be gone. Maybe someone had discovered he was dead. There was no reason anyone would think to let the Russells know about his passing. Uncle Paul and he were friends, but it wasn't like they were relatives.

Even as he pushed the door open and stepped in, he knew Bernie was still here. He could feel it. He almost turned and ran. But there wasn't any reason to be afraid. He hadn't been scared of Bernie when he was alive. Why should he be now that his friend was dead?

It wasn't like he believed in ghosts. Sure, everyone talked about them a lot around here, but only a few weirdoes actually believed they existed. Pastor Ray insisted when a person died their spirit went to be with God. Reed still wasn't sure about the God thing, but it was better than thinking about ghosts haunting a house.

Giving himself a shake, he started looking for the journal. He was in the kitchen, so that's where he started. He knew it wasn't likely to be there, but just looking in drawers by the narrow beam of his penlight gave him courage to move to the next room.

From the kitchen he went into the living room. He'd already checked the loose brick, so now he shone his light on the cluttered coffee table, in the magazine basket, and on the bookcase with its few books. Not there. That left the bedroom and the even smaller room Bernie called his office.

Reed shuddered as he thought of what lay in the doorway to the office. Clenching his hands, he started toward the office. Reed told himself he didn't have to be afraid. He wasn't going to be shocked this time. He knew exactly what was in the doorway, and he didn't have to see it all at one time. His flashlight would guide him around the body. He didn't have to look at the face.

A lump formed in his throat, and he tried to swallow. The still form wasn't Bernie, not who—*it*. Putting his hands on his knees, he bent over and breathed slowly like the basketball coach showed them when they got the wind knocked out. After a minute, the lump relaxed and the spots disappeared from his vision.

Taking a deep breath, he switched his flashlight back on, and headed for the office. The body lay exactly where he knew it would, half in the study and half out. The feet in their worn house shoes were straight up, almost like they were frozen. Rigor mortis? He'd heard the term on TV shows and in movies, but he'd never seen it. And he didn't want to touch one of the feet to see if it was stiff.

Shining the thin beam of his light carefully to avoid Bernie's face, he stepped around the body and went to the desk. The journal, a worn blue volume, wasn't on the surface of the desk which was clean of clutter like Bernie always kept it. One of the drawers of the desk was big enough to file things in, so Reed opened it and began to sort through. Nothing bulky like the journal. The office was tiny. Just big enough for the desk and the small drafting table where Bernie drew the designs for the wooden toys he made in the workshop.

The workshop! Why hadn't he thought of that earlier? Bernie had promised to make a special box for Reed to keep the journal in until Reed inherited it. Reed had thought it was a joke. But maybe not. If Bernie had written it in his will, the journal was his now.

His heart kicked up as he moved to the drafting table and shone his light on the diagram that lay there. It didn't take long to realize he was looking at a drawing of a box. Bernie had been serious.

Moving as quickly as he could without stumbling over Bernie's body, Reed left the office. Deciding to skip the bedroom until after he checked the workshop, he moved back through the house following the thin yellow light.

The workshop was in a separate building. It wasn't big enough to have been a stable, even for one or two horses, and Bernie had always joked about it being a cross between a deluxe outhouse and a pitiful storage shed. Reed reached for the door, hoping it wasn't locked. The knob turned easily, and he slipped inside. Pulling his cell phone out of his pocket, he checked the time. Four-fifteen. He would have to hurry. The sun came up early in July, and Marty and Paul usually got up to watch the sunrise.

But the journal would either be here, or it wouldn't. There was no reason for Bernie to hide it. He always said it wasn't worth anything without the stories that went with it. Which is why he'd taken so much time to tell Reed the stories. When Reed tried to write them down, Bernie had shaken his head. "Nope! These stories are what your Dr. Russell calls oral history. Passed down grandfather to grandson. Just like I'm passing them down to you. You keep them in oral history. Once you write these stories down, they get changed. Details get lost. They die."

The workshop didn't have any windows, so he switched on the light. He blinked. As dim as the bulb was, it was lighter than his eyes had had to work with in the last several hours. But it had been worth it. As soon as his eyes adjusted, he spotted the tattered blue journal lying in a rough box with a bottom and three sides, fitting perfectly. The other side of the box waited on the table, as if it expected Bernie to come out of the house any minute now and fit it in with the special hinges the old guy used on his antique reproductions. Something had interrupted his friend, and he'd gone inside to die. Even as Reed wondered what it could have been, he snatched up the journal and opened it.

It was the first time, he'd seen inside. Bernie had always opened it and read to him from it, saying, "Oh yes. This entry is dated October. My granddad said that was when ..."

The writing looked like gibberish, and Reed wondered if it was written in another language. He fervently hoped not. He thought Bernie's people came from Ireland, but it would take him forever to find someone to translate Irish. Shining his light on the page, he slowed down. The first entry, dated October 1897, was a summary of the writer's day: "Bought a shovel from a peddler who came to camp, made bread with the last of the baking soda, went to the creek to wash my shirt."

Reed flipped to the middle of the book. Another summary: "Spent 6 hours digging for gold, found copper." The back of the book was the same. The last entry was dated August 1919. Now the description sounded more like the town of Jerome that Reed knew. "Went to the saloon for a beer, stayed at Little Daisy hotel for eight hours, back to the UV for next shift."

No wonder Bernie said this book wasn't worth anything without the stories. How many of the stories he told about the entries were true? But he couldn't go there. He had to believe Bernie's gold doubloon story. Too much depended on it for it to be a tall tale. Flipping back to the beginning, he put his finger in the middle of the page and dragged down, checking each item. He found the reference on the third page, almost at the bottom. "Went to Yavapai camp. Traded a broken pickax for a gold coin on a seed necklace." That had to be the doubloon Bernie talked about.

The coin had disappeared sometime in the fifty years between when the journal was written and when Bernie's grandfather inherited it, but the story was intact. Reed remembered it word for word. That story was the first step on the path that would take him to earning the money he needed to get to the college he knew would carry him to a future far away from Lloyd Harper, Sr.

5

"Thanks, Marty!" Scott was out of the pickup almost before it stopped. With a wave over his shoulder, he headed up the path he knew so well. He knew his goodbye was too quick, almost rude. He should have taken the time to thank Marty properly and call Carly for a ride to Marty's showroom when he was done, but he felt guilty enough about abandoning the job Marty had made just for him a year and a half ago. He didn't want to prolong his time with her. Besides, he wasn't quitting, just changing his status to part-time. She understood his future was in geology, not in antiques.

At just before 8 a.m., Montezuma Well National Monument was deserted. Only a fraction of the tourists who visited Montezuma Castle came here anyway. The blacktop path stretched ahead, empty of visitors. He could have taken his time, but it helped to run as if he were late for a specific appointment. He passed the ancient pit house ruins without even a glance and headed up the left side of the loop. At the top, he paused and looked down into what history had dubbed "the well."

No matter how many times he came here, first with his dad and now sometimes with Reed, the sight always captivated him. Ten stories below where he stood, the shimmering blue-green pool reflected the images of prickly pear and pock-marked rocks that circled it. Today the scene had changed. A canopy was set up on the left side directly above a small cliff dwelling. Dr. Jessie and a younger woman stood outside the shelter, heads bent over something Dr. Jessie was holding. Scott didn't know much about Dr. Dexter, but he knew he wasn't a young woman.

A swallow darted from its nest in the cliff several hundred feet to the right of where the women stood and swooped across the pool toward a target only the bird could see. As he watched, movement lower down caught his eye. A man, probably Dr. Dexter, stepped out from under a second canopy set up on the right side of the pool.

From his many visits, Scott knew the paved walkway down led to a narrow passage that followed an irrigation ditch flowing with cold water and lined with ferns. The geoarchaeologist must have gotten permission to create his own path. Now to find it.

Sure enough, where the blacktop turned toward the irrigation ditch, a double line of two-by-fours headed through the prickly pear for what had to be Dr. Dexter's camp. As he stepped over a thin chain with a *No Entry, Archaeological Work in Progress* sign, a voice behind him shouted, "Stop!"

Scott turned to see a thin Yavapai man with a yellow do-rag and two long braids striding him, waving his arms. Dressed in jeans and a red T-shirt, he looked young, only a few years older than Reed.

"Didn't you see the sign, man—or do you think it applies to everyone but you?"

Scott held up his hands. "I need to speak to Dr. Dexter."

"You can't go down there! That man shouldn't be down there either." He practically spat the words *that man*. "This is sacred ground, *my* sacred ground. Those archaeologists should be run off our land!"

Scott felt his temper rising, but he knew getting mad would make things worse. And worse might be a punch thrown. The guy wasn't thin—he was wiry. And he looked strong. Scott was in good enough shape, but he didn't like the idea of a shoving match. "This site is a national monument," he said. "It belongs to all Americans, not just to the Yavapai."

"Only because *your* ancestors slaughtered *my* ancestors. This *site*, as you call it, was an important place to the Ones Who Came Before. It's an outrage to disturb it!"

"Look, buddy. I'm not going to disturb anything. I just need to talk to Dr. Dexter."

"What's going on up here, Jackson?" The shout came from a man on the plank path behind Scott. Older than Dad, but younger than the gray-haired principal of his junior high, the newcomer had to be Dr. Dexter.

"*Wassaja* to you, *Bilagaana*!"

Scott recognized the Navajo word for *white man* that had crossed into general usage. Not a neutral word, a serious insult.

"A person gets one name, *Jackson*! The name your parents gave you, the name Mina calls you is good enough for me."

Before Wassaja could escalate the argument, Scott blurted, "Dr. Dexter, I'm Scott Russell ..."

The man's eyes passed over Scott, as if he weren't there.

"Russell," Scott repeated, saying the name more slowly.

Still without looking at him Dr. Dexter said, "I don't care who you are. You're not allowed here. No unauthorized visitors."

"You're the one who's unauthorized!" shouted Wassaja.

"The Council didn't give you permission to come here and dig up the bones of my ancestors."

Dr. Dexter stepped over the chain and moved around Scott. "For the last time, Jackson Henry, we're not digging up bones." He enunciated each word clearly—not yelling but with a force that made Scott cringe. Maybe working for this guy wasn't such a great idea after all. Maybe he should stick to antiques this summer.

The geoarchaeologist turned abruptly back to Scott. "Did you say *Russell*?" The older man's blue eyes, so surprising with his thatch of black hair and closely trimmed beard focused on Scott.

"Yes sir. My dad is Dr. Paul Russell. He and Dr. Jessie are friends. She told me you might need help this summer and to come around eight o'clock to talk to you."

"Come along, then. I'm headed over to talk to her now." Dr. Dexter climbed the last few feet to the top, stepped over another "no entry" sign, and started following another path of planks that circled the well.

Scott followed, and Wassaja fell into step behind him.

Without halting, Dr. Dexter said, "You're not invited, Jackson."

"I don't need an invitation from you! Dr. Jessie told me I was welcome to see Mina anytime."

Dexter stopped so suddenly Scott had to step off the makeshift walkway to keep from running into him. "Stay on the boards," the older man snapped.

Scott started to object, then closed his mouth. The geoarchaeologist was annoyed with him but getting angrier at Wassaja by the minute. Better to keep it that way.

"On one condition, Jackson."

"Yeah, yeah. On one condition. I haven't forgotten."

"Explain to our new friend, then. He might need the same sort of reminder."

Wassaja transferred his scowl from Dr. Dexter to Scott. "I'm welcome as long as I keep my opinions to myself."

"Because ..." prompted Dr. Dexter.

Wassaja's eyes narrowed. "Because no one is interested. I'm preaching to the wrong crowd. I need to drum up more support for my viewpoint if I expect to get anywhere."

Dexter gave a satisfied nod. Transferring his attention to Scott, he said, "That goes for you, too, young man. If you're going to work with me, you'll do it on my terms."

Scott held out his hands, palms up. "No problem, sir. I'm here to learn. I don't know enough about geoarchaeology to have an opinion. I only heard of the discipline last night." He started to add that he knew something about the geology of the land around here, but seeing the older man's attention shift yet again, he decided to keep that information to himself for the moment.

Seemingly satisfied, Dr. Dexter turned and marched on.

Scott stepped back onto the path and tried to match his speed with that of the older man. Behind him, Wassaja growled, "Don't think this is settled, *Bilagaana*. I may not be able to do anything about Dexter and Jones, but I'm not going to stand by and ignore the fact that they're expanding their team."

They rounded the far end of the well and approached Dr. Jessie's camp. Wassaja pushed around the other two and went to meet the young woman Scott had seen talking to Dr. Jessie earlier. Dr. Jessie was nowhere in sight.

"Mina," Dr. Dexter growled, "where's Jessie?"

Skin the color of Manzanita bark, shining black hair pulled into a single braid that hung well below her shoulders, and a smile that reached laughing black eyes. A double strand of silver and turquoise beads around her neck stood out against her red smock. She was Yavapai like Wassaja. His girlfriend?

As if to confirm the guess, Wassaja draped a proprietary arm around her shoulders.

"Good morning, Dr. Dexter." Her soft voice reflected the amusement in her eyes. Because Dexter was always grouchy? For the second time Scott wondered if it would be smarter to continue working for Marty full-time.

Mina slipped out from under Wassaja's arm and nodded at the edge of the sinkhole. "Dr. Jessie's at the dwelling checking out an idea she had during the night. Did she forget a meeting?"

Dexter shook his head. "This kid showed up this morning, claiming Jessie told him I would hire him for summer work. I need to discuss it with her."

When Scott started to object that he wasn't expecting to be paid, Mina turned her smile on him, somehow conveying sympathy and welcome. Scott decided Mina was more than pretty—she was beautiful. "Do you want me to get her for you, Dr. Dexter?"

"No need. I'll go down."

As Dexter headed toward a ladder at the edge of the sinkhole, Wassaja said, "Come home with me, Mina. The art fair starts today. Grandfather decided yesterday that he isn't up to selling this year. He gave me his booth. In exchange for selling his coiled baskets, I can put out a few of my carvings to sell. I need your help setting up."

Mina's smile disappeared. She shook off Wassaja's arm. "I've got work to do, Jackson."

"You don't want to be part of this destructive *Bilagaana* work, Mina."

"We've had this discussion before. You know perfectly well I'm doing this to satisfy my independent study credits. Besides, it will help toward the degree in Anthropology I'm going to get after Yavapai Community College."

"But it goes against everything we stand for."

"Maybe it goes against what you stand for, Jackson. From my perspective it fits in very nicely. Dr. Jessie and Dr. Dexter are working to discover how our ancestors lived—how they managed to feed the large population in the Verde Valley with this tiny settlement by the Well."

"By digging everything up? Better to preserve things as they are."

Mina put her hands on her hips. "Aren't you even a little bit curious about how The Ones Who Came Before lived? They had a thriving civilization, and then they just disappeared. Why? They wouldn't have left this valley because of the drought that chased other people from their ancestral homes. Wikiup Creek may have dried up, but The Well and Wet Beaver Creek kept running. Dr. Dexter has already established that much with his work. So why did they leave?"

"You know the stories as well as I do! They had a prophecy about white men coming with destruction. They followed the prophecy and left." Wassaja made a sweeping gesture that took in the canopies, the parking lot, and the road that led down into McGuireville.

"If you're going to spout that tired theory, at least get your facts straight. That prophecy came a hundred years too early."

"Not so early in the length of history."

"In human terms, that was three or maybe four generations back in those days. That's a little early to pack up and abandon this lush valley for the dusty mesas of Hopiland. Now go away and let me get my work done. I'll stop by the fair on my way home."

As Mina turned away, Wassaja grasped her by the arm. "What you're doing here is wrong, Mina!"

She shook him off. Putting a finger in the middle of his chest, she said, "No. What you're doing is wrong. You're trespassing. Now, get off the land that's off limits!"

"Or you'll what? Refuse to see me again? You tried that once before."

The fight suddenly seemed to go out of Mina. Reaching up, she put a gentle hand on Wassaja's face. "I love you," she whispered. "Even if we disagree about some pretty important ideas. I give you the room to believe something different than I do. It's your turn to give me the same room." Turning Wassaja toward the plank path, she gave him a little shove. "Now go set up your booth so you can sell lots for your grandfather and at least two or three carvings for our wedding account. I'm earning my part this summer. It's about time you made a deposit."

Wassaja turned back. Grabbing her shoulders, he leaned down and kissed her. "You'll see it my way one of these days."

She laughed softly. "Not today. Now, go on. I have work to do. And so do you."

Wassaja made a sound somewhere between a laugh and a growl and loped away.

Mina turned to Scott. Are you a student at Yavapai Community too?"

Scott's face grew warm. He hated it that he still blushed like a little boy—or worse—a girl. "I'll be a sophomore at Cottonwood High School this year."

She laughed, a friendly, welcoming laugh. "Don't be embarrassed. I just finished my freshman year at Yavapai. You'll be in college in no time."

For the first time since he asked Marty to drop him off, Scott relaxed. It would be nice to have someone close to his own age here.

Mina motioned to Scott to come with her. "Let me show

you what I'm doing and give you an overview of Dr. Jessie's project."

Scott followed her along a short plank path to a large wooden tripod. A 4-by-4 frame holding wire mesh about the size of window screen hung suspended by four ropes. "First, Dr. Jessie digs out a plotted area of the floor in the dwelling, picking out the larger artifacts by hand. Then she brings the dirt that's left up here, and I sift it."

She grasped the screen and shook it from side to side. Dirt fell through to the ground below. Using a trowel, she sorted through the pebbles that were left. Picking out one, she handed it to him. "This is a bead. It was probably made from a fragment of pottery. If I hadn't sifted the dirt, we would have missed it."

Scott turned the tiny pebble in his hand, held it up to examine better. Ordinary clay, but tiny bits of color clung to the surface, remnants of faded paint. "Okay," he said. "But I want to learn the geology end of what Dr. Dexter does. Dr. Jessie said he's a geoarchaeologist. I want to work with him." He grinned. "Not that what you're doing isn't important."

Mina returned his smile. "You don't have to worry about my feelings. You're more interested in where the creek ran back then and if the spring that feeds the Well was already active."

Scott nodded. No wonder Wassaja wanted to marry Mina. Beautiful, sure of herself, and nice—kind.

"Dr. Dexter has been complaining that I work for Dr. Jessie, but he doesn't have anyone. I don't think you have to worry."

"No offense, but why isn't he showing me what he does?"

"Because you offered him an opportunity to come talk to Dr. Jessie. He's sweet on her. Of course, she doesn't know he exists—like that, I mean."

Scott frowned. "I thought Dr. Jessie was married."

"She was. Until about a year ago. Of course, that was before

I started working for her, but she's let a few comments slip through. Her husband left her for a younger woman."

"You're kidding! She's beautiful."

"Men are crazy." Mina blushed suddenly. "Sorry. I didn't mean anything ..."

Scott grinned. "Forget it. Guys think women are nuts too. So, Dr. Dexter's not married either?"

"Also divorced."

"They both like the same kind of work. Why don't they get together?"

"You know romance doesn't work like that, Scott. Just because you like someone as a friend doesn't mean you want to go out with her. Besides, Dr. Dexter is too old for Dr. Jessie. She likes him as a coworker. She's grateful he thinks enough of her theory to help her try to prove it. He's been around a few years, and he has more publications than she does. His name on her project will help a lot."

Scott studied the bead in his hand. "What's she trying to prove—I mean what's her hypothesis?"

"That Coronado and his gang had contact with the Ancestral Puebloans who lived in the Verde Valley."

"But like Wassaja said, I thought they followed their prophecy and moved out a hundred years before Coronado showed up."

"That's the current theory. Dr. Jessie is trying to make her mark. She's an associate professor, but she wants to become a full professor. That means she has to publish original work, preferably something that either extends or contradicts a current theory. She's looking for evidence of a Spanish presence here in the pueblo. Since Montezuma Castle has been thoroughly excavated, she's digging here at the Well."

"A gold doubloon would prove her theory."

"It would be perfect." She gave him a curious look. "What do you know about gold doubloons?"

"We have a legend ..."

Mina held up her hand. "Wait. Here they come. I think Dr. Jessie will be interested in your legend."

The two archaeologists were deep in some discussion. Scott caught the words *pottery* and *shard*.

Mina joined them. "Did you find something new?"

Dr. Jessie shook her head.

Dr. Dexter said, "Yes."

They looked at each other and laughed. "That would be a maybe," said Dr. Jessie. "Scott, it's good to see you this morning. How's everyone at your house?"

Scott felt suddenly shy. "Great!"

Before he had to say more, Mina came to his rescue. "Scott was about to tell me a story about gold doubloons."

Both archaeologists looked at him.

"It's just a legend. It's probably not true."

Dr. Jessie waved away his apology. "Don't underestimate legends. It might have its roots in truth."

"That's what my brother Reed keeps telling me, but I think this one is pretty far-fetched. Gold doubloons have been found in shipwrecks, not inland like we are."

Dr. Dexter nodded. "Even so, we want to hear any local talk about gold doubloons."

Scott shrugged. "Some of the old-timers around here say the conquistadors hid a bag of gold somewhere in these mountains when they came through the Verde Valley looking for the Seven Cities of Cibola. The legend doesn't say why they did it. It's not like the local inhabitants would have had any use for gold coins."

Dr. Jessie looked thoughtful. "Don't be so sure about that. We know they had a gold mine of sorts up around Jerome."

The geoarchaeologist frowned. "Have any coins been found?"

"Not one—ever. But that doesn't keep people from hoping." As soon as he said the words, he wished he could take them back.

Dr. Jessie looked annoyed. "We know Coronado came through here."

Scott made a helpless gesture. "I didn't mean there isn't any reason to keep looking."

Dr. Dexter pointed across the Well. "Come on, Russell. Let's go look at some rocks before you get yourself tossed out of this dig before you start work."

Scott followed the geoarchaeologist along the plank path. He was going to have to keep his opinions to himself. He didn't want to be classified with Wassaja/Jackson or whatever his name was.

As they walked, Dr. Dexter said, "So, Russell, you're interested in geoarchaeology. What do you know about the field?"

"To be honest, not much. I'm curious. I've been studying geology since I was a little kid, and it's hard to live in this area without developing an interest in archaeology. But I don't really know how the two fields dovetail."

They started down the path to Dr. Dexter's camp. "I'm focused on two basic questions at the Well," Dr. Dexter said. "The site formation history and the environmental conditions when the Sinagua lived in the area. If you're a budding geologist, I'd expect you to know something about that first area."

"I know the Well is an old sinkhole fed by a spring that never dries up, even in the middle of summer."

"Technically, it's a collapsed carbonate cauldron fed by a

limonene spring, a relatively rare phenomenon on our Colorado Plateau."

Different words, Scott thought, same basic idea. But he didn't say it. If he wanted Dr. Dexter to take him on, he didn't need to come across as a smart-aleck know-it-all.

"The pool is interesting in its own right. It's a closed system with water that has a high concentration of arsenic. Scientists have discovered a number of endemic, or unique, species in this pool that haven't been seen before—or anywhere else."

Scott nodded at a pair of small black ducks floating on the pond. "Those coots aren't unique. What are they doing here?"

"I've never heard a satisfactory explanation. I know they show up on a pretty regular basis and root around in the pondweed. But I've never seen any other ducks here. The species discovered here don't appeal to ducks."

Scott wasn't interested in pond dwellers, but he knew Dr. Dexter expected a question. "What have they found no one has seen anywhere else?"

"They've identified five or six new ones so far. Among them a spring snail, a new type of water scorpion, and a new species of leech."

"Ugh. I hate leeches."

"Don't come here at night then. They stay in the slime on the bottom during the day and surface at night to find food."

Time to change the subject. "You said environmental factors."

Dr. Dexter nodded. "I'm primarily interested in the climate and vegetation in the 1500s. I'm looking for evidence that the climate at the Well was still conducive to human habitation at least up until the middle 1500s."

"To support Dr. Jessie's theory that the Sinagua were still here when Coronado came through?"

Dr. Dexter studied him. "You listen on more levels than one, don't you, Russell?"

"I try to, sir." It was easy to superimpose Dr. Jessie's time frame on Dr. Dexter's investigation. But why would a scientist of his standing collect evidence to support someone else's theory? He thought scientists waited to form a theory until they had amassed as much evidence as they could.

Scott decided not to ask. He needed to gather his own facts to answer that question.

6

Reed pushed the door open and walked into Spook Hall just after 8:30. He'd hoped to be here by 8:00, but he hadn't wanted to face anyone this morning. He was sure one of them would be able to tell something was wrong, and he didn't have any answers to the questions they were sure to ask. That was one downside of having a family that actually cared about you—they noticed things.

The big room where he'd interviewed the afternoon before was empty except for an old man folding chairs and putting them on a dolly. Bernie?

Reed gave himself an internal shake. Not Bernie. Bernie was dead. "Excuse me," he said.

The old man ignored him. More likely didn't hear him. His voice had come out shaky and sort of soft. "Excuse me!" This time he shouted.

The old man dropped two of the metal chairs with a crash. When he turned Reed saw he wasn't really an old man, not as old as Bernie anyway. "I'm not deaf. What do you want?"

"I'm looking for the Seven Cities Adventure Tours. They were in here last night."

"And left a mess for me to clean up."

"Do you know where they are now?"

"Probably in the back office the Council voted to let them rent for the summer." But no good's going to come of that outfit. We've got enough tourists. Don't need more."

"Sorry," Reed said. "Where's the back office?"

The janitor nodded to the left. "Down that hall. Third door on the right."

"Thanks."

The old guy ignored him, reached for a broom leaning against the wall.

Reed took a deep breath and headed for the hallway.

It was dim and dusty, making Reed sneeze. The door to the office stood open, and he could hear voices. Were they expecting him? Would they even remember? Reed touched the bottom of his backpack where he'd stashed the journal.

Reed knocked on the door frame. The two men he'd seen the night before looked at him. "If it isn't our boy with the gold doubloon," said the one Reed had identified as the boss, Mr. Parnell. "Did you bring it with you?"

Reed took a step back. He hadn't promised to bring it, had he? He'd never even seen it himself.

Mr. Parnell laughed. "Relax, kid. You didn't promise me the doubloon, but you promised me a journal entry describing it. You also promised me your friend has it."

His dead friend. But Reed didn't say it. That would come out of its own accord. Later. After he had the job. Reed took off his backpack and opened it. "I have next best thing. I've got Bernie's great-grandfather's journal. It tells about buying a doubloon *necklace* from a Yavapai trader."

Mr. Parnell stood up and moved closer. "Let me have a look."

Reed pulled the journal out but didn't hand it to the man. "The story isn't written down. It's a piece of oral history."

The other man, Freddie, said, "I told you so, boss. The kid is just hot air. He wants a job, so he makes up a tall tale to go with the legend we heard."

"I did not make it up! Oral history is a legitimate form of history. If you don't believe me, you can ask Uncle Paul."

Freddie snorted. "Uncle Paul? Is he like Uncle Sam?"

"He used to be a history professor at the university. Now he's with the Park Service. He's collecting oral history of the mining era for a book."

"Simmer down, kid." Mr. Parnell held out his hand. "Give me what you've got. Let me see for myself if it will help us."

Reluctantly, Reed handed him the journal.

Mr. Parnell opened it, flipped through several pages and closed it. "Is this your idea of a joke, kid? This isn't a journal. It's nothing but an expense ledger."

"If you'll look on the page with the yellow sticky note, sir, you'll see the entry I was talking about. Three-quarters of the way down the page. It says, "Spanish gold coin strung on leather thong.""

"I see it. So what?"

"So, it proves Uncle Bernie's ancestor had at least one genuine doubloon. If he had one, there must be more around here. I can find them for you." Reed was improvising now, but he was desperate. He could feel the tide turning against him. He had to have this job.

Mr. Parnell went back to his chair, carrying the journal with him. "What have you got in mind, Ron?"

"Reed, sir. My name is Reed."

"Okay, Reed. Convince me."

"My uncle Bernie has a map of all the places he's searched for the missing treasure. He's also mapped out the other likely hiding places that he hasn't searched. He promised me I could have the map. Don't you see? I've got a start. We know the doubloons legend is more than just a story because of the journal entry and Uncle Bernie's doubloon."

Freddie looked skeptical. "You've sure got a lot of uncles,"

Reed ignored him. It was true, but he didn't want to get into that.

Mr. Parnell looked impatient. "Let's say you find the doubloons. What good does that do me?"

Reed stopped. None. It took care of Reed's problem, eliminating the need for the job. Time to improvise. "While I'm looking, I could take some of your clients along with me." He could hunt at night, make sure the targeted site was clear, and then take a tourist or two along with him. It wouldn't be cheating. He needed the treasure to get to college. These guys were exploiting the old story to get their business going. It wasn't the same thing.

"I've got a better idea," Mr. Parnell said. "How badly do you want this job?"

"I need this job, sir. I want to go to college, and I don't have enough money to pay for it."

Freddie winked. "None of your uncles can help you out?"

Mr. Parnell frowned. "Give us some privacy, Freddie. This young man and I are about to make a deal."

The way the boss of Seven Cities said the word *deal* made Reed nervous. He didn't want a deal—he wanted a job.

Freddie didn't budge. "You and I are partners, Don. Whatever arrangement you think you're going to make, don't forget I'm part of it."

"Sure, sure. I just want our young friend to feel comfortable. Too many bosses can make a guy nervous. Go to the cafe and get us some coffee. We'll be done by the time you get back. I'll tell you all about it."

Freddie shot Reed a considering look and then got slowly to his feet. "You want some coffee, kid?"

What Reed wanted was a cigarette. He'd promised Aunt Marty seven weeks and three days ago to quit smoking. So far he hadn't broken that promise. But right now ... He shook his head. "Thanks, but I've got to be at the hardware store by ten."

"Have a cup before you come back, Freddie. And be sure to close the door on your way out."

Freddie growled something Reed couldn't understand and left the room. The door didn't exactly slam, but Reed jumped.

Mr. Parnell made a dismissive gesture. "Don't worry about Freddie. He's a bit of a hot head, but he's great with numbers."

Reed nodded.

Mr. Parnell tipped his chair back and considered Reed. "I've been wondering how to make my company stand out, and your visit last night got me thinking in an entirely new direction. A treasure of gold doubloons might be just what I'm looking for. Anyone with a fifth-grade education knows Coronado didn't find any cities of gold because there never was such a thing. But gold fever is a powerful driver. Coronado's friend Antonio de Mendoza caught gold fever and outfitted an expedition to the New World to follow the story of the Seven Cities of Gold. Then Coronado marched from dusty Native villages to barren mesas across New Mexico and Arizona. It drew three hundred thousand people into the California territory after the discovery of gold at Sutter's Mill in 1848. It's even what put Jerome on the map. The miners found copper, but they were looking for gold."

He paused. "With me so far, young man?"

"Yes, sir." Reed wasn't sure where the guy was going with this train of thought, but what he was saying made sense.

"All right, then. We can't give these tourists a city of gold. We *can* give them your gold doubloons."

"What if I don't find the treasure?"

Parnell waved a hand in dismissal. "It's hope that fuels gold fever. We give them hope with the legend."

"It's more than a legend. That journal proves there are doubloons. Uncle Bernie has the one mentioned in the journal. He just hasn't given it to me yet."

"Fine. Fine. Meantime, I've got a business to get going. All it would take is a few coins. We don't need the treasure to fuel the hope. All we need is a spark to light the fire. And I know how to get the kindling. It will be your job to toss the match."

Reed shifted uncomfortably. He never liked it when people started talking in riddles. Sometimes they slipped something by you. "Sorry, Mr. Parnell. You lost me."

The boss let his chair down on all four legs. "I know where to get gold doubloons. Not real ones, of course. That would be too expensive, but excellent reproductions only an expert could tell aren't the real thing. You're going to scatter a few of these little beauties where my tourists can find them."

MARTY PARKED in the driveway that ran beside the 1920s bungalow. Most days she almost floated around back on a cloud of mild surprise. Today, however, she sat in her pickup and remembered. More than an antiques showroom, *Old and Treasured* was her dream come true. She'd bought it as a residence and workshop when she moved to Clarkdale and struck out on her own in the antiques business she'd learned in Virginia.

Had that been only eighteen months ago? So much had happened since that it seemed like much longer. She'd married

Paul, acquired a stepson and a foster son, begun building a new home with the three of them, and moved into a workshop on the side of Cleopatra Hill. The little family added an unexpected dimension to her life she could no longer imagine living without.

The picture of Paul and Scott sitting with Jessie in the living room of that new home flashed in her mind. Had she let herself feel too secure too quickly?

Shaking herself loose from the doubts she'd been avoiding all morning, Marty got out and started around to the back door she used as her entrance to what was now more a showroom than a workroom. As she rounded the corner, she glanced at *The Treasure Trove*, the old stable-garage Carly used to house an ongoing rummage sale. Was her partner-in-training here this morning? Or was she off on a treasure hunt, as she called her regular trips to thrift stores?

As if in answer, the small door they used to enter the garage when they weren't transporting cast-off furniture opened, and Carly burst out into the sunny backyard, her ginger curls bouncing around her face as she hurried toward Marty. As always, Marty marveled at Carly's boundless energy. Yes, she was ten years younger, but she raced from one task to the next as if they were all urgent. One of these days she'd have to slow down. Or would she?

"Marty! You're later than usual. I was starting to wonder if you were taking the day off."

"Just running a little late."

"Did you still want to inventory the supplies this morning? I've got a couple of hours to spare before I have to head for the estate sales in Sedona."

Marty had forgotten about the inventory, possibly because spending the morning with the enthusiastic Carly was the last thing she wanted to do. She shook her head. "I've got other things I need to do this morning. We can put that off for a few more days."

Carly nodded, taking the change of plans in stride the way she took every unexpected turn of events. "Where's Scott? If we're not doing the inventory, I can use his help."

Scott, of course, was at Montezuma Well, sucked into Jessie's orbit as surely as Paul had been. But she didn't say that. "He's following a lead on a job that can give him geology field experience." No need to mention the foray into geoarchaeology, a discipline no one in the family had ever heard of before yesterday. "I'm afraid we're on our own if he gets the job."

Carly shrugged. "Good for Scott. He's not really into antiques."

No, Scott was working here because Marty had given him a job. And maybe because Paul insisted. Enough. Carly was right. Antiques weren't Scott's idea of fascinating work. She brought herself firmly back to *Old and Treasured*.

"Carly," she said, "you go on with whatever you were doing. I'm getting close on the table I have in my workshop, and I want to find a buyer." She marched herself into the house, and into her tiny office. She kept a list of prospective buyers on her computer, categorized by the kind of antique she thought she could interest them in.

Opening up the file, she scanned the list of customers just starting out with antiques, still on a budget, but wanting the real thing. Even though the table was going to be repaired rather than restored to its original condition, one of these customers would be interested in a genuine Duncan Phyfe.

Priscilla Edwards was a possibility. A first-year history teacher at the high school with a special interest in early American history. Blonde and outgoing. Like Linda. She'd probably been a cheerleader. No doubt had a best friend like Jessie.

Marty jerked her attention back to her task and wrote Priscilla's name and phone number on a sticky note.

Did Priscilla need a dining room table? She had to be using something. But if it was something she'd picked up at a garage sale, maybe Carly could take the current table for *The Treasure Trove*, and Marty could offer Priscilla a trade-in credit on the price of the Duncan Phyfe.

The screen door banged open, and Carly called out, "Look what I found! You'll never believe it!"

Marty swallowed a groan. Why now? Just when she was getting somewhere. To be fair, Carly was sure to burst in sometime, why *not* now? Maybe she'd found a genuine antique this time.

"Look at this footstool, Marty! Doesn't it look like real Stickley Arts and Crafts? I saw a chair and footstool almost exactly like this one online listed at—get this—$20,000!"

"Down, girl. At that price, the set was signed, a real rarity."

"Still ..."

"Where's the chair?"

"No idea." Carly's face fell. "But it's mission oak and in pretty good shape. You could show me how to restore it. I don't think it would take much work."

Not for the first time, Marty wondered what Carly considered *not much work*.

Getting to her feet, Marty took the square stool with the cracked leather cushion from her partner and set it upside down on her desk. She knew immediately that it was just one step removed from the dump, but she didn't want to completely discourage Carly. She hoped Jessie's partner, Dr. Dexter maybe, would be as considerate of Scott's feelings.

Forcing her mind back to Clarkdale and her own partner,

she said, "I don't know. See this lengthwise crack? The wood split years ago. But keep looking."

"Oh, well. One of these days, I'll find something worth restoring. What luck have you had? Found a buyer for your table yet?"

"Priscilla Edwards might be interested."

"Might be? Have you called her?"

"She's in class."

"Earth to Marty. This is July. Summer vacation. Priscilla is remodeling her house. This is the perfect time to tempt her."

Marty blinked. Of course, Carly was right. Why hadn't she called? To cover for herself, she said, "Oscar Rodriguez might be interested in purchasing it for his wife's birthday." They were retired, coming late to the fascination with antiques, but perhaps ready to step up from Carly's collectible what-nots to a piece of furniture.

"Oscar and Dominique are in Alaska. Fiftieth wedding anniversary, remember?"

Marty managed to keep from groaning. She forced a smile. "You're right! It just slipped my mind."

Carly put her hands on her hips and studied Marty. "What's with you, boss lady? You remember these details better than I do. You always tell me how important it is to think of our customers as people with lives beyond antiques."

"I've got a lot on my mind this morning."

"Scott takes a new job in the middle of the summer. What's up with that?"

"He's a teenager. His priorities are on his future, not on current commitments. Scott's a good kid, but he's still a teenager."

"Granted. Then what? Paul!"

Marty started to deny it, but the look of discovery on Carly's face told her she'd be wasting her time.

"Time for a therapeutic cup of coffee. You need to tell me what's going on in your head."

Marty did not want to have this conversation with Carly. Not only was it not her business, but she read Marty too well. "I've already had two cups of coffee. I don't need a third."

"Then nibble on some crackers or peanuts while I have a cup."

Marty was about to tell her that her private life was just that, but Carly was gone. With characteristic speed, Carly was already in the kitchen. Marty sighed and followed her. She might as well get this over with. Maybe she could steer the conversation back to Scott. He wasn't coming back, and Carly was going to have to find a replacement little brother.

She should have known better. As she entered the kitchen, Carly said, "It's that woman, isn't it?"

Jerome was a small town, but surely gossip about Jessie hadn't already made its way down the hill to Clarkdale. She tried to pretend she didn't know what Carly was talking about. "What woman?"

Carly pulled out a chair for Marty and handed her a package of cheese and peanut butter crackers. "That archaeologist, of course. The one Paul dated back in college."

"Who on earth told you that?"

Carly put her cup of coffee down on the table and snapped her fingers. "Jessie! That's the name."

"Who told you about Jessie?"

"Someone who knows Jorge."

"Whoever it was ought to get the facts straight. Jessie was Linda's high school friend."

"It doesn't matter. Whoever she is or was, my friend says Jorge told him it's clear there's history there. And it might not all be in the past."

Marty winced. What if Jorge was right? She stood up. "We

both have work to do. We don't have time to worry about third-hand gossip."

"You know you won't be able to concentrate."

"Don't worry about me. Isn't this your day for combing the thrift shops in Sedona?"

Marty didn't wait for an answer, but Carly's voice followed her as she left the room. "You don't want to talk to me. I get it. So go talk to Sofia. You need to face facts, girlfriend."

Marty pretended not to hear. Carly—or Jorge—didn't know Paul like she did. Paul was her husband. He was committed to her. That was when a little voice in her head whispered, *Linda was Paul's wife before you. What if Jessie reminds him of Linda too much?*

Marty sighed. Maybe talking to Sofia wasn't such a bad idea.

But not yet.

7

Paul took his eyes off the road long enough to glance at Jessie. He wasn't sure agreeing to take her to interview her Yavapai assistant's grandmother was a good idea. But when she'd asked, he'd decided he could combine her trip to the reservation with his visit to George Henry. Not a high priority, but a good reason to go. This morning Jessie's blonde hair was loose on her shoulders. Slender and tanned, she didn't look much older than when they were in college. She still knew what colors to wear. Her purple T-shirt brought out the blue of her eyes. She leaned close to adjust the air conditioner, and he caught a whiff of sweet cinnamon, the same perfume she'd always worn.

Suddenly he was twenty years younger, driving his ancient Ford pickup on the Skyline Drive. The University of Virginia was behind them, Big Meadows picnic area just ahead. Jessie sat in the passenger seat, a flowered tablecloth his mother had loaned them on her lap and a picnic basket beside her feet. Like now, she was talking enthusiastically, gesturing to emphasize important points. Instead of speculating on Coronado's visit to the Verde Valley, she was reviewing a guest lecture on Thomas Jefferson's early years she'd attended the night before. Because of his work schedule at the movie theater, he'd missed the event.

Paul pulled himself back into the present. Not autumn, summer. Not a colorful tree-lined road climbing gently. Flat, dusty blacktop, cutting straight across the desert.

He cleared his throat. "Let me stop you there, Jessie. It sounds like you and I have different purposes this morning. We need to decide who's going to take the lead in our conversation with Winola."

She went suddenly quiet, and for a moment, he was afraid he'd insulted her. He had, after all, interrupted her mid-sentence.

But before he could apologize, she laughed. "Same old Paul. I see Linda didn't manage to teach you any manners."

He started to respond, to say that Linda had nothing to do with this. But Jessie added, "Never mind. Your manners didn't bother me when I first met you, and they don't bother me now."

Paul ignored the tempting rabbit trail. "I want to give Mina's grandmother the opportunity to tell us whatever she remembers from her grandmother's stories. You want to ask her specific questions about Coronado."

Jessie laughed. "Lighten up, Romeo. I promise I'll let you have your turn asking questions. Didn't I always make sure you had a chance to make your points? I know Linda sometimes got frustrated, but I'm not Linda." She paused and then added, "Or Marty."

He glanced at her. She was smiling. He must have imagined the barb.

Jessie rested her hand on his arm. Not Linda, not Marty, all right. Jessie had always been a woman who touched. She didn't mean anything by it. He remembered her slipping her hand in his whenever they walked side-by-side. She finally stopped when Linda announced, "Back off, Jess! Paul is mine now, and I don't intend to share him with you. Sharing a room is one thing, a boyfriend is something entirely different."

At the time he was flattered. After Jessie married and Linda's jealousy focused on a woman he'd known since childhood, he was annoyed. But he'd explained it away as part of Linda's drive for perfection. When Linda started complaining about the time he spent working on a paper with a female colleague, he'd wondered if he should have taken that long-ago anger at Jessie as a warning sign. Maybe if he'd stood up to Linda when she'd accused Jessie of trying to take him away, he could have saved them both from the one area that caused serious friction in their marriage.

Now, Jessie patted his arm. "Does this bother you, Paul? Would it worry Marty? We both know what Linda would say."

"Marty isn't Linda. And since Linda is dead, she shouldn't enter into our conversation."

Jessie made a clucking sound. "Why are you getting so defensive about the women in your life, Paul?"

He knew she was teasing, but jealousy had taken a toll on his first marriage. Marty wasn't the jealous type, but he didn't want to joke about a keg of dynamite. "I'm not defensive. I just don't want to talk about either of my wives with you. Our friendship is something between us. Neither Linda nor Marty has anything to do with it."

"You are defensive! And for good reason. I predict you're going to regret your second marriage as much as you regretted your first."

"I never regretted marrying Linda, and I won't regret marrying Marty."

"Come on, Paul. This is me you're talking to. It's impossible to be married to someone for as many years as you were married to Linda without a moment's regret. Now you're repeating the pattern with Marty."

"What pattern? I met Linda in college. We had a classic young adult romance. Marty was a neighbor in trouble. That was a friendship that deepened into something more."

Jessie took her hand back and put it in her lap. "On the surface. But the underlying process was the same. You fell in love with Linda at first sight and rushed into a relationship. If you're honest with yourself, I'm guessing the same thing happened with Marty. She was your neighbor, but weren't you drawn to her from the first time you saw her?"

Paul shifted uncomfortably. He remembered Marty running from Lois's house calling for help. She had quite literally fallen into his arms. But that didn't mean he'd fallen in love with her then. He ignored the question.

But Jessie wasn't through. "How long had you known Marty before you got married?"

"A year. I don't call that rushing into a relationship. "

"How much of that year did you to spend dating?"

"Good grief, Jessie. Marty and I were both mature adults when we met. Dating didn't enter into it."

"That's my point. It probably should have. But leaving that question to the side, how many months of the year did the two of you spend together?"

Paul did a swift calculation in his head. The summer break was half gone when they met. At the end of the summer, he'd gone back to teaching, and Marty had gone back to Virginia to decide what to do with Lois's bequest. She moved to Clarkdale and started her antique business after Christmas. They married at the end of the following summer.

That added up to a little less than nine months. But he didn't say that. He wanted to be done with this conversation. "Long enough that we both knew what we were getting into."

But had they? With Scott's disappearance and Reed's appearance, those months had been tumultuous, to say the least.

He wasn't about to give Jessie those details, though he suspected she already knew them. Who had given her the details of his relationship with Marty? More likely, who had she pumped?

Before he could ask, Jessie touched his arm again. "Look at that! It says *Yavapai-Apache reservation.*"

Paul didn't need to look at the stone signpost that displayed the pink and yellow Great Seal of the Yavapai-Apache Nation to know where they were. But he was grateful it had distracted Jessie from her cross-examination.

Mina's directions were excellent, and in less than ten minutes, they were pulling into the driveway of her grandmother's cookie cutter government-issue house. The frame structure would have looked at home in the middle of a handkerchief-sized lawn anywhere in the Midwest. Surrounded by desert dotted with prickly pear cactus and tumbleweed, the house looked like it had been plucked from an alien planet.

"It doesn't fit, does it?" Jessie's words echoed his thought. "Stone would be so much better. It would stand up under the wind and be cooler in the summer and warmer in the winter. The ancestors knew what they were doing when they built their homes in cliffs."

"Or adobe. Don't forget the apartment structure of Tuzigoot. Or the ruins just beyond Montezuma Well."

"I wonder if the contractors who built this housing development had ever even been to Arizona before taking this project, much less on this reservation." As she made the comment, Jessie released her seatbelt and opened her door.

Paul put a restraining hand on her arm. "Wait, Rap ..." Just in time he caught himself. *Rapunzel* had been his nickname for Jessie until he met and fell for Linda, who had the same golden hair.

Jessie punched his arm playfully. "Almost slipped up there, didn't you, Romeo?"

Paul chuckled. His roommate had teased him about having two girlfriends, Linda and Jessie. One of them had heard it, and the joke had stuck.

"Understandable," Jessie murmured. "In so many ways this morning has felt like twenty years ago."

Paul unbuckled his seatbelt. "But it's not. You and I are middle-aged professionals here to gather information for our respective research projects."

"Speak for yourself, Dr. Russell. I don't consider myself middle-aged. I might be reaching the end of youth, but I'm not there yet."

Paul reached over and ruffled her hair. "If I remember correctly, you're only two years younger than I am. That makes you thirty-seven."

"Thirty-six! My birthday isn't until September. I'm crushed that you forgot."

"Thirty-six times two is seventy-two. Like it or not, you've reached middle age."

She frowned. "Not funny, doc. Age is a matter of attitude. It's spending your life with kids that makes you feel middle-aged."

Paul let that pass. The last thing he wanted was to defend Marty's age to Jessie. He opened his door. "Let me take the lead with Winola. I'd like to set up our meeting so that she does the talking."

"Nope. Mina is the link between Grandma and us. And while I respect the cultural right to circular thinking, our time is limited. Since we only have a couple of hours, we need a little bit of direct-line communication."

"I'm not going to argue, but believe me, you'll get more information if you allow Winola to talk to us in her own way. No doubt Mina has told her what we want. I'm sure she understands. She'll get to the information you're after more quickly if you approach her on her own terms. Remember, this is her home."

Jessie got out. "Don't underestimate her. Grandma she may be, but I'm positive this is one old lady who's used to dealing with researchers. Her granddaughter is thoroughly acculturated."

Paul didn't agree, but he decided to let Jessie find out for herself. Before Jessie could knock, the door opened. No doubt Mina's grandmother had heard the SUV pull into her driveway. A woman with a wrinkled face but still largely black hair stood in the doorway, a closed expression on her face. Wearing a long light blue cotton dress with circular white bands reaching from her knees to the hem, she could have been fifty or eighty, or any age in-between.

When the older woman didn't speak, Jessie said, "I'm Dr. Jensen, the archaeologist in charge of the dig where your granddaughter Mina is working this summer. This is my colleague Dr. Paul Russell. We'd like to come in and talk with you."

When the woman didn't move, Paul said gently, "I think you are Winola Tewa. Perhaps your granddaughter told us we might come to see you."

Mina's grandmother shifted her gaze from Jessie to him. Obeying the unspoken command, he took Jessie's arm and drew her back a few steps. Then he smiled. When Jessie started to speak again, he squeezed her arm and shook his head slightly.

Winola studied them for a moment. Then she nodded and

stepped out of the doorway. They followed her into a sparsely-furnished square room. With one hand she gestured at a much-worn sofa. As they sat down, she lowered herself into an overstuffed armchair to the right of the sofa.

Almost immediately Jessie said, "I'm sure Mina told you about our work. It's important to my research that we find evidence the Spanish conquistadors visited Montezuma Castle while it was occupied. I'd like to hear from you what stories your grandparents might have told you from those long-ago days."

"That's not where our story begins."

"I understand, but that's the part of the story I'm interested in. Please tell us anything you've heard."

Winola didn't reply. They waited, but still she didn't speak. Jessie stirred impatiently.

For a second time, Paul put a restraining hand on her arm. Looking at Winola, he said, "I know stories must start at the beginning. Please tell us where the story of the Yavapai begins."

The old woman leaned back in her chair and threaded her fingers together. "Long time ago, the ones-who-went-before lived in a place where no rain came for a long time. So long they couldn't grow any food. Back then, the people and animals could talk to each other. So when the people knew they were going to die, they asked Hummingbird, or Mina Mina, to find a new place where they could grow food. Mina Mina flew until he found a great tree growing up through a hole in the sky. Curious, he flew into the hole.

"He came out into an upper world where he found plants growing. When he saw how rich the earth was, he knew he had found a place where the people could grow food. He flew back down through the hole and told the people. When they heard the good news, the people and the animals climbed the tree, coming out in the area you people call *Montezuma Well*."

"You named your granddaughter for Hummingbird!"

Jessie's outburst made Winola blink.

Paul murmured, "I apologize for my friend."

"Okay. The name on my granddaughter's birth certificate is *Gabriela*. I gave her the name Mina Mina when she found a hole in the sky and went to college. She liked it and took it for her own. She says she's in that new world looking for answers about the Ones Who Went Before."

The old woman fell silent, and Paul wondered if she would go on with her story. He'd heard variations of this creation account but never about Hummingbird. Jessie stirred beside him. Before she could get to her feet, Paul said, "Please continue, Grandmother."

Jessie frowned but didn't get to her feet.

Winola hesitated. After another moment had passed, she said, "The People made one bad mistake when they climbed that tree. They forgot about the frog people and left them down below. At first the crops grew, they had plenty to eat, and the people and the animals got healthy and strong. Then one day water started pouring from the hole where the tree grew.

"Pretty soon, the people could see there was going to be a huge flood. They knew they would all drown. So they got a tree, hollowed it out, and made a canoe. Then they took a young girl and put her in the canoe with plenty of food. The flood came, and, as they feared, all the people drowned, except the girl in the canoe. When the water receded, she found her canoe resting on the red rocks in Sedona. She climbed out and became First Woman.

"First Woman had many adventures with Father Sun and Brother Moon—too many to tell. One day she bore a daughter. Her daughter bore children. They all came to live at the place where you and my granddaughter are digging."

Winola folded her hands in her lap and looked at them.

"Thank you for the story, Grandmother," Paul said. "Your people are right to entrust you with this story."

Jessie shifted impatiently, "What happened when the Spanish came?"

"That's not my story."

"What do you mean?"

When the older woman didn't answer, Jessie looked at Paul. He ignored her.

"I don't know that story," the old woman said. "Talk to that crazy kid Jackson's grandfather. He knows stories about the people and the white men." She got to her feet. The interview was over.

8

The sun was headed toward the western horizon when Reed finally made it to Montezuma Well. As much as he'd wanted to get here before five, he hadn't had the nerve to ask Mr. O'Riley to let him go early again. He was lucky the boss had ignored Denny's suggestion to fire him. Reed started up the path to the Well's rim. From the top he could find Scott. He wasn't sure what he thought about scattering the fake doubloons where Mr. Parnell's tourists would find them. But that was a bridge he would cross after the guy got them—if he even could. Secretly Reed hoped he wouldn't be able to get them.

But this part of his job, making contact with the authorities in the historical places Mr. Parnell wanted to show his tourists, was fine. Montezuma Castle, Tuzigoot, and Montezuma Well were the three places his boss had specified. Reed had decided to start with the Well, hoping Scott might still be here. Reed scanned the scene spread out before him, looking for Scott's blond hair. It always stood out, a lighter spot against the dark background.

His brother was still here, not down below where Reed expected him to be. A man he assumed was the geoarchaeologist Scott was working for packed up gear and stowed it under a canvas canopy. Instead of helping him, Scott was across the wide expanse of lake up on the rim directly across from where Reed stood. He seemed to be in intense conversation with a girl with a black braid that hung to the middle of her back. He wondered how long her hair would be free of the constricting braid. But all this observing and wondering wasn't getting him anywhere with the task at hand.

Even though he hadn't actually promised to scatter the doubloons, he had agreed to look for likely spots. He was supposed to make friends with someone he could drop by to visit so when he came to hide the reproductions no one would notice him. That was the part of the plan that made him nervous. If there was nothing wrong with what he was doing, why did Mr. Parnell want him to go unnoticed?

Reed pushed aside the uncomfortable thought and concentrated on how he could get to Scott. His foster brother was a built-in friend, but he had to let the others here know who he was so he could start dropping by. Maybe Scott could introduce him to someone who could be a contact at Montezuma Castle. Maybe Uncle Paul knew someone at Tuzigoot. Reed also intended to create a map of some of the caves and canyons around Jerome that Bernie had explored. All he had were his memories of those stories, but he'd listened closely once he'd understood the importance of the treasure.

As he scanned the area, he spotted a sort of sidewalk made from planks that skirted the top of the Well. Because he couldn't see any other way around, Reed headed for it. When he reached the end of the paved trail, he encountered a no-entry sign hanging on a chain. A quick look around showed him that he was alone. Stepping over the chain, he moved toward Scott and the girl.

That was when he realized he hadn't come up with a reason for being here. He couldn't say Mr. Parnell wanted him to look around. The uneasy feeling settled in the pit of his stomach. He ignored it. He was almost in shouting distance when he suddenly wondered how Scott had gotten here. The only transportation he had was a bicycle—not very practical for the trip from Jerome to the Well. So someone had given him a ride—either Uncle Paul or Aunt Marty. He would simply offer to give Scott a ride home.

Scott saw him and waved. "Reed! Come meet Mina."

If Mina was the girl standing beside Scott, Reed was ready. She was beautiful in a different way than he'd ever seen in a girl. Her skin was the color so many girls laid out in the sun to get, and her hair was so black it was almost blue. Her black eyes welcomed him, and her smile showed even white teeth. Suddenly Reed realized this girl didn't know anything about him. She didn't know who his father was, why the Russells had taken him in, or even that he had a tattoo on his back. It was like stepping into a new world. All he had to do was watch his temper. As he registered the friendly welcome in her eyes, he decided that would be easy.

"Mina," Scott said, "this is my brother Reed."

He hadn't even said foster brother. She would think he was a Russell. Until she found out his last name, but maybe by that time he could have impressed her so that she wouldn't be curious about the Harpers.

Reed held out his hand. "Hi Mina. It's nice to meet you."

She put her small warm hand in his larger one, and he knew he would never be able to be angry with her. He wouldn't treat her like his father had his mother. Not in a million years. No matter what.

Mina gave him another one of her smiles. "It's nice to meet you too. Sorry that my hand is a bit grimy. Archaeologists dig around in the dirt."

"Not a problem. I get wood dust on my hands all the time."

Mina blushed ever so slightly, and Reed realized he was still holding her hand. He released it, but he didn't think she'd minded. Did she have a boyfriend? It didn't matter. She didn't have on a ring, so she wasn't married or engaged or anything like that. If she had a boyfriend, he was about to get some competition.

Scott cleared his throat. "I hope you came to give me a ride home," Scott said.

Reed pulled his attention away from Mina and tried to get back on track. He was here to find an excuse to come and hang out once in a while. He'd thought Scott was it, but now he had a real reason to show up. "Sure thing, buddy. After I left the hardware store, I decided to run over and see what your new job looks like."

"So, what do you think?"

Reed looked at Mina. He tried not to, but he couldn't help himself. He grinned. "It looks good to me."

Mina blushed again. But she smiled at him. She was interested, all right. It had been a while since he'd had a girlfriend, but he hadn't forgotten the signs. Of course, his last two girlfriends had been losers—like he was back then. But things were turning around for him now. He could feel it. He had two jobs, an excuse to really search for the gold doubloons, and now, a chance at a girlfriend.

"Better than interesting. I've only been here one day, and I'm hooked. It makes sense that geology and archaeology would intersect, but it's like a new world. I may have found a specialty."

"Mina! You're late!"

Reed turned at the harsh tone, ready to call the newcomer out. A couple of years older than he was, the guy was Yavapai like Mina. Her brother?"

"I'm just about ready, Jackson." Mina's voice was soft and conciliatory. "Can't you see we have a visitor?"

"How did he get here? No one's supposed to be back here but authorized personnel."

Scott moved to stand beside Reed. "This is my brother, Reed. He's got as much right to visit me as you have to visit your girlfriend."

"Wrong, *Bilagaana*. I have permission. Does he?"

Reed clenched his fist. "Not yet," Reed said. "But I met Dr. Jessie last night at our house. She knows me." Just saying the words *at our house* gave him a boost of confidence. He belonged here. And this guy obviously didn't know how to treat a lady. It wouldn't be that hard to convince Mina she deserved better.

"Come on, Reed. Let's go home. Marty wants to have supper together. She said seven, at the latest."

"Sure." Reed directed his best smile at Mina. "See you around."

The guy she'd called Jackson stepped in front of him and poked a finger in the middle of his chest. "Mina is my girl. We've been together since junior high. We're going to get married right after college."

"Jackson!" Mina pulled on his arm. "Let Reed alone. He just meant he'll be up here to see Scott once in a while. Forget him. Help me stow the gear so I can leave."

Reed took a deep breath. He'd meant more than that, and he was pretty sure Mina knew it.

"Come on, Reed," Scott said. "We've got to get going."

Reed was about to tell Scott to mind his own business, but he suddenly remembered his vow not to lose his temper around Mina. She already had one hot-headed boyfriend. She certainly didn't need another one. Without another word, he stepped around his competition and followed Scott toward home.

SCOTT WAS RELIEVED to get Reed away from Wassaja. Five more minutes, and there would have been a fist fight. He knew Reed's temper, and he'd already seen two displays from Wassaja. He was pretty sure Reed had fallen for Mina. Usually, Reed kept his distance from girls, didn't even try to talk to them. But he'd made eye contact, smiled at her, and even stood up to Jackson. Just the fact Reed was even attracted to Mina surprised him. She was in college, so she was probably older. But even if they were the same age, she didn't seem the type Reed would like. He claimed not to go for what he called "brainy" girls.

"Slow down, buddy! We're not going to a fire."

Scott realized he'd been practically running. The danger was past, and Reed sounded back to his normal self. That was the thing about Reed. He got mad, but it was over almost as soon as it started. His brother had admitted to him that he was trying to break the habit of getting angry before he thought, but it was pretty ingrained, from what Scott could see. Not a surprise, knowing what Mr. Harper was like. It was hard thinking of the man as Reed's dad. Anybody who would beat up his own kid ...

Reed's voice cut into his thoughts. "I got the job."

Scott turned and held up his hand for a high-five. Walking backward so they could keep moving, he said, "Good for you, bro! I knew you could do it. Was it your good looks that tipped the balance?"

Reed rolled his eyes. "No way. It was my brains." The sarcasm in Reed's voice made Scott wince.

The thing was, Reed was a good-looking kid and plenty smart. But he didn't know it, wouldn't believe it when Scott or his dad tried to encourage him. Scott knew of at least one girl at church who wanted to ask Reed out, but her parents were furious when they saw her talking to him after a youth group meeting. When Reed got to college, no one would know about Mr. Harper or Reed's past. Suddenly Scott understood Reed's desire to go far away from here. The University of Virginia seemed like an impossible goal, but if that's what Reed wanted to do, he was going to help him any way he could. He knew his dad and Marty were saving all the money Reed insisted on paying each month. They were going to give it to him, probably with more added, when he graduated from high school. But UVA was expensive. As he thought about it, this second job sounded like a good idea.

"When do you start, bro?"

"I just did."

"What? Did Mr. O'Riley fire you for going to the interview yesterday?"

Reed shook his head. "I was afraid he would because of Denny. But Mr. O'Riley was great. He told Denny that he'd given me his word that I could go, and he was still the boss. He even told Denny never, ever to call me B.T. again. He was really mad that Denny did it over the intercom."

"He seriously made a reference to your bat tattoo over the intercom? That's low! How did Mr. O'Riley find out? Did you tell him?"

"No way. Somebody who was there heard it."

"Maybe that guy in lumber who likes you. He's stood up for you before, hasn't he?"

"Yeah. Pete was a friend of my dad's. I think he saw Pa take a swing at me a couple of times. You better look where you're going, buddy. You're about to trip over that chain."

Scott turned just in time.

When they were back on the paved path, Scott fell into step beside Reed. "So how did you start today if you still have your job at the hardware store? Did Mr. O'Riley cut your hours?"

"No. This job is extra income, not in place of what I'm already making."

Scott didn't say anything, just waited for Reed to explain. The silence stretched until they were almost at the pit house exhibit. Then Reed said, "I'm supposed to make contact with the official sites where the tour is going to stop. Montezuma Well is one of them. I decided to start here since I knew you had this job."

Scott stopped walking. "How did you know? I didn't know myself until about nine o'clock this morning."

"You had an in with the boss lady. Can you imagine anyone saying no to her, a good-looking woman like that?"

"You're right about that. Dr. Dexter was pretty vague about everything until we talked with Dr. Jessie. I think he's got a crush on her."

"A crush? Come on, Scott. She's as old as your dad. Grown-ups don't have crushes. They fall in love."

"Yeah, well, whatever. So, what does 'make contact' mean? And why are you supposed to do it?"

"Mr. Parnell says he needs the good will of the people who run these places. He says sometimes they're not too excited about having large, enthusiastic groups showing up—especially these little parks where there aren't many rangers around to keep an eye out on what the guests are doing."

"Makes sense. But nobody in Dr. Jessie's project qualifies as an official of the park. The only one at the Well stays in that trailer they use as a visitor's center. And she leaves at 5:00 when the park closes."

"I know. I checked before I came to find you. I'll come back tomorrow morning before I go to the hardware store. But you're a connection."

"And Mina." Scott punched Reed in the shoulder.

Reed grinned. "One I intend to follow up on."

"I don't know. That Wassaja is trouble. You heard him warn you off."

"Mina's a big girl. She can make up her own mind."

"Where'd you park? They put the gate down soon."

Reed didn't answer. He had turned around and was staring back up the paved trail that went from the parking lot to the rim of the Well.

"Hey, bro!" Scott tapped Reed on the shoulder. "Did you forget something?"

Reed started. "No. Let's go." His tone was sharp as if he'd been interrupted while thinking through some complicated problem.

Scott studied Reed. Something was wrong. Not anything huge. But something. "What?"

"Nothing."

"Yes. Something."

Reed gave Scott an annoyed look.

Scott stared back. "What?"

Reed scanned the area almost guiltily. Then he started walking toward the road. "There's a little more to the job Mr. Parnell wants me to do than just be a liaison."

Scott kept quiet. It was hard to get Reed to talk, but once he started, you didn't want to interrupt him or he'd never get going again.

"He's got the idea that he can use the story about the gold doubloons hidden around here to get his tourists excited. He wants me to hide a few reproduction doubloons where a really observant person might find them. Not anything obvious, you know. He wants it to be a challenge." Reed stopped walking and looked at Scott.

"I don't know, bro. That sounds tricky to me."

"Why?"

"It's like salting a mine when there's no real ore to dig out."

"Who says there aren't any real doubloons to find?"

Just in time, Scott caught himself from repeating his error from the night before. He couldn't make fun of Reed's belief again. "People have been looking for them for years. Why haven't they been found?"

Reed started walking again. "No one has looked in the right place. That's the other thing about this job. While Mr. Parnell is paying me to find good hiding places, I'm going to be looking for the real treasure. Bernie's journal has a list of sites his family has checked over the years. I know there's nothing at those places. Bernie told me their search still left a lot of territory out there. The caves were here when Coronado marched through."

"And so were the pueblo ruins." Scott grabbed Reed's arm, forcing him to stop. "You can't put any of the fake coins in the ruins! Promise me you won't do that."

"But Mr. Parnell wanted me to hide a few at Montezuma Castle, the Well, and Tuzigoot. They're perfect!"

Scott shook his head. "No way. Those are protected archaeological sites. People can't take anything out and they can't add anything." He wondered if he should tell Reed about Dr. Jessie's project. Reproduction doubloons would ruin her entire study.

"I don't see what it would hurt. If they find them, the doubloons are out of there. If they don't, I'll come back and get them after the tour group leaves."

"You can't! Promise me you won't."

Reed took a deep breath. "You don't understand, Scott. I have to."

Something about the way he said it caught Scott off guard. Gentling his tone, he said, "Why?"

"First, I need the money. Second, Parnell's got Bernie's journal. He said I can have it back after he knows for sure I'm up to doing the job. He's going to find that out by looking here at the Well to see if he can find one I hid. That's what I was doing a while ago. Looking for a good place to hide a couple. I was thinking the pit house ruin would be good."

"You can't. Dr. Jessie is looking for proof the Spaniards had contact with the people of the Castle and the Well. She's trying to change the way people look at that section of Coronado's march. It would literally change the history books if she finds what she's looking for."

"So, if I hid one, and she or one of her team found it, they might think it was genuine."

Scott nodded.

Reed ran his fingers through his hair. "What am I going to do? I've got to get the journal back so I don't look in places that have already been searched."

"Dad—"

"No! Please, Scott. Please don't tell Uncle Paul. All I want to do is get this job and earn extra money to put in my college account."

Scott looked at his brother. He didn't like sneaking around behind his dad's back, but Reed had a point. "Okay. I won't talk to him. I'll help you, but you have to promise me you won't hide any doubloons at archaeological sites."

Reed let out a long breath. "I promise. But you'll have to help me figure out what to say to Mr. Parnell. I have to get the journal back."

Scott nodded. "We'll think of something."

They had reached the road and were headed for Reed's

motorcycle when the Sheriff's car pulled up. Sheriff Winston got out. "Lloyd Harper, Jr."

Scott cringed at the name. Reed was doing everything he could to escape that name and the image that went with it. Whatever was happening, it wasn't good.

Reed stiffened. "I changed my name. It's *Reed* Harper now."

"Until you have it changed in a court of law, you're still Lloyd Harper Jr., and I'm required to use your legal name for what I'm about to do."

Scott held his breath.

The Sheriff opened the back door of the SUV. "I have a warrant to bring you in for questioning in the death of Bernard Lyons."

REED STARED AT THE SHERIFF. Questions slammed against each other in his head so fast, he couldn't sort them out. Did the sheriff think he'd killed Bernie? Had that nosy neighbor been prowling around last night and seen him go in Bernie's house? What should he say? Should he tell the truth?

That question slapped him back into reality. This was Sheriff Winston, the guy who hated Lloyd Harper, Sr. These days he always thought of his dad as *Lloyd Harper*. It hurt too much to even think of him as *Dad*. A dad didn't just leave town and never look back. Paul Russell was a dad—not only to Scott. He was more of a dad to Reed than Lloyd Harper had ever been.

"Quit staring at me like I'm speaking a different language, B.T. Get in the car. We're going for a little ride."

The reference to his bat tattoo snapped him out of it. "I told you, my name is Reed now."

The sheriff snorted. "And I told you, until you change it legally, it isn't."

Reed started to tell him B.T. was a kid's nickname, that it wasn't what was on his birth certificate. But that brought him full circle. His birth certificate said "Lloyd Harper, Jr."

Scott's voice came so suddenly, Reed started. He'd actually forgotten Scott was here. The humiliation started in his gut and climbed into his chest and up to his throat. Scott thought he had turned over a new leaf. What would he think if he knew the truth? Knew Reed had left Bernie dead so he could go back and steal that journal? He had to redirect this, convince Scott he didn't know anything about it. He grabbed at the first rule he'd used in the old days—don't admit you know the crime has been committed. Back then it was trashing mailboxes, keying a car, or stealing a beer from a six-pack when no one was looking. Nothing like murder. But the rule would still work.

"What do you mean *Bernie's death*, Sheriff? I'm supposed to go to his house this evening after supper."

The sheriff studied him. He stood there and took it. He'd been studied by cops a lot tougher than Larry Winston. Beside him he felt Scott squirm. Second rule—stay calm and look them in the eye. If you drop your eyes, cops think you're guilty. If you stand your ground, you might be able to plant a little doubt about your guilt.

Sure enough, Sheriff Winston stared at him, looking for a chink in his armor probably. He wouldn't find one. Reed had too much to lose. Besides, no one could know anything. He'd been careful.

"Get in the car," the sheriff said. "The parking lot is no place for this conversation."

"Don't you have to read him his rights?" Scott's voice was too loud and a little shaky. He was going to have to give his brother a crash course in the rules of survival.

The sheriff transferred his attention to Scott. "No, boy. As a matter of fact, I don't. I'm just asking your friend to go with me and answer a few questions."

"My brother." Scott's voice had dropped to a more normal pitch, but it still sounded shaky.

"Your *brother*? Aren't you Scott Russell? This boy is Lloyd Harper, Jr. Brothers don't usually have different last names."

"My parents adopted Reed." He stepped closer, almost as if the two of them could send the sheriff packing by joining forces. "And don't you have to call my parents before you question him? Don't kids have the right to have their parents there if they get arrested?"

Reed's throat closed up. He couldn't cry. He just couldn't.

The sheriff took a step closer to Scott. "For someone who seems to be so familiar with the Miranda law, it seems like you've got some things to learn. First, I'm not required to call a kid's parents just to question him. If I put him in Juvie, that's a different matter. But no one said anything about Juvie—" He looked at Reed. "Yet. Second, your 'parents,' as you call them, consist of your father and your stepmother. That isn't quite the same thing. Last, your father is fostering Lloyd. He didn't adopt him. That's an entirely different legal relationship."

Reed stole a glance at Scott. He was holding up pretty well, considering, but his neck was red, letting Reed know Scott was getting angry. That was a good thing, as long as he kept cool and didn't blow up. Anger was a lot better than fear.

The sheriff reached for Reed's arm. "Time to go. I was supposed to get off work an hour and a half ago. We've got to get this interrogation going."

Reed didn't like the idea of getting in the sheriff's car. He'd had enough of cop cars from his days in L.A. "What about my motorcycle? I can follow you."

The sheriff stared at him like he couldn't believe his ears.

"Follow me? You mean take off into the hills so I'd have to chase you down."

Reed shook his head. "No, sir. I'm just worried about my motorcycle. I can't just leave it here by the side of the road. If you want me to go first, you can follow me and make sure I don't take off."

The sheriff tugged him toward the car. "Not happening," the sheriff said. "Come on."

Reed jerked free. "That's my only transportation! If someone steals my motorcycle, I lose both my jobs."

Scott held out his hand. "I'll take it home," Scott said. "Give me your keys."

Reed started to object. Scott didn't have a license, but when he looked at his friend—brother—whatever he was, Reed realized Scott needed something to do. He knew how to ride it. They'd had plenty of lessons, and Scott needed a way home. Without saying anything else, he took the keys out of his pocket and tossed them to Scott.

The sheriff grabbed his arm again, and this time Reed didn't object. What was the point?

As the back door slammed, Reed remembered the first rule of survival: *Don't Care.* Just acting like you didn't care wouldn't work. You had to really not care. He learned that one before he joined the gang. He learned on his own when he was a little kid. When his mom left.

The sheriff climbed in the front seat and slammed his own door. Reed stared at the back of Larry's head through the Plexiglas divider. From this angle he could see how thin the guy's hair was getting. Little bald spots peeked through faded orange hair. That helped. No reason to care what an old guy like that thought.

Then Bernie's face popped into his mind, wrinkled with a black mole on his nose. Bernie was balder than Larry, a lot older. He cared what Bernie thought. That brought the grief to the surface, grief he'd been doing his best to pretend wasn't there. Bernie was gone. No more afternoon cups of instant coffee after school. No more Saturday mornings in the workshop. No more stories about the old days. Reed's throat closed up again. He couldn't cry. Especially not in the back of a cop car.

What was wrong with him? When had he started caring? Why did he even have to remind himself of that first rule of survival? The first rule meant he needed it to live by.

Not what was wrong with him. *Who.* Scott. And then Uncle Paul. Reed reminded himself that Scott's dad wasn't his uncle. But then he remembered that conversation in Uncle Paul's study. He said everyone was a child of God. He said that made him and Reed's dad brothers. If they were brothers, he was Reed's uncle.

The car started up the switchbacks. Reed looked out the window. He only had a few minutes to get himself under control. He didn't care. He didn't care. He didn't care. A whisper in his heart tried to start an argument with his thoughts. "Shut up," he muttered.

"You say something, B.T.?"

The growl from the front seat slapped some sense back into him. Reed gritted his teeth and went numb. Outside, it began to rain. Yesterday he welcomed the rain. Today he didn't care. He repeated it to himself. He didn't care. Not about the rain, or the girl. Not about Scott or Uncle Paul. He didn't even care about getting arrested.

9

Marty punched Paul's number into her phone. When it connected, it went straight to voicemail. She swallowed her frustration. "Scott and I have a problem we need your help with. The sheriff arrested Reed. I need to talk to you. Call me back as soon as you get this." Marty punched her phone off and looked at Scott. "Same thing you got. No answer. Where can he be?"

"Maybe he turned off the ringer. He does that sometimes when he's writing."

"Surely he checks it. How long ago did you call him?"

"As soon as the sheriff drove off. When I didn't get an answer, I came home. I thought maybe he was on his way. Dad won't even look at who's calling when he's driving."

"I don't know what to do. Larry Winston and I aren't exactly friends. Paul needs to deal with this."

"We can't leave Reed at the sheriff's office! If it gets late, he'll take him down to Juvie."

Marty looked at Scott's worried face. She pulled him into a quick hug. "Of course not, honey." Releasing him, she turned off the heat under the chicken stir fry she was making for dinner. It didn't matter that she had no idea what to do. She just had to take it one thing at a time. First was to find out what was going on.

Crossing out of the kitchen, she went to the line of hooks they'd screwed into the wall at the bottom of the stairs and grabbed her shoulder bag. "Come on. Let's go see Sheriff Winston. I'm sure as soon as your dad gets our messages, he'll head to the sheriff's office. He might beat us there." It was more a prayer than a hope. Where could Paul be?

Scott was already by the front door. Holding it open for her, he said, "It's a horrible mistake. Reed didn't even know Bernie was dead. He's going to miss his afternoons with Bernie."

Marty knew it was true. She and Paul had both been glad to see the unlikely friendship develop between the unhappy teen and the old man. It was good for both of them. Reed even called Bernie "Uncle Bernie."

They hurried to her little pickup. As she buckled her seatbelt, she wondered what she was going to say to Larry. The man seemed to live with the assumption that people went around killing other people. The first time she met him, he'd practically accused her of killing her grandmother. Now this. If a person believed other people solved their problems by killing someone, she could see how he might have jumped to the conclusion that she'd pushed Grannie down the steps to get her legacy. But this. What possible motive could he think Reed had for killing Bernie Lyons?

She glanced at Scott. "What happened to Bernie?"

"No idea. The sheriff didn't say."

They reached the Catholic Church at the bottom of the hill. Marty stopped, but traffic was light. Most of the shops had closed for the day. A few restaurants were still open, but by now the tourists were headed for Sedona or Flagstaff. She turned right. Less than a block away, just beyond the old concrete amphitheater, she found a parking place two doors from the sheriff's office. No sign of Paul's SUV. Worse, the office looked closed.

Scott went straight to the bottom line. "What if they've already gone to Juvie?"

"Let's don't assume the worst until we know for sure." Marty opened her door and got out.

Scott ran ahead. Marty watched as he knocked on the door and then tried to turn the knob. As she reached the office, he turned. "No one's here."

Marty nodded. Now what?

Scott had his phone out. He punched in a number and then held the phone to his ear. She could hear the rings and then the voicemail greeting. "Dad! Where are you? Call me back. Please!"

Marty moved around him and looked at the glass door. A number for normal business hours, but no alternative for after hours—just instructions to call 9-1-1 in case of emergency. Taking out her own cell, she punched in the normal hours number. Surely Larry would know they were worried about Reed. "Come on," she muttered. "Pick up." It didn't even ring, went straight to an announcement that repeated the information on the door.

"What do we do?" Scott's voice was tight. "We have to find Reed."

"Your dad knows Larry better than I do. He'll know what to do."

"There's no telling where Dad is! He must have left his phone somewhere. He used to do that when Mom was alive. After she died, he was sure to keep it with him in case I needed him." He looked at Marty. "I guess he feels like he's got you as backup now. He probably just forgot. It's probably in his office or in his briefcase. No telling where he is. Maybe in a meeting."

Marty took a deep breath. If Scott was right, she was on her own. She decided to take the plunge. "Where is Juvie?"

"Prescott. The jail is closer. It's in Camp Verde. What if the sheriff took Reed to jail? He's almost eighteen."

That would be like Larry. Take the easiest way out. Besides it would scare Reed even more than he already was. She took a deep breath. "Come on. We'll go to the jail. Call your dad again and ask him to meet us there ASAP."

The sun was low in a blazing western sky as they headed down the switchbacks. Marty braked for the first hairpin turn. "I know how to get to Camp Verde, but where's the jail?"

"I'll Google it." After a minute he said, "After the turn onto 260, it's nine miles. You turn right on Cherry Creek Road and then right again on Commonwealth. It says no one under twenty-one is allowed on the campus."

"You're certainly not twenty-one. When we get to the gas station at the bottom of the mountain, I'll turn around and take you home. Then I'll go. Surely by then your dad will get the message."

Scott shook his head. "No way. Now that I look at the directions I remember. I know exactly where the jail is. It's by the Out of Africa Wildlife Park. You pass the turnoff for the jail before you get to the Park. I guess I just sort of ignored the jail. It's set back from the road."

"You've been to the Wildlife Park?"

"Mom and Dad took me every summer when I was a kid. Last spring, the church youth group went. One of the seniors has a part-time job there, and he got us passes. You can drop me off. I'll walk over there. When you're done, you or Dad can come get me."

They rounded the last switchback. The gas station wasn't

far. Marty slowed. "You're sure you don't want me to take you home? It could be a long wait."

"I don't care. If they close the park, I'll find a place to sit and wait. I have to know what's happening to Reed!"

Marty nodded, ignored the knot in her stomach. Not only did she have to do this, she had to do it alone. Not that it was right to think that Scott would help her. He would just have been a familiar face. And it would have reassured Reed.

But there was no use in wishing for what couldn't be. They reached the bottom of the hill. She stopped at the sign and then turned right. She needed to focus to the meeting ahead. "Scott, tell me exactly what happened with the sheriff again. Try to remember everything."

Scott took a deep breath. "It was crazy! Reed and I were in the parking lot at the Well, headed for his motorcycle to go home. The sheriff pulled up. He couldn't come in because the gate was already down. He got out of his car and told Reed he was taking him in for questioning in Bernie's death."

"What did Reed do?"

"Nothing. I think he was in shock. He just stared at the sheriff."

"Was Reed cooperative?" Which in Larry Winston's vocabulary meant, "Did he grovel?" Maybe Reed had been scared enough.

"Until the sheriff called him *B.T.* That made him mad."

Marty suppressed a groan. Reed had a temper, and that old nickname was a trigger. Reed was working on his anger, but it was still there, simmering just below the surface. Not that she blamed him. She and Paul—and Scott—were all doing their best, but it was unimaginable that a father would just walk out, even an abusive father. "Did Reed yell at the sheriff?"

"Nah. He clammed up. It was like he just froze. Before I found out his dad beat him, if I ever asked anything about how things were going at home, he used to freeze like that. I learned not to ask."

"How did you find out what was going on at home?"

"I sort of figured it out. The first time I saw him with a black eye, I asked him who did it. He told me it was some kid he didn't know. Gave me a story about driving too close behind the guy on his motorcycle. I thought it was fishy, but I let it go."

"But eventually you found out the truth."

"Yeah. About the third time I asked him what happened, he just said to forget it. That's when I knew he'd lied to me before. His dad was the only one who he'd protect like that." Scott looked out the window. "One day he showed up with a backpack and a bunch of bruises. I worked up my courage and confronted him. He admitted he was running away. I couldn't just let him do that. So, I asked Dad, and he said B.T.—Reed—could have our guest room as long as he stayed in school. You remember when he moved in with me and dad. You guys were dating."

Marty remembered. Though she'd loved Paul for his big heart when he took in the abused boy, his action scared her so badly she almost walked away from the relationship. She hadn't felt prepared for teenage boys. She'd been right. It suddenly occurred to her that she had no idea what she was walking into at a jail. "Have you ever been to a jail, Scott?"

"Who me—studious, rule-abiding rock collector?"

Marty shot him a quick grin. "I didn't mean, 'Have you ever been arrested?' I'm pretty sure your dad would have told me that kind of nefarious history before we got married, and I took you on as a ..." She hesitated. *Stepson* sounded so cold.

"*Son* is okay," Scott murmured.

"Okay. Anyway, he never told me anything like that."

"I've never even been inside a juvenile detention center, much less a jail." Scott sounded defensive.

"I didn't mean to imply that you had. I was just wondering. I don't know what to expect."

"No clue. Do you mind if I put in my earphones and listen to some music?"

"No. Of course not." She'd done it now. Made things worse by transferring her fright to Scott. This was exactly what she'd been afraid of. She'd told Paul she didn't know anything about teenagers. This was a perfect example. She'd never been inside a jail either. She shouldn't have asked Scott about it.

The nine miles passed too quickly. She followed the signs to the Out of Africa Wildlife Park, noting where the turn was for the jail. No wonder Scott hadn't paid much attention to it. It was set back from the road, a compound of square buildings painted mud brown.

Scott took off his headphones. "You and Dad have got to get him out of there. He'll go nuts if he has to spend the night. He spent the night in Juvie one time in L.A., and he said it was the worst night of his life."

With a jolt, Marty realized she'd never taken the time to actually sit down and ask Reed about his life before coming to them. Not that it would have been easy. The boy seemed to freeze whenever anything came up about his earlier life. Still, that didn't excuse her. She should have pushed. She wondered if he'd told Paul anything.

They reached the entrance to the Park. Scott said, "Just let me out here. No need for you to go in."

"What about money? You'll have to pay an entrance fee. And you might want a snack."

Scott gave her a disgusted look. "I'm not a little kid, Mom *Too*. I've got enough money."

The name he'd chosen for her had turned out to be a mixed blessing. Depending on the way he said "Too," she could always tell when she was over the line. Obviously, she'd made another mistake with him. "I didn't mean ..."

Scott leaned over and gave her a quick kiss on the cheek. "I know. You're getting used to this whole teenager thing. I'm just jumpy. I wish I could go in there with you."

She nodded, wishing whole-heartedly he could go with her too. "Any word from your dad?" It was a useless hope. Paul would have called. But Scott checked his phone for text messages. "*Nada*. Maybe he's already over there."

Before she could respond, Scott was out of the vehicle. "See you soon."

She nodded, hoping it would be true. As he headed through the wide entrance under the archway, she could hear the trumpeting of an elephant. Africa would be a great place to be right now. Taking a deep breath, she turned the car around and headed to the jail.

Up close it was even more forbidding than it had been from the road. Not a window anywhere. An automatic arm that said "Stop" kept her from entering the parking lot until she took a ticket. She wondered if they would charge her for parking. Emblazoned on the side of the building straight ahead were the words "Yavapai County Detention Center." Just to the right, a glass door was labeled with the words "Jail lobby." She wished they could make up their minds. Was it a detention center or a jail? What was the difference anyway?

She scanned the parking lot for any sign of Paul's SUV, but it wasn't there. Parking her pickup, she grabbed her purse and got out. From habit she locked the doors, though surely no one would steal a car from the jail parking lot. Unless they were trying to make a getaway. Absurd. Marty stopped and took a deep breath. Then another. And another. She had to be calm, or at least appear calm. And confident. Like she knew what she was doing. She was here to take her foster son home. He wasn't eighteen, which meant he was a minor. She didn't know the laws about such things, but she was about to find out.

Setting her jaw, she marched toward the glass door. She could do this. So what if it was new? Paul had swept her into one new experience after another—marriage, instant motherhood, foster parenting, building a house. She'd been fine every time. Paul might not be here right now, but he would come. For now, she would handle the situation. She pulled open the door and stepped into the lobby. A standard-issue waiting room, receptionist—or whatever title they used for the stony-face woman in a police uniform sitting behind a counter with a sign-in pad. Chairs lined up along one wall. Reed sat huddled in a corner, looking somehow defiant and miserable all at the same time. Her heart went out to him, and now she knew she could do this. She signed her name and time in and looked at the woman.

"My name is Marty Russell," she said in her most confident voice. "I'm Reed Harper's foster mother, and I'm here to take him home."

"Not so fast, Missy."

Marty turned to see Larry Winston come through a door that no doubt led to offices. How did he know she was here? Cameras, probably. "My name isn't *Missy*, Sheriff Winston. As you well know. You can call me Mrs. Russell."

He raised an eyebrow and looked down at her. He wasn't as tall as Paul, but he was still several inches taller than she was. "All right, Mrs. Russell, slow down. For starters, you don't even seem to know the name of your so-called foster son. It's Lloyd Harper, Jr."

Marty shook her head. "Read the agreement papers, Sheriff. They say, 'Lloyd Harper, Jr. aka Reed Harper.' It's all perfectly legal for a person to choose a name. Soon enough, we'll get to the courthouse and get it changed officially. I'm here to take Reed home. I don't know what you think he's done, but he's a minor, and this isn't the Juvenile Detention Center. You have no right to detain him here." She had no idea if that was true or not, but it sounded good enough. If Larry didn't back down, she would get a lawyer. Brad Lockridge had faced him down when he'd been determined to take her in on a ridiculous charge of murdering her grandmother.

Larry snorted. "If you really knew the law, you'd know a seventeen-year-old can be held and tried as an adult on a serious enough charge."

"Just what is this serious charge?"

"At the least it's criminal negligence in the death of Bernie Lyons. At the worst murder. In between, accidental death. Lots of ways to interpret the evidence."

Marty knew she was out of her depth now. "I demand a lawyer. We have the right to advice."

Larry laughed, a humorless sound. "No need. Junior has already demanded one. He'll be here once we track him down."

Now Marty's temper was fraying. The man was playing games. Where was Paul? He could always handle Larry.

As if in answer to her question, the lobby door opened, and Paul walked in. He caught her eye and gave her a reassuring smile that somehow communicated pride in her. She took a deep breath, thankful the ability they seemed to have to read each other's minds was still intact.

He turned his attention to the sheriff. "What's going on, Larry?" His tone was calm, curious even, not in the least combative.

It was the right chord to strike. Larry relaxed. "We've got a complicated problem. Unfortunately, Lloyd Junior has put us at a standstill by demanding a lawyer. Unfortunately, everybody seems to be at supper."

Paul ignored the outrageous statement as if it were totally

reasonable. "Is there an office where you and I and Reed might talk for a few minutes? Maybe we can find another way out."

The receptionist spoke, surprising Marty. The stony expression had relaxed just enough that the lines around her mouth had disappeared. "You can have Conference Room Three. Down the hall to the right."

Paul put his hand on Reed's shoulder. "Good. Come on, son."

Marty saw Reed sit up straighter. Paul had that effect on people. Somehow his large, calm presence communicated a way through even the tightest line of scrimmage. Before she could ask, he came to her. Giving her a quick kiss on the cheek, he whispered, "Sorry. Talk later." Aloud, he said, "I picked up Scott and parked on the shoulder just outside the campus. You can take him on home. Start up the grill. I'm pretty sure, we'll be able to work something out and be home in time to do the burgers."

She wanted to throw her arms around his neck and pull his face down next to hers and give him a real kiss. From the wink he gave her, she thought he probably knew what was in her mind. Instead, she said, "Sure thing." Catching Reed's eye, she said, "See you soon."

"It might not be that easy," the sheriff grumbled.

But Marty knew he was already giving in. As she started for the door, the receptionist said, "If you would, sign out, ma'am."

Marty nodded. As she paid for parking, the door closed behind the sheriff, Reed, and Paul.

"Good luck, Mrs. Russell."

Startled, Marty looked up into a smiling face. "Thanks."

"Larry can be a real pain sometimes. He's not a mean man, just disappointed. But it looks like your husband knows how to handle him. It's going to be all right."

Marty studied the woman: brown hair, just starting to show gray at the hairline, friendly brown eyes, short well-manicured fingernails, gold wedding ring. Kate, according to the name plate on her desk. She was the first person she'd encountered who seemed to like the sheriff.

"Kate, may I ask you a question about Larry?"

"Ask away. I might answer, or I might not."

"Why does he hate Reed?"

"Reed?"

"Officially, he's Lloyd Harper, Jr. Reed is the name he chose for himself."

Recognition dawned. "It's not the kid as much as the name. Larry holds Lloyd Harper, Sr. responsible for his sister's death."

Marty went from puzzled to mystified.

"Larry's younger sister, Barbara, dated Lloyd, Sr. seriously for about six months. When he left without even saying good-bye, she was crushed. She tried calling his cell, but he blocked her. At first she was angry. But Barb wasn't one to stay mad. Her anger turned into depression. Six months after Lloyd left, she swallowed a bottle of sleeping pills. Larry found her body two days later."

Marty remembered the headline, *Sheriff's Sister Dead from Overdose.* "The newspaper article made it sound like an accident."

Kate nodded. "Larry made sure of that. But she left a note."

"How sad."

"It hasn't been a year yet. Larry refuses to go to a grief group. He's got all that bottled up inside. I don't think he's aware he's taking it out on the son."

"Could you point it out to him? Reed is doing everything he can to be different from the alcoholic father who beat him. He hates the name at least as much as Larry does—maybe more."

Kate gave Marty a sympathetic look. "I'll watch for an

opening, but Larry isn't one to take personal comments. He'll figure it out. Give him time."

Marty managed a smile, but time was something Reed didn't have.

PAUL OPENED the jail lobby door and held it for Reed. As they stepped out into the dark parking lot, Paul said, "I parked on Cherry Creek Road."

Reed didn't respond.

"Scott was with me. Since he's not twenty-one, he couldn't come onto the campus."

Voice tight, Reed said, "So Scott's waiting for us?"

Puzzled by Reed's evident reluctance to see Scott, Paul looked at the boy. Reed's whole body was tense from clenched fists to dragging feet. "No. I asked Marty to pick him up and take him home so they could get the grill going. I wanted a few minutes with you."

Reed stopped walking. Not looking at Paul he said, "You're mad at me."

Taking the boy gently by the shoulders, Paul turned Reed to him. "Of course not. Why on earth would you think I'd be angry?"

Reed didn't relax. "Okay. I used the wrong word. You're disappointed in me."

"No. I'm not disappointed either. What's behind this Reed? I'm on your side. No matter what's happened. You couldn't tell that by the way I convinced Larry Winston that he was jumping to ridiculous conclusions thinking you had anything to do with Bernie's death?"

"But you had to get me out of jail! Doesn't that make you ashamed of me?"

"It makes me curious—not angry or ashamed." He let the boy go and started walking again. Reed remained silent until they reached Commonwealth Road.

"What if I did something wrong and got sent to jail for it?"

Paul wondered if Reed knew more about Bernie's death than he'd admitted. But this wasn't the time to show anything but support. "You're my son, Reed. I'd still be on your side."

They turned onto Cherry Creek Road and headed for the SUV. As Paul clicked the button to unlock the doors, Reed said, "I'm not your son, Dr. Russell. I'm Lloyd Harper's son. You gave me a place to live when I ran away from Lloyd because you're a good man."

Keeping his disappointment out of his voice, Paul said, "All right then, you're my nephew. We decided that when we were looking for what you would call me."

Reed shook his head. "No, sir. I'm not part of your family. I'm just a friend of Scott's."

Paul didn't reply, glad he had a couple of minutes to move around the front of the SUV, get in, and put the key into the ignition. He had no idea what was going on, but this was a serious setback. Before he started the engine, he turned on the inside light and looked at Reed. Teeth clenched and arms crossed, the boy stared straight ahead. Paul touched his shoulder gently. "Look at me, Reed."

He had to wait, but finally the boy turned just enough to look at him, though he still wouldn't meet Paul's eyes. "We've been down this road. Remember what I told you? We're all God's children, which makes me and your birth father brothers. That makes me your uncle. One day, if you'd like, Marty and I want to adopt you. That would make you our son."

The statement clearly startled Reed. He unfolded his arms and stared at Paul. "You pick me up from the jail and offer to adopt me?"

"Whenever you're ready, say the word." Paul wanted to pull the boy into a hug but decided it wasn't the right time. He was on Reed's side, but he needed to know what that side was.

Paul started the engine. Keeping his voice gentle, he said, "I know Bernie was your friend. When did you find out he had died?"

Reed looked out his window even though it was too dark to see anything. "When the sheriff arrested me to take me in for questioning."

Paul's gut told him Reed wasn't telling him the truth, but instead of confronting the issue, he said, "Larry told me a neighbor saw you at Bernie's the day before anyone discovered Bernie had died. He told me the coroner is guessing Bernie died the day before he was found. It was a leap, but the sheriff claims that puts you at what he calls 'the scene of the crime' at the right time."

"Nobody killed Bernie. It was an accident."

Paul accepted the statement without pointing out that the opinion implied previous knowledge of his friend's death. "What makes you think that?"

Reed hesitated—realizing his own slip? "The sheriff said they found Bernie in the doorway of his study. There's a difference in the height of that room and the hall. I saw Bernie trip on it more than once. If he fell backwards and hit his head on the wood stove, the fall might have killed him. I kept telling him to fix that. I offered to bring some lumber from the hardware store and fix it for him ..."

Reed broke off, and Paul was sure he was fighting tears. Whatever had happened and whatever Reed knew, the boy was innocent of any part in the old man's death. Paul was certain of that.

He waited a minute to give Reed a chance to regain control.

Then he said, "What were you doing at Bernie's that afternoon?"

"I went by to pick up a family diary Bernie offered to loan me so I could get a job with the Seven Cities Adventure Tours."

Paul glanced at Reed, but the boy was staring out at the night again. "I didn't know you were looking for a job. What happened at the hardware store?"

"Nothing. I need a second job."

"For?"

"So I can go to the University of Virginia. I haven't got the grades for a scholarship, and it's expensive. I looked online."

It was an evening for surprises. Paul knew Reed was determined to go to a four-year college, but this was the first he'd heard about his alma mater. "Why UVA? If you go to Northern Arizona or Arizona State, you get in-state tuition. That would save quite a bit."

Reed turned to look at him. "I thought you knew that's where I want to go. You went there, and you wound up as a university professor. I want to be someone when I grow up, Uncle Paul." He paused, looked back out the window, and muttered, "Not like my loser father."

Paul thought about that. Layer on layer to unpack. He decided Reed needed to know a little more about his path to UVA. "UVA wasn't my first choice for school."

"You're kidding, right? I thought that was your dream school."

Paul turned off Highway 260 onto 89A. "Nope. I wanted to go to UCLA because it has a great history department and because it's in California. I'd never been west of the Mississippi, and I was hungry to see the West. My father was a sportswriter who wanted me to follow in his footsteps. He picked out the University of Missouri at Columbia for me. The University of Virginia never entered our conversations."

Reed turned away from the window. "What changed your mind?"

Paul stopped at the stop sign at the bottom of the switchbacks. "I didn't change my mind. My circumstances changed."

Paul drove the steady incline in silence. As they started up the switchbacks, he said, "A few days before Christmas my senior year of high school my dad was killed in a hit-and-run. My mother was born with a heart defect that kept her from working, so when Dad died, our finances took a serious hit. An out-of-state-school was out of the question, and UVA had offered me a football scholarship. I hadn't wanted to take it because I was pretty well done with football, but suddenly it was my best chance to go to college."

They topped the last switchback. "I could live at home to take care of my mother and save a bunch of money at the same time. It still wasn't quite enough, so I got a work-study grant to make up the difference."

"Couldn't you have gotten a football scholarship and a work-study grant at UCLA?"

Paul laughed. "Nope. I was a local boy, good enough to play for the home team but not in the league of UCLA."

"Tough luck."

"Life hands out tough breaks no matter who you are. No one escapes. At least not permanently."

They drove through the quiet, dark town in silence. As he made the last turn toward their house, Paul said, "You can go to college anywhere and still make good career choices."

This was a case of do-as-I-say, not do-as-I-did. Teaching at a university hadn't turned out to be a good fit for him. He'd wasted a good bit of time and money getting a doctorate he didn't need for the career path that fit him better. But Paul didn't point that out—another conversation for another time.

"You can do what I did, Reed. Start out at Yavapai and live at home, keep working at the hardware store. After you've got your two years of basic classes behind you and some money saved up, you can go to NAU or ASU or U of A and major in whatever you've decided on. If you work hard at Yavapai and at whichever Arizona four-year school you choose, you can have your grades up so you can get a teaching assistantship wherever you want to go for grad school. If you still want to go to UVA, you'll be able to do it. Part-time teaching will pay for your tuition."

Paul opened the garage door with the remote, pulled into the garage, and turned off the motor.

In the sudden silence, Reed said, "I still want to start at UVA like you did." Opening his door, he got out.

Paul sat in the car, feeling like he'd flunked "serious conversation lab" with Reed. Not only had he not gotten through on the college issue, but he also hadn't found out everything Reed knew about Bernie's death. He couldn't put his finger on what Reed wasn't telling him. But he was holding something back. Paul was sure of it.

10

S cott got up from the picnic table. "Great burgers, M2. Is it okay if I take one up to Reed?"

She was looking at his dad. For a minute he thought she hadn't even heard him. He was about to repeat the question when she shifted her gaze. "Sure. Promise him we're going to figure this out together."

Lifting the lid of the grill to retrieve the last burger, he placed it on a paper plate and went about fixing the bun the way Reed liked it—no ketchup, heavy on the mustard, lettuce and pickles, but no tomato. As Scott turned to go, his dad said, "Tell him we want to have a family meeting in the morning before you two head off to work. We're a family. We'll deal with this together."

A family meeting ... Scott mulled that over in his mind. The last time—the only time—they'd had a family meeting was when the four of them decided his dad and M2 should apply for legal foster parent status. He took the stairs up to the huge loft two at a time. Like the night before, Reed's door was closed.

Placing the soda on the floor and balancing the paper plate in one hand, Scott knocked twice and then opened the door.

"I've got your burger. Fixed just like you like it."

Reed was lying on his bed staring at the ceiling. Without turning his head, he said, "I'm not hungry."

Scott retrieved the soda and went in. Closing the door with his foot, he went to the desk and put the food on top of Reed's closed sketch pad. Straddling the desk chair backwards, he said, "We're all on your side. You don't have to hide up here."

"I know."

"You're not acting like it."

Reed sat up and swung his legs over the side of the bed. "What do you know about how I should act after practically being locked up in jail? You ever been hauled around in the back of a cop car?"

Scott was so surprised at the fury in Reed's voice, he didn't take it personally. "Hey, bro! I come in peace. You don't have to yell." He held out the soda.

Reed stared at it, and Scott wondered if he was going to refuse to take it. Finally, the older boy sighed and took it. Popping the top, he took a long drink. "I'm tired, Scott. It's not much fun being treated like a murderer."

"Why did the sheriff accuse you of killing Bernie? He was your friend."

Reed took another drink. "Go away, Scott. I don't want to talk about it."

Scott studied foster brother. What was he supposed to do? He knew Reed was in big trouble, and he wanted to help. But he couldn't do anything if he didn't even know what was going on. "Why did the sheriff take you to the jail?"

"Larry Winston hates my father, so he hates me. I knew Bernie. That's enough for him."

"Come on, Reed. I know Larry hates your dad, but he had some reason."

"Some old biddy said she heard me roaring up the hill—those were her words 'roaring up the hill.' All I did was drive up there after work. It's not like cars are quiet. Motorcycles just have a different sound."

"So, the sheriff thinks Bernie was killed yesterday afternoon?"

Reed drained the soda can and crushed it in his hand. "Like I told your dad, no one killed Bernie. He died from an accident."

"How do you know?"

"Because the sheriff told me they found him in the doorway of the study. That floor's uneven. I've been after Bernie for the last three months to let me level it so this wouldn't happen. I've seen him almost fall there. Now it's happened."

"You sound like you know that for sure."

Reed aimed his can at the trash can and tossed it. The can missed and clattered to the floor. "They don't know when Bernie died, but since I was the last one anyone saw going to his house and I'm Lloyd Harper's son, the sheriff is sure I must have killed Bernie."

"Why would you kill him?"

Reed put his face in his hands and bent double. He muttered something so low Scott couldn't make out what he was saying. All he heard for sure was *B.T.*

Scott sat down on the bed beside Reed. "What's your nickname got to do with it?"

"Go away, Scott. I don't want to talk about it."

"I'm not going to go away. You're my brother, and I'm on your side. No matter what. But I can't help if you don't level with me."

Reed sat up, wiped his eyes on his sleeve, and turned to

look at Scott. "If I tell you, you've got to promise me you won't tell your dad."

Scott stared at Reed. Whatever he was expecting to hear, this wasn't it. What should he do? He had never directly lied to his dad. Sure, he'd skipped pieces of the truth or changed the subject when he didn't want to level, but his dad usually got the truth out of him. He was Reed's brother, but he was Dad's son. Should he, could he, keep something Reed told him from Dad?

Reed broke eye contact, and Scott knew he had to decide. Right then. He took a deep breath. "I promise I won't tell Dad unless something happens that makes me think he has to know —but only to help you. I promise I won't tell him just to hurt you."

Reed turned his head and studied Scott so long Scott had to make himself maintain eye contact. Finally Reed said, "Fair enough."

"What's your bat tattoo got to do with it?"

"Not yet." Reed got up and went to his dresser. Opening the top drawer, he pulled out a rope bracelet. "You remember this?"

"Sure." It was the bracelet he'd made for Reed for Dad and M2's wedding.

"You still got the one I made you?"

"You bet."

"Go get it."

Scott nodded. "Back in a flash."

As he crossed to his own room, he knew what was in Reed's mind. They were going to repeat their promise to be brothers until they died. He took a deep breath. If this was what it meant to be a brother, he was in. The bracelet Reed had made for him was in the drawer of his desk. He pulled it out and went back to Reed's room. Everything was quiet down below. Dad and M2 were either downstairs in their room or on a walk.

Either way, it was just as well. He didn't think he and Reed needed to be interrupted right now. Whatever Reed's secret was, it wasn't something that was going to be that easy to keep to himself.

Reed was standing at his window, staring out at the side yard. Not much to see out there in the dark. He turned when he heard Scott close the door. "We put them back on," he said.

Scott complied. Guessing at the next step, he said, "Now we do our handshake."

Reed nodded and offered Scott his hand. In silence they repeated the secret handshake they had made up for the occasion. It was odd, feeling Reed's warm hand in his again. It felt harder than before. He wondered if his own did too. They'd both done a lot of physical labor in the year since the wedding.

Without needing a cue, together they both said, "We promise to be brothers until we die."

On an impulse, Scott grabbed Reed and gave him a rough hug. They both turned away at the same time. Scott swallowed hard. It would be stupid to cry. When he had the impulse under control, he straddled the desk chair again. Putting his arms across the back, he rested his chin on his arms. "Okay, brother. What's the story?"

Instead of returning to the bed and sitting down, Reed went back to the window. Looking out, he said, "I never told you why I got that tattoo."

When he didn't say anymore, Scott decided he had to say something. "I just figured some of your friends in L.A. dared you to go with them to get a tattoo, and you decided on a bat."

Reed turned to look at Scott. "We all got that bat tattoo. I was in a gang. That was our symbol."

A gang? Reed was such a loner Scott hadn't ever thought of him as the gang type. Still, he remembered the old Reed. B.T. had been into smoking pot. He'd even pushed it on Scott—and almost succeeded. But his dad ... Scott pushed away the memories.

"Did your gang do more than marijuana?"

Reed sat on the end of the bed, facing Scott. "Nah. We were just a bunch of unhappy junior high kids. I don't think we had a mother between us. A couple of the guys were living with their grandparents. A couple of them had fathers like mine. We were too young to get a license for a motorcycle, so we borrowed a few and rode after dark. That's why we called ourselves *The Bats*."

"I get why you want to leave that behind, but what's it got to do with the sheriff?"

Reed stood up again and went back to the window. Scott wondered if he should suggest they take a walk. He hated watching his brother act like a caged animal.

Before he could say anything, Reed turned to look at him again. "I left L.A. when I was thirteen, but The Bats stayed together. Somebody sent me a newspaper article a year ago— anonymously. It said The Bats was one of the gangs the cops were targeting." Reed sat back down on the bed, bent double, and put his head in his hands. In a voice so low Scott could barely hear him, he said, "They made killing a requirement for membership. If the sheriff knows that ..."

PAUL KNOCKED on the doorframe of Marty's workshop. He didn't like to interrupt her, but it was ten p.m., an hour after their agreed-upon time to quit working, even on deadline. She must not have heard his knock over the whine of the sander.

"Marty! "Still no response. Not wanting to scare her, he stood for a minute and watched. Her concentration was complete, and he wondered what she was thinking about as she moved the sander an inch at a time, working to reclaim the signed but badly damaged Duncan Phyfe table she'd found in the back of Lou Springer's garage. Not Reed. They'd talked that over at the table after Scott took Reed his hamburger.

If he knew his Marty, she'd escaped to her workshop for a much-needed break from family business. She'd told him once she had fun imagining the original owners of pieces she was working on.

The Scottish cabinet maker, Paul knew, had worked in New York in the early 1800s, so the buyers would have been wealthy city dwellers. The drop leaf dining room table would seat eight or ten comfortably, so it would have belonged to a family. Possibly the family of a lawyer or a British landowner who had immigrated to the young nation had sat around that table.

Paul shook himself out of his reverie. "Marty!" Even though he was closer, she still didn't answer. He went to the wall and unplugged the sander.

Surprised, she turned. When she saw him standing there, plug in hand, instead of returning his smile he expected, she frowned. "I'm really busy, Paul. As you can see."

He nodded and offered the smile she hadn't given him. "You've lost track of time, sweetheart. It's ten—past quitting time."

"I know what time it is. Priscilla Edwards wants this table, and I need to get it finished."

"I'm sure Priscilla wouldn't want you to wear yourself out." Closing the distance

between them, Paul dropped his hands on her shoulders and started to massage the tight muscles. "It's been a long day, and with everything that happened with Reed we missed our afternoon check-in."

Before he could say more, Marty pulled away. "Long and

busy, and it's not over. I need to finish this side before I quit for the day, even if that means this day ends after midnight." Taking the plug from him, she started toward the wall.

Her flat refusal to stop work surprised Paul as much as her rejection of the shoulder rub had. "It's a big table, Mart. You're not going finish it today. Come sit on the swing with me. I have a lot to tell you."

She started to shake her head, but Paul didn't intend to take *no* for an answer. At least not for something as routine as a piece of furniture she wanted to finish. Grabbing her hand, he drew her toward the door. "That table will still be here tomorrow morning. But neither one of us will have time to talk then."

She sighed but came with him. When they were sitting side-by-side, he set the porch swing in motion with a gentle push with his foot. "I'm sure you can imagine how odd it felt spending the day with Jessie again. It's been so many years. I kept expecting to see Linda. Jessie is so much like Linda in so many ways."

"How did Jessie react to the reservation?"

Marty's question caught Paul off-guard. They'd had an understanding that whoever was talking had the floor until he or she got to a stopping place.

But he answered easily. "Understandably, Jessie isn't used to the rules of communication among Native Americans. She kept trying to hurry the conversation along. She had a single burning question she wanted answered, and I think she was frustrated waiting for Winola and George to finish their stories."

When Marty didn't reply, he went back to his own story. "Winola told us the Yavapai emergence story. I hadn't realized how important Montezuma Well is to their understanding of the universe. Winola said it's their place of emergence. Other than that, the story is much like the Hopi tale. It contains a drought, a flood, and a young woman who escapes to carry on the bloodline. The biggest difference is there is only one previous earth or land of the ancestors."

Paul could tell Marty wasn't interested. "What was your day like, sweetheart?"

"Not nearly as interesting as yours. I went to Priscilla's house to measure her dining room and then I came back here to work."

"How is Priscilla?"

"She's enjoying her summer. Recharging her batteries after a tough year. About what you'd expect from a high school teacher."

Okay. That was a non-starter. He tried again. "Did you go into the show room?"

"No showings scheduled today. No casual lookers. I spent a few minutes in my office.

Paul tried another focus. "How's Carly?"

"Fine."

Paul turned on the swing to study his wife. She looked tired. Maybe she'd stood too long sanding the table. Even with an electric tool, sanding damaged wood was hard work.

Since she didn't seem to want to talk, Paul went back to his own story. "I'm afraid Jessie was frustrated with our day, but I got some excellent information from Jackson's grandfather. It's overwhelming hearing the details of a disturbing oral history like the Yavapai have. Because George was repeating the memories of his grandparents rather than memories of stories, the impact of our bungling government was pretty overwhelming.

"Even now, the government has never acknowledged that the Yavapai and the Apache are two separate tribes with very different cultures. It's absurd that each tribe doesn't have its own reservation."

Marty didn't speak.

Paul soldiered on. "Unfortunately, George's memories don't go back as far as the Conquistadors."

"Still, I'm sure Jessie enjoyed the trip down memory lane with you."

Marty's sarcasm surprised Paul. No matter the issue, they always found a better way to communicate with each other.

Stung, he said, "Where on earth did that come from? Jessie and I are friends. Surely you don't object to two old friends reminiscing."

Marty stood up abruptly, causing the swing to jerk to a stop. "I need to close up the workshop."

She was angry. But instead of catching her hand and insisting that she tell him why as he normally would have done, Paul let her go. Jealousy was something he wasn't prepared to face—or forgive.

11

Reed cut the engine on the motorcycle.

Scott climbed off the back and handed Reed his helmet. "Thanks for the ride. I know this leaves you with a couple of hours to kill before you're due at work."

"No problem. I've got some things I'm going to do."

"Not in the park, right?"

"I promised you I wouldn't. Besides, I want to check out a few possible caves I found on the topo map."

"I wish I could go with you. You know how dangerous it is to go in alone."

"No worries. I don't have enough time this morning to check and see if the hills have caves." Reed dismounted, locked the motorcycle, and clipped the two helmets to his backpack. Keeping his voice as casual as he could, he said, "I think I'll go with you to where you're working and then go on up and say hi to Mina."

"I don't think Jackson is anyone you want to tangle with. He's older, and he's mean."

Reed kept walking. "I'm just going to say hi. Besides, I don't think he'll be at work with her."

"He comes over sometimes."

"I've had experience with mean dudes."

"Mina's older than you are."

"So? She can't be much more than a year or two older. I'm about to turn eighteen. I bet she's only nineteen. Even if she's twenty, so what? Girls date younger guys all the time."

"I thought you were just going to say hi."

Reed stopped at the top of the hill. "Don't worry about me. It's no big deal. You go on down where Dexter is and find out what he wants you to do today. I'll go on around." He pointed across the sunken lake. "There's Mina. Working alone. No big bad Jackson Henry."

"Whatever." Scott started down without as much as a 'See-you-later.'

Evidently, he'd made his brother mad, but Scott would get over it. He always did. Just to make sure Scott knew it really wasn't a deal, he said it. "See you later, bro."

Scott raised his hand in acknowledgment but didn't look back. Reed went on. The sky was a clear blue this morning, the kind that made a guy from smoggy L.A. want to whistle. He was still a good one hundred yards from the archaeology camp when Mina spotted him. She smiled, and by the time he got to her, he was having a tough time keeping that whistle inside. He didn't think he'd ever met anyone with hair that black or skin that exact warm color. Her black eyes sparkled, and her smile took his breath away. He knew she wasn't faking it. She was glad to see him. He'd been right to come. She didn't know anything about the Bats or Sheriff Winston or even Bernie.

As soon as he was in range, he called, "Morning, beautiful."

She looked up at the sky. "Another gorgeous summer morning."

She was teasing him. That was good. Reed took a deep breath. "That's not what I meant, and you know it."

She turned that smile on him. "Good morning, Reed. I'm glad you came over. What's up?"

The opportunity was suddenly there, and he didn't know what to do with it. He'd expected to make small talk first, maybe find out what her job was. He tried to get back on track. "I'm interested in your side of the dig. Scott told me all sorts of things about Dr. Dexter's search for the original path of the river. But you're up here with the ruins. What are you and Dr. Jensen trying to find out?"

She cocked her head. "You're sure that's what you want to talk about?"

Reed stiffened his resolve. He didn't want her to think all he'd come for was to ask her out. To prove his point, he slid his backpack off and dropped it. "I'm sure—if you have time. I know it's something about Coronado. I'm interested in his march through the Verde Valley for other reasons." That much was true, and it wasn't even small talk. They were the ones rumored to have left the doubloons.

Mina shrugged. "Okay. You can be my audience. I have to give an oral report to my advisor next week. Pull up a stool and prepare to listen to my talk. Feel free to stop me if something doesn't make sense."

Reed grabbed the camp stool she pointed at and opened it. He relaxed. This was more like it. Get her to realize he was interested in what she did, not just in her pretty—make that gorgeous—face.

"Good morning, Dr. Snow." She caught his eye and winked.

For some reason, he felt himself flush. Oh, brother. He was

trying to be cool and now he was blushing like a little kid. Thankfully, she ignored his reaction.

"I want to give you an overview of the work we're doing up at Montezuma Well. Dr. Jensen chose the site because it's the one dwelling that wasn't found by early trophy hunters who came to Montezuma Castle and did so much damage. She's hoping to unearth evidence that proves beyond a shadow of a doubt that Coronado made contact with inhabitants, thus beginning the name of this entire area."

"Hey!" Reed twisted toward the sound of the angry male voice.

Jackson Henry was on the path, almost even with the camp. "What's going on here? I thought I told you, punk. Mina's my girl!"

Reed stood, ready to say Mina could talk to anyone she wanted to. But before he could get the words out, Mina stepped between them.

"What is this?" roared another male voice, Dexter's. "It doesn't look like any work is going on here! Mina—explain!"

"Just a minute, Ken!" Dr. Jensen's sharp tone made Reed jump. He turned so quickly, he knocked over his backpack. As he knelt to pick it up, Dr. Jensen said, "Mina's my assistant, not yours."

Dexter said something, but Reed didn't hear. Two of Parnell's doubloons had tumbled out of his pack onto the ground. Horrified, he realized he must not have zipped the baggie all the way across. Without daring to look up, he scooped then into his hand and shoved them in the pocket where he'd stowed the baggie.

"She is," Dexter growled. "But Mr. Henry has no business here. Nor does this other boy."

Reed forced himself not to react. Taking his time putting

his arms through the straps, he made sure to keep the pack upright as he slid it on his back.

Her voice calm, Mina said, "It's all right, Dr. Dexter. Reed just stopped by to invite me to meet him for coffee tomorrow morning before work. I have no idea why Jackson is here."

Startled, Reed looked at Mina. Had she seen? But she didn't look at him. Maybe she was just trying to send Jackson a message.

"It's a free country!" Jackson shouted.

Dexter didn't respond. Just grabbed the young man by the arm and turned him toward the path. "Get out of here. Now! You don't have any legitimate reason to be here. Visit with your girlfriend when she's off work. I told you the next time I caught you on site I'd report you. Consider yourself reported. If you have any sense, you'll be long gone by the time I get to my walkie talkie and call the ranger."

Under the cover of the confrontation, Mina stepped closer. "Starbucks. Seven sharp," she hissed. "We have to talk."

MARTY CLIMBED the four steps to Sofia's gallery. The bright yellow sign on the door read, *In Studio. Ring.* Marty pushed the bell and waited. Sofia moved like a woman younger than her late seventies. People who didn't know guessed her to be in her sixties. Still, it would take a few minutes before she came to the door. Marty wondered if she should have come.

Why bother Sofia with marital problems that were probably all in her head? But she knew she'd worry until someone who had known Paul much longer than she had reassured her. She needed to stop worrying before she created a problem that didn't exist.

Sofia flung open the door, arms wide and face lit with her

warm smile. Marty returned the smile, knowing she'd made the right decision. Sofia would tell her there was nothing to worry about, she would believe her, and that would be the end of her doubts about Paul and Jessie.

"Come in, Amiga! I was trying to avoid taking a much-needed break, and here you are to rescue me from my workaholic sins."

Marty stepped into the hug. She smiled, looking down at the tiny woman. "Is working too much a sin? I think God wants us to work."

"Sí, sí. As long as we keep our priorities straight. Work was given to sustain us, not to define us. But never mind all that. Come and have a cup of warmed-over coffee and at least two cinnamon *ojarascas* with me."

"Don't tempt me."

"What else am I supposed to do? If you don't help me, I will eat them all myself."

As Marty was swept along in Sofia's welcome, she decided she didn't need to bring up her doubts. Sofia would tell her Paul was a dedicated Christian who would never look at another woman, even if she appeared from the past he'd lost when Linda died. But when she was seated at Sofia's minuscule table in her tiny kitchen, her hands around a warm pottery mug, Sofia said, "I think you have something on your mind, *amiga.*"

"What makes you think I wasn't at a lull in the shop and decided to come visit my adopted granny for no reason except that I miss her?"

"That certainly. But there's more. I can tell by the tiny crease between your eyes. It's deeper than usual. That means you've been thinking too much."

Marty smiled. "Guilty as charged. You know me too well."

"I'm learning that's what grannies are for. Tell me what is troubling you."

Marty wondered who else in the family had been to see Sofia, but with Sofia's attention focused on her, she plunged in. "It's Paul."

"Of course. One year into this marriage. It's bound to happen."

"What's bound to happen?"

"You run into something unexpected in the other person, something that makes you wonder if you knew this man you married as well as you thought you did, that makes you question your decision to promise to spend the rest of your life with him."

Marty laughed softly. "I thought you were never married."

"Once, many, many years ago. It's a story I don't often tell. Some day, but not today. Today is for your story. What have you discovered about my friend Paul Russell?"

"You're going to think I'm crazy."

Sofia shook her head.

"It's not so much that I wonder if I've made a mistake. I guess I'm afraid he thinks he made a mistake marrying me. I'm so much younger. I don't have any ties to his past. He loved Linda, and they were happy together. If not for that terrible car wreck, they would have been one of those couples who celebrate fifty or sixty years of marriage." She trailed off.

"That's true. It means Paul is a faithful man. Is that a surprise to you?"

"No, of course not. It's just that I'm so different from Linda."

"Yes. But Paul knew those things when he asked you to marry him. He is a man of many facets. He has the ability to be happy in many different ways. You saw that when he invited

Scott's troubled friend into his family. I think you were the one who was afraid of that change."

Marty smiled. "Guilty again. I thought I was too young to be a mother of an angry teenager. I was scared enough of Scott without throwing Reed into the mix."

"And now you're afraid you're too young to be a good wife to Paul. Is that it, *amiga?*"

Was that it? Or was it that she was afraid Jessie was a better match than she was, that Jessie could round out Paul's family in ways she couldn't? It didn't really matter. Either way led to the same conclusion. Marty sipped at her lukewarm coffee. She put down the mug. "It's Jessie."

"The archaeologist, Linda's friend?"

"Not just Linda's friend—Paul's friend. She was the one who introduced Paul and Linda—when I was in elementary school, as Scott pointed out."

Sofia reached for the coffee pot and refilled both their mugs. "I'm sure Scott didn't mean anything."

"Of course not, which is what makes his comment so devastating."

Sofia reached for a piece of the shortbread and pushed the plate toward Marty. "So, Paul and Jessie have college in common."

"And Linda."

"*Sí.* And Linda. But Paul didn't turn to Jessie when Linda died. I'm sure I would have known about that. Paul and I first became good friends after Linda's death. He never mentioned Jessie once. The first time I heard of her was when Jessie came to visit you."

"Paul wouldn't have turned to her then. Jessie was married when Linda died."

"And now she's not?"

"No. She was in the middle of a divorce when Paul and I got married. That's why she wasn't at our wedding."

Sofia picked up a blue and white pitcher shaped like a cat and poured milk into her coffee. "What's happened to worry you?"

Marty searched for a concrete example to explain her uneasiness. Nothing big, just an accumulation of moments—the interrupted phone call, the day with Jessie he'd been so enthusiastic about, the lack of interest whenever she talked about her work.

When the words came, they came in a rush. "I love Paul so much I don't think I could bear it if he felt like he'd made a mistake marrying me. Until Jessie came, I was the happiest I've ever been. I know he was happy too. We had lots to laugh about. He whistled and sang in the shower. But I'm afraid he doesn't feel the same way now. I know he misses Linda. How could he not? She was Scott's mother, and Scott looks like her. Before we were married, I told him I didn't expect him to pretend like Linda never existed.

"This is different. Jessie looks so much like Linda! And she keeps reminding him about thing the three of them did. He has to be thinking about what it would be like if Linda hadn't died.

"If he had married Jessie, his life would have had a loss, but it would have gone on much the same. Jessie could have recreated the life Paul and Linda dreamed of. When Paul married me, his life took a dramatic turn. Sometimes Paul looks with confusion. I don't have to remind him I'm not Linda anymore, but is that a good thing? Maybe he just quit commenting on how Linda used to do things. Maybe he still wishes for the way Linda built their life together."

Sofia's soft voice echoed her fears. "You're right, *amiga*. You're not Linda."

"That's the problem. Paul is missing Linda."

"Maybe so. Do you ever miss your grandmother Lois?"

"Practically every day. "

"Does that mean you wish Paul were Lois?"

"Of course not."

"Why not?"

Marty considered. "Because Paul adds something to my life that Granny Lois never could." She paused. "That's your point, isn't it, Sofia? I add something to Paul's life that Linda couldn't."

"Paul loves you, Marty. I see it in his eyes. I hear it in his voice."

"But what if love isn't enough?" There it was. That's what she was afraid of. She loved Paul. She knew he loved her. She could even accept that she offered Paul something Linda hadn't. Still, Jessie offered Paul a link to his past, a comfortable continuity to his experience. She, on the other hand, represented a challenge every day.

"Love *isn't* enough." Sophia picked up the worn Bible that always sat on her table, opened it, and began turning pages three-quarters of the way through. "I love the verse from first Corinthians thirteen that you and Paul chose for your family motto."

Marty didn't need to hear verse thirteen. She knew it by heart. "*Faith, hope, and love abide, these three But the greatest of these is love.* I do love Paul. You're saying I need to have faith in him and in our future together."

"Give him some time. That's what *abide* means in this verse. Faith, hope, and love last through time. My friend Paul is processing a lot right now, but I know him. He'll find his way through the confusion."

12

Paul switched off the small recorder he'd used when he and Jessie interviewed Jackson Henry's grandfather George. In spite of all he knew about the shameful treatment Native Americans had suffered at the hands of Anglo settlers, the old man's story upset him. He hadn't known how much the Yavapai had suffered or how close they had come to being wiped out.

From the beginning of outside contact in the 1500s with the Spanish, the tiny peace-loving tribe had been mistakenly identified with the Apache. By 1860, individual random killings of Yavapai had become governmental policy. With a shake of his head, Paul began jotting notes to get the chronology straight.

George Henry's account had started where his great-grandfather's stories began, after the Civil War. If the tribe's oral history went as far back as the Coronado like Jessie hoped, George didn't know about it. As far as Paul was concerned, 1871 was far enough. The contradiction in official policy toward the Yavapai couldn't have been clearer.

General Crook, the face of the U.S. Army in the Verde Valley, ordered his troops to kill on sight "all roving Apache," the mistaken identification of the Yavapai. That same year, President Grant established the Rio Verde Reservation for the Yavapai. The next year, 1872, troops fired on men, women, and children hiding in an ancestral cave above the Salt River. No soldiers were killed, but seventy-six Yavapai died.

Paul took his hands off the keyboard and massaged the back of his neck. The day before, he'd listened dispassionately to George's monotone recitation of the story. Now he wondered how he'd done it. He supposed sitting in a lawn chair on his host's handkerchief-sized patio, watching the afternoon monsoon clouds build up on the horizon had helped keep him grounded in the present.

This afternoon, reviewing the information in his closet-sized office gave him a headache. He needed two aspirin and a cup of coffee. Pushing back his desk chair, he headed for the minuscule kitchen that served as a break room for the administrative offices of the Jerome State Historic Park. Chipped mug in hand, Paul opened the door and stepped out onto the walled section of flat roof that provided access to outside to the second floor.

He was too restless to sit at the ancient Formica-topped table. Jorge's voice drifted up from the walkway below. Curious, he went to stand beside the waist-high wall.

"... a great audience," Jorge was saying. "You're on your own now. I hope you'll take a few minutes to look at the vehicles we have in the garage. As many of you will no doubt recognize, the garage was once a stable. Remember that when Douglas built his mansion overlooking the Little Daisy Mine, the mode of transportation for the wealthy was the horse and buggy."

Jorge was doing a great job. Paul made a mental note to

compliment him. He sounded relaxed and in command of his information. No wonder he'd had a great audience.

"Be sure to check out the ore cars displayed along the front walk. And before you leave the park, take a few minutes to stop and look at the old mineshaft."

Paul shifted his attention to a white panel truck headed to the eight-bedroom, seven-bath mansion that had once been the Little Daisy Hotel. He couldn't read the lettering on the side of the truck as it made its way up the long winding driveway, but he'd heard the new owners were redecorating. Whoever had bought the $6.2 million reclaimed structure had to have plenty of money to do whatever they wanted.

A different experience than when he and Linda had redecorated the house they bought while he was still in grad school. Jessie had come to help transform the run-down two-bedroom, one bath bungalow into a home. A picture of two young women, enough alike to be sisters, flashed into his mind —two blonde heads bent over a list of window measurements and a bolt of fabric Linda had picked up on sale.

Despite the fact that she'd never so much as threaded a needle, his wife was determined to make curtains on a borrowed sewing machine. When he insisted they could afford to buy curtains, she'd dismissed the idea. "We can't afford the ones I really want," she said. "I can do this. You just wait and see." And she had. Some kind of shiny fabric.

When it came time to hang the curtains, he put his foot through the orange crate he used as a stepstool. Jessie teased him about football players who run to fat when they stopped playing. He caught her in a headlock and demanded an apology. Linda's flash of jealousy caught him off guard. He reacted poorly.

"Andrew Joseph Walker—get off that wall!" A woman's shout from down below dumped Paul back into the present.

He swallowed the last of his cold coffee. What was he doing? He had work to do. Back in his office the computer had gone to sleep. The file he'd been working on was still open. He scanned what he'd written so far. He'd stopped at 1872.

The next date George Thomas talked about was 1875. That year three thousand men, women, children, and elders were forced to march one hundred eighty miles from the Rio Verde reservation to the San Carlos reservation. Fifteen hundred died on the trail. Two months later, President Grant rescinded the promise of the Rio Verde reservation, returning the land to the public domain available for sale.

Paul leaned back in his chair. No wonder Jackson was angry enough to reject his Anglo name and reach back into history for the name of an early Indian rights champion. After being captured by Anglo invaders when he was five years old, Wassaja became a doctor. Barring non-natives from the Montezuma Castle wouldn't balance the books, but after hearing the stories Jackson grew up with, Paul understood the young man's desire for acknowledgment of historical ownership.

The first few bars of a harpsichord minuet made him blink. Marty. Here he was off task again, and she was calling to chat. Usually he enjoyed their afternoon catch up, but today was different. The phone started to repeat the snatch of Mozart. Paul considered letting the call go to voicemail. But that tactic was sure to prompt another call in fifteen or twenty minutes. He would just have to keep it short today.

He picked up the phone. "Hello, Marty. What's up?"

"Just checking in. Four o'clock is our usual time. I've had quite a day."

"Excuse me, Paul." Another voice, Jorge's voice came from over his shoulder. "Can I talk to you for a minute?"

Paul put his feet on the floor and swiveled to see his friend standing in the doorway. "Come in. As soon as he said it, he felt guilty. He'd rather talk to Jorge than Marty. "Hang on a minute, buddy. Let me take care of this phone call."

He planned to say, "I'll have to call you back," but Marty was gone.

"If this is a bad time ..."

"No. It's fine." Paul put his phone face down on the desk and swiveled to face his friend. He felt awkward sitting while Jorge stood. "Should we go into the break room?"

"This will be quick. All I want is to ask you if it's okay for me to ask Jessie to dinner."

"It's a great idea. I imagine she's bored with nothing to do except work."

Jorge studied him. "You're sure."

"Of course. I can't promise she'll say *yes*, but I'm sure she'll appreciate the gesture."

"That's a given with any woman. I just want to make sure I'm not stepping on any toes."

"Stepping on toes?"

"You and Jessie obviously had a relationship in the past. I wondered if it was over."

"Jessie and I were friends, twenty years ago. We're still friends. We dated casually before I met Linda, but we were never romantically involved."

"Okay. Whatever you say."

Paul could tell Jorge wasn't convinced, but he didn't want to argue. "She likes fancy restaurants. I'm guessing she'd love a night out in Sedona."

Jorge looked surprised. "I thought archaeologists didn't like to dress up. "

Paul grinned. "This one does. She hasn't always been an archaeologist."

"The Mariposa? Great food, spectacular views of the red rocks, and star-gazing."

"Perfect, but don't forget your wallet."

Paul started to turn back to his work, but Jorge made no move to leave.

After a moment, his friend said, "You're sure about this? The last thing I want is to stick my nose into your love life."

Paul felt the side of his neck grow warm. "It's nothing like that. I'm happily married to Marty. Jessie belongs to my past."

"I don't judge."

"Jessie was Linda's friend. I promise you, that's all there is to it. Go have a good time. Jessie can be a lot of fun." As soon as the words were out of his mouth, Paul wished he could take them back. He hoped Jorge didn't take them the wrong way.

When Jorge grinned, Paul's heart sank.

He considered what to say. But everything he thought of would make things worse.

"As long as it's over between you."

"It's over. I mean it never was." Paul wished his neck would quit making him look guilty. "Just go call her, man. I've got to get back to work."

Still grinning, Jorge said, "You got it." But he left.

Paul ran his hands through his hair. What on earth was going on? Marty was mad enough to hang up on him, and Jorge thought he had to ask permission to invite Jessie to dinner. Jessie reminded him of Linda. That's all there was to it. Even as he moved the mouse to wake up the computer, he wondered. Was looking back with Jessie playing with fire?

13

Thursday

Reed wanted to take off his helmet as he followed 260 toward the Days Inn exit off I-17. Whenever he was nervous, feeling the wind in his hair reassured him that he was free and could exit any situation he didn't like. But he'd promised Uncle Paul never to ride without a helmet. He was determined his word would be good, even when no one was there to see it.

Across the freeway a statue of Kokopelli, the flute player of the ancient petroglyphs, beckoned to him. Almost as tall as the pole that held the Starbucks logo, the statue was touted to be the largest in the world. Reed didn't doubt it. Why the food plaza that surrounded Starbucks chose Kokopelli to draw customers was a mystery. The restaurants weren't on the Yavapai-Apache reservation, though they were close by. Of course, tourists coming from Phoenix would likely never have seen such a symbol before.

Reed shook off the nervous speculation. He should focus on Mina. He was more nervous than he should be. After all, she was the one who had initiated the coffee, spelling out the time and place—and publicly too. It wasn't like they were sneaking around behind Jackson's back. At first, he'd been thrilled. Then as he considered it, he wondered if Mina were using him to teach Jackson or Wassaja or whatever his name was that he didn't own her. Their relationship seemed pretty complicated, more intense on his side than on hers. But even if that was her motive, what did it matter? It wasn't like he was ready to ask her to marry him or anything.

All he wanted was to spend time with a beautiful girl who didn't know anything about his past. But that was getting complicate. What if she heard the sheriff had questioned him regarding Bernie's death? But why would she? Bernie wasn't exactly a celebrity, and his death was an accident, pure and simple. Why Sheriff Winston wanted to blow it into murder puzzled Reed. He wasn't surprised at being picked on, but why a murder? Maybe he wanted to make a big splash—a little cop in a tiny town frustrated at his anonymity.

He followed the exit road past Denny's to the small strip mall where Starbucks was the first store. A line of cars at the drive-thru window told him 7:00 a.m. was a prime time for coffee and snacks. As he cut the engine on his motorcycle, he wondered if they would even find a table. Locking his motorcycle and taking his helmet and backpack with him, Reed opened the glass door and stepped into the air-conditioning. Even this early in the day, it was welcome. Things had been so dry this summer. The monsoons should have started by now, but so far not a drop of rain.

He spotted Mina at the end of a long bench that served as the back for a row of little tables. Not exactly booths, but the same idea. A painting of a Starbucks coffee shop surrounded with cactus in bloom hung on the wall behind the bench. Some artist's idea of what Arizona looked like, an artist who hadn't ever been in the state, no doubt.

Reminding himself Mina had taken the lead, Reed took a deep breath and did his best to look confident.

When he got close enough, he said, "Good morning, beautiful."

She rolled her eyes. "That sounds like something out of an old black and white movie."

He grinned and sat down in the chair across from her. "In case you can't tell, I don't date much. I don't have any idea what the cool kids say to gorgeous girls."

"'Hi there' will do for a start."

"Okay. Hi there, Mina. Thanks for meeting me."

She gave him a look he couldn't interpret. "Let's just say I have a few questions for you."

He wondered again if she'd seen the fake doubloons. But even if she had, would she know what they were? It wasn't like you learned about stuff like that in school.

"Let me get us some coffee, first." He stood up so fast, he almost turned his chair over. What was he going to tell her? He should have thought this possibility through more carefully, decided on how to explain. But he'd let his imagination run away with him, convinced himself she wanted to break up with Jackson and use him to do it. "What do you want to drink?"

"A tall latte." She reached for her bag and started to open it.

"On me. Do you want a pastry or something to go with it?"

She smiled, and he relaxed a little. She couldn't think he was a crook or something and give him a smile like that. Still, he had to think fast.

"You pick something. I'll split it with you."

He went to the counter and caught the eye of one of the three baristas wearing black tee-shirts, black jeans, and green aprons. The young man, probably about his age, pushed his black-rimmed glasses up on his nose. "What are you having?"

"Two tall lattes and one of those pastries."

"Raspberry or blueberry?"

Why not splurge? He had enough money. If he were going to date Mina, he'd have to start turning loose of a little of it. "One of each." As he waited, a plan came to him. He would take control of the conversation. Get her to talk about herself. Maybe she would forget about the fake coins or decide they didn't mean anything.

He exchanged bills for a cardboard tray, including a tip for the barista. About six steps and he was back at the table. As he handed Mina a latte, he said, "How did you get interested in archaeology?"

She looked surprised, but she answered. "Dr. Jessie made a presentation at Montezuma Castle Visitor Center about what she intended to accomplish with her dig. Jackson wanted to go because he wants to stop any digging on lands the Ones Who Went Before occupied. What she said about exploring the past to remember made sense to me."

Reed offered her the two pastries. "You choose."

She gave him that smile. "Let's split them."

"Good idea. You do the honors." As she cut them with the little plastic knife, he said, "Is that when you asked Dr. J if you could work with her?"

"It was." She put half of the blueberry on the raspberry plate and transferred the raspberry to the blueberry plate. "I cut. You choose now."

He winked. "Like five-year-old kids."

"My sister has me trained."

He took one of the plates and sampled the blueberry. It

melted in his mouth. No wonder the things were so expensive. "You have a little sister?"

Mina hesitated. When he looked up, he saw sad eyes. He had the sinking feeling he'd brought up a painful subject. "Listen. I'm nosy. You don't have to answer every question I ask."

She sighed and slid a bite of pastry on her fork. "My sister is two-years-older than I am, but she has Down Syndrome. She functions like a small child."

Reed felt like he'd stumbled and lost his balance. He'd never imagined something like that. Reed was quiet for a moment, trying to decide how to put what he was feeling into words. "It's not like that, though. For some reason I feel comfortable with you. I was just thinking how hard it would be to have a sister who never grew up. I've always wished for a brother or a sister, but I never stopped to think it might be hard."

She gave him a curious look. "I thought Scott was your brother."

Too late. He'd given himself away. And here he'd planned for her to think he was a normal dude. He shrugged. "I guess one family secret deserves another. Not that it's a secret. Scott is my foster brother. My family sort of went to pieces, and the Russells gave me a home. Scott and I were just friends until ..." He swallowed hard. He was not going to cry. The emotions snuck up on him at the worst times.

She reached across the table to touch his hand. "I don't know what happened to your family, but my family hasn't exactly been normal, and not just because of Janet's disability. My dad came back from Iraq pretty messed up. He drank a lot, and then one day he just didn't come home. We have no idea where he is. Mom doesn't even know whether he's alive or not."

"Oh man. That's tough." He took her hand in his and

held it, warm and soft. "My dad is a drinker too." He cleared his throat. What was he doing, telling her all the things he didn't want her to know about him? But he had started, he might as well finish it. "He got mean when he was drunk. My mom left when I was just a kid, six or seven. Then I moved out almost two years ago." He caught himself just in time. Instead of saying 'Lloyd left,' he said, "My dad left town a couple of months after I moved in with Scott and Uncle Paul."

"My dad was never mean. Just quiet. Except when he had a nightmare." Mina gave his hand a little squeeze, and then released it. "We'd better eat these goodies. What time do you have to be at work?"

Reed glanced at the hands of a clock set into the wall. A little after 8:00. "Not until ten. What about you?"

"I'm usually there by now, but Dr. J told me to enjoy my coffee. I think she likes your family. She went to college with your foster parents, didn't she?"

"Just Uncle Paul. His first wife, Scott's mom, died a few years ago. Aunt Marty is Uncle Paul's second wife. She's younger."

"I think Dr. J. said she went to college with *Paul and Linda.*"

"Yeah. Linda was Scott's mom."

They ate in silence for a few minutes, but it was a comfortable silence. Then Mina put down her fork and looked directly at him. "I've got a question I have to ask you, Reed."

Here it came. But maybe not. He held his breath and did his best to look curious.

"Where did you get gold doubloons?"

Man. That was the worst question she could ask. Should he tell her the truth? Reed almost kicked himself. He was trying to break his habit of lying for no good reason. It was one thing to lie to keep from getting hit. But it wasn't right to lie just because he wasn't comfortable with the truth. "I can explain."

"I hope so."

"I'm trying to save up enough money to go to college in a couple of years. My job at the hardware store doesn't pay enough."

She raised an eyebrow.

"Too much information?"

"For now. Just tell me where you got those coins."

"Have you heard of the Seven Cities Adventure Tours?"

"Just that they're coming to the area. My grandmother is a member of the tribal council. They're trying to decide whether to cooperate with the company and invite their tours to visit the reservation."

"Mr. Parnell is the head of the company. At least he's in charge of this region. He gave me a few replicas of gold doubloons to sort of use for a treasure hunt for his customers."

"So those weren't real."

Reed took a sip of his cold coffee. What he really wanted was a big glass of water. "I wish. If the ones he gave me were real, I'd be carrying around close to fifty thousand dollars."

She frowned. "That means you have at least ten fakes."

"Yeah."

"Where do you plan to hide them?" Her tone was icy.

He wanted to lie again, tell her they were all going in a bag in a cave off of 89A out of town on the way to Prescott. He fought the urge. "Not on any national land. Scott already made me promise that. I'm going to look for some caves or something. Nothing dangerous. Mr. Parnell doesn't want anyone to get hurt."

"Will they know they're looking for fakes, or are you using the legend that one of Coronado's men stashed a bag of doubloons around here to sell tickets?"

"Hey! It's not my idea. I'm just the hired help. I don't know what Mr. Parnell is thinking." That was a lie, but he couldn't help it. Evidently Mina was more worried about this scheme than Scott was. He didn't want her to think he was some kind of crook.

"Okay. That wasn't fair. But don't you realize that a scheme like that could ruin Dr. J's research? She's not really counting on the legend, but she's doing her best to prove there was interaction between the people who lived here with Coronado and his men. Just one gold doubloon in the right place would go a long way to proving her theory. If it turned out to be a fake ..."

"It would look like Dr. J planted it."

She nodded. "It would do more than stop this project. It would ruin her reputation."

REED CLOSED the driver's side door on Mina's Dodge pickup. As she put her key into the ignition, he touched her arm. "This was fun." *Fun* wasn't the right word for the intense conversation, but he didn't know what word to use. "I mean, can we do this again sometime?"

Pushing her shining black hair off her face, she turned to study him. "It was interesting, Reed. I'd like to get to know you better."

He felt a rush of pleasure, but before he had a chance to make a specific invitation, she added, "On one condition."

Before she could spell it out, he interrupted. "I promise. I'll find out what Mr. Parnell has planned, and I'll make sure it won't interfere with Dr. Jessie's research."

She studied him. "If what you're doing won't hurt her work, we can go out again."

"What about Jackson?" The words were out before he even thought. But it was just as well. She was putting her cards on the table. He had a right to do the same.

"Jackson is a friend who goes back to high school. He wants me to marry him, but I've known for a long time it would never work out between us. Every time I tried to pull back, he got so angry it wasn't worth the fight." She fingered the turquoise and silver beads at her neck. "Just because I don't love him doesn't mean I don't want to keep him as a friend." She touched Reed's arm. "Does that make sense?"

At her touch Reed's heart kicked up a notch. He nodded dumbly. Frustrated, he clenched his fist until his fingernails dug into his palm. The pain jolted him into speech. "I understand. I like this one girl at church as a friend. I know she wants me to ask her out, but I don't feel that way about her."

Mina gave him a shy smile. "Thanks for understanding. I care about Jackson, but I don't want to marry him. Until I met you, the confrontation just wasn't worth it." She crossed her arms over her chest. "I'll tell him tonight. I'll let him know I'm moving on."

Moving on—with him. Reed's heart kicked up a notch. He'd hoped, but he hadn't really thought it could happen. "Maybe we could grab a pizza tonight. I can tell you what I find out from Mr. Parnell." Not exactly a lie, but he would figure out what to say between now and then.

"That would be fun. But first I need to talk to Jackson. Text me so I'll have your number. I'll text you when I'm leaving."

"If you need more time to talk to him, we can go tomorrow night."

She shook her head. "Tonight. A date will give me an excuse to keep it short. He's had to know this day was coming."

Reed stepped back from the pickup. "See you soon!"

Tonight they could talk about something besides gold doubloons. More than anything, he wanted to get to know this girl.

Mina gave him the smile that made the world look a little bit brighter. Then she put the pickup in gear and backed out of the parking place.

He stood watching until she was disappeared into the traffic on the freeway heading north toward Montezuma Castle and Well. Then he put on his helmet, slid his arms into his backpack, and got on his motorcycle. He had an hour and a half before he had to be at the hardware store.

Reed decided to take the long way and go by the Cornville Road. It followed Oak Creek for a while, and this time of morning it should be deserted. The residents who worked in Flagstaff or Cottonwood would already have left for work. The ones who were retired or worked from home would be lingering over coffee. He had to think, and that road winding beside the vineyards on the rocky side and lush green pastures on the other, always helped him relax and see things from a different perspective. He had to decide what he was going to do about his job with Seven Cities.

He followed the access road that ran along the freeway a short distance and then turned west along the Cornville Road. As he'd hoped, the two-lane road was practically deserted. He was skirting the truth with Mina. He hadn't actually lied when he'd said he didn't know what Parnell was planning. He didn't know the details of the treasure hunt the boss had in mind, but he knew more than he'd let on.

For one thing, he knew for sure that Parnell was not planning to tell them they were looking for replicas of doubloons. He was hoping whoever found the bag of coins would be so pleased with the prize—whatever that was going to be—they'd forget about the small deception. By participating in the hoax, he was as bad as Parnell.

He could hardly get his head around the conversation with Mina. Instead of hiding behind the fact she didn't know him or his background to build a new relationship, he'd been more honest with her than he had been with anyone but the Russells —first Scott and then Uncle Paul and Aunt Marty. Of course, there was more she didn't know, but none of it would shock her. The rest was pretty much expected given what he'd told her.

And she hadn't pulled away. More than that, she'd shared her life with him. Been honest about a sister she could have kept hidden, told him about her struggle with her mother to get free, even her reason for wanting to be an archaeologist.

He passed a green open space where two proud chestnut horses grazed. Parnell was overestimating the gullibility of some of his "contestants" and underestimating how long it would take that large a coordinated group to find the stash—no matter how well-hidden. He would be caught in the crossfire, a fact which Parnell had to be aware of. Reed didn't want to be like Parnell. He wanted to be like Uncle Paul. He wanted the kind of relationship Uncle Paul and Aunt Marty had. They might not agree on every single detail of life, but they could talk about it. He couldn't imagine either of them doing something to hurt the other one the way he'd watched his father deliberately hurt his mother—and then him when Mom couldn't take anymore.

He sat at the junction of the Cornville Road and the connector road that fed onto 89A headed for Cottonwood. He knew what he had to do. It wasn't going to be easy. Maybe the hardest thing he'd done since shoving his things in his backpack and agreeing to let Scott take him to his house. Whatever it took, he had to get loose from Parnell and his shady scheme. He could still look for the real doubloons on his own. He wouldn't be getting paid for looking for them, and he wouldn't have the same amount of time, but that didn't matter. What mattered was being able to look Mina in the eyes and tell her he would have nothing to do with any fake doubloons. He might even take it another step further and tell Dr. J or Dr. D what Parnell was planning. They could stop him.

As the passed the bank in Cottonwood, the clock told him it was 8:45. He had enough time to get up to Jerome, hand over the doubloons to Parnell, and get to the hardware store on time. It would be tight, but that would keep the conversation short. The best way to do this anyway. Setting his jaw, he took the turn and headed for Jerome.

This early in the morning traffic was light, almost nonexistent, going up toward Jerome. Tourists would start flowing into town by 9:30, and by 10:00, when most of the shops opened, drivers would have a tough time finding a parking place. But for now, Reed made good time. He was in front of Spook Hall before he had figured out exactly what he was going to say. But that didn't matter. The main thing was to get the doubloons back to Parnell and retrieve Bernie's family journal. Uncle Paul could show it to Dr. J. Maybe the reference to the doubloon necklace would mean something to her and she could follow up on it.

He locked his motorcycle, shouldered his pack, and took the bag of doubloons out of the outside pocket. Before he could back out of his plan, he opened the outside door to Spook Hall and went in. The large gathering room was empty, and his sneakers squeaked as he crossed the wood floor. Maybe Parnell wasn't in yet. He couldn't remember the other guy's name, but what he had to say had to be said to Parnell, so it didn't matter. As he started down the hall, he could almost hear his dad shout, 'You stupid kid! You're throwing away good money for a girl who practically admitted she's using you to get rid of her boyfriend.'

Reed shook his head. He had to think of what Uncle Paul would say. Lloyd couldn't tell him what to do anymore. Uncle Paul would be ashamed to know he'd taken the doubloons in the first place, but he'd be proud of him for getting rid of them. A new idea struck Reed. Maybe Uncle Paul would want to look at Bernie's journal. It was sort of an oral history. Even if he didn't want it, he would know who would. Taking another deep breath, he sneezed. Suddenly he wanted to laugh. He was making a big deal out of nothing. He would just tell Parnell he'd decided he didn't want the job.

The door with the sign that said Seven Cities Adventure Tours was closed. He knocked, halfway expecting not to get an answer. But the answer came all too quickly. "Come in, Fred."

Parnell was there alone. He had a ledger open on the desk which he closed when he saw who it was. He frowned. "What are you doing here, kid? You're supposed to be out hiding the doubloons. They may not be real, but they cost me a pretty penny, and you'd better put them where people can find them."

Reed put the bag of coins on the desk. "I've decided I don't want the job. Here they are. I want Uncle Bernie's journal."

Parnell leaned back in his chair and looked up at Reed. "You already took the job. No backing out."

"No sir. I didn't sign a contract, and you haven't paid me anything. I thought about it, but it's not a good idea. There's a research project going on at Montezuma Well. I could get in trouble with the law for doing this job." Surely the man would understand that.

Parnell got to his feet. Not much taller than Reed but a lot heavier. His face turned an ugly shade of red, and Reed wondered if the man would hit him. "I'm telling you. You can't back out. How do I know you won't go and tell everyone my plan? You could ruin me in this town."

Reed took a step back. "I don't care about your company. I won't tell anyone because it would make me look bad. What you're doing isn't honest. There are your doubloons. Now give me my journal."

"Or what?"

"Or I'll go to the sheriff and tell him what you're doing and that you stole my journal." That was a bluff because the sheriff would want to know how he got the journal, but Parnell couldn't know that. Parnell looked him up and down as if trying to decide if he would do it or not.

"I'll do it!" Reed used the tone his father had used whenever he threatened Reed with a beating. He didn't want to face Sheriff Winston, but if he had to, he would. He held his breath.

After what seemed like an hour but was probably not even a minute, Parnell shrugged. "It's not like your journal is worth anything. Just a list of stuff. Who knows what that necklace really was?" He opened a bottom drawer of the desk and pulled out the journal. Reed reached for it.

"Not so fast, kid." Parnell dumped the coins on the desk.

They looked so real. What had Scott said? It would take acid or enough water to see if it would float or sink. He hadn't tried either of those tests. Maybe they were real. But that was ridiculous. Scott had told him each real gold doubloon would be worth at least $6,000.

Parnell spread them out, placing them in pairs. "Nine!" he roared. "I gave you ten! Where's the other one?

"I ... I don't know. It should be there." Reed stared stupidly at the coins. He hadn't taken them out of their bag. Then he remembered spilling them while Dexter yelled at Jackson. But he'd gotten them all. Hadn't he?

No one had had access to his pack. No one except Scott, but Scott would never take something of his.

Then he remembered. Mina at Starbucks. She'd been alone with his pack when he went for their coffees; she'd seen the doubloons when he spilled them. But she wouldn't have taken one—would she?

He lunged at Parnell. "I'll get it back!" Snatching the journal, he ran.

14

Paul looked in the open door of Marty's workshop. She was still working on the Duncan Phyfe table, but she had progressed to the other side. Even so, he knew she wouldn't hear his knock over the buzz of the electric sander. He shouted "Marty!" Because she was facing the door, he expected her to see him, but she didn't look up.

Was she ignoring him? Since Jessie's arrival, Marty had been tense. She'd pulled away from him when he tried to massage her shoulders. She'd missed their daily afternoon check-in. She'd even pretended to be asleep when he came to bed. He knew it was his fault. He'd wallowed in the past and let Jessie lure him into going out to the reservation without Marty.

The last conversation they'd had in this workshop hadn't ended well. He was sure she didn't want a repeat of that talk. Even so, it wasn't like Marty to ignore what was in front of her, even if it was difficult or unpleasant. He considered pulling out the plug as he had once before, but he wanted to avoid any action that would seem like repeat of that earlier scene. He waved his arms and shouted again, "Marty!"

This time, whether because of the movement or because she decided he wasn't going away, she looked up. She frowned, but she turned off the sander.

When she didn't greet him, he said, "Sorry to interrupt your work, but we need to talk—about Jessie."

"Now isn't a good time. I'm not at a good stopping place."

"Come on, Mart. Any place is as good as another with sanding. We need to have this conversation, unpleasant as it may be for both of us."

For a moment he thought she was going to refuse. Then she sighed. "I guess we might as well get it over with."

With a stab of guilt, he realized not only was she reluctant to discuss Jessie. She was dreading the conversation. He wanted to reassure her, but he decided it would be better stick to his prepared speech. "Come on, hon. Let's go out on the porch."

When they were sitting side by side on the swing, Paul took her hand. "I never meant to hurt you, Marty. It's just that Jessie reminds me of Linda. I'm sorry."

Instead of looking at him and saying, *Why?* or *I understand,* or even *How ridiculous,* she stared at the horizon. He decided to skip the part on silly sentimentality. "I want you to know how much you've added to my life. Mine and Scott's."

Still, she didn't look at him, just kept staring at the jagged blue line of the mountains in the distance. Needing a response, Paul turned her toward him.

Marty put her hands up to her face, but not before he saw the tears.

Taken off guard, Paul took her in his arms. Ridicule, anger, frustration—he'd been prepared for any of those reactions. He didn't know what to do with sorrow. Why did his gratitude make her cry?

Sobbing now, she leaned her head against his chest.

When her sobs finally stopped, he said, "I don't understand. Why are you crying?"

"Oh Paul! How can you ask me that? I thought you and I would be together until one of us died."

"We will be. I'm not going anywhere. I'm just being honest with you."

When silent tears started down her face again, he couldn't think of anything more to say. Unable to bear the sadness on her face, he kissed her.

When he let her go, she rested her head on his shoulder. He held her gently, waiting for her to explain.

In a minute, she took a deep breath and sat up. Taking his face in her hands, she said, "That's very noble of you, Paul, but I want you to be happy. I don't want you to stay with me out of guilt. If Jessie is a better fit for you and Scott ..." She broke off as he started to laugh.

He knew it was the wrong reaction. He tried his best to stop, but the outrage on her face made him laugh even harder. Part relief, part surprise—whatever he had expected her to say, this wasn't it.

"What's so funny?" she demanded.

"You, honey. You're so *not* Linda!"

"You don't have to rub it in!"

Her words stopped his laughter as completely as a slap would have. She truly didn't understand. On top of breaking her heart, she thought he was insulting her. "I need to start over," he said. "I've made a complete botch of what was supposed to be a heartfelt apology." He got to his feet and held out his hand. "Come with me. Maybe I can show you what I was trying to say."

He led her to the side of the house where the extra lumber they needed to finish the project was stacked. Putting his arm around her shoulders, he said, "I loved Linda deeply. She was a wonderful wife, and she gave me Scott."

She pulled away. "I get it, Paul!"

"No, you don't. You think you do because I'm still not explaining things right. Linda was wonderful, but she was sure of how our corner of the world should be. She wanted everything just so, and she was willing to work hard and contribute more than half to achieve her vision. But she wasn't flexible. She wouldn't have wanted to build a house ourselves. She'd have taken an extra job to make sure we could hire the builder she thought would deliver the best product. It would've been a lovely home, but it wouldn't have been this house.

"You're a different person than Linda was, Marty. When I said how much you've added to my life, I didn't mean that to be in the past. You add a new dimension—now. You'll add a new dimension in the future. Maybe it's your ability to see the possibilities of a broken-down antique and your willingness to tackle the job, no matter how difficult, that makes you able to take these huge surprises I keep springing on you. Sometimes I think you got a broken-down antique when you married me."

Marty studied him with a bemused expression. Then, shaking her head, she started to laugh.

"What?"

"You! How can you think that?"

"Jessie kept pointing out the age difference between us ..."

"She was putting me down, Paul! Not you."

Paul studied Marty. She was serious. His carefully planned speech was useless. Knowing she remembered their wedding with as much wonder as he did, he began to whistle *Ode to Joy*.

REED LOOKED AT HIS PHONE. Should he call Mina? She'd told him she'd call after she talked to Jackson, but it was nine o'clock. Surely it wouldn't take that long to tell him she just wanted to be friends. He'd expected to hear from her an hour ago. He wanted to tell her about giving the doubloons back to Parnell and ask her to look for the missing one. She could do it without arousing any suspicion. He couldn't do it because if he showed up again so soon, Dr. Dexter would send him packing, probably before he got around the rim to Dr. Jessie's camp.

The suspicion he didn't want to think about tugged at him. He sighed. What if Mina had taken it? He didn't think she'd squatted down as he scooped them up, but he'd been so rattled he wasn't totally sure. She could have leaned over and swiped one, especially if it had landed away from the main pile. Or she could have taken one from his pack while he went for their coffees.

Should he call her? Maybe she wasn't calling him because she felt guilty. Or decided she didn't want to break up with Jackson. Or decided he was a loser after all.

Reed wasn't used to worrying. Usually, he just acted and went along with wherever the road took him. Which was why he'd gotten involved with the Bats. And why he was a year behind in school. It was also why he'd taken the job salting the doubloons in the first place and why he hadn't listened to Scott when Scott told him salting fake doubloons was a terrible idea.

He shoved his phone in his pocket and headed for the door. He had to talk to Scott. This was weird. He couldn't remember needing reassurance from a friend since he left California He was a loner, had been ever since Lloyd moved them to Cottonwood. He'd decided no more gangs, and since all his friends had been in the Bats with him, he'd been left him on his own.

He'd never confided in Scott about anything except Lloyd—and then the gang. Maybe this new road he was on would include more than being honest with Mina. Maybe it would mean letting Scott in. Before he could talk himself out of it, he opened his door and headed for Scott's room. As he went across, he looked downstairs. Uncle Paul and Aunt Marty were sitting on the couch reading. She had taken off her shoes and had her feet in Paul's lap. He was idly rubbing her toes as he turned the pages in his book. It was a calm picture, like nothing he'd ever seen in his old home.

"Hey, buddy!" Uncle Paul looked up from his book. "You doing okay? You were quiet at supper."

Reed jumped. He didn't want them to think he was spying or anything. But Uncle Paul didn't look angry, just concerned. He wasn't ready to talk to Uncle Paul, especially now with Aunt Marty there. Not sure exactly what to say, he shrugged and said the first thing that came into his mind. "Just thinking about Uncle Bernie. I thought I'd go talk to Scott." It was true. Bernie was never far from his mind. He missed the old guy. Uncle Paul was turning into a father, but Bernie was the grandfather he'd never known.

"Good idea. It's always best to share what's on your mind. We're family, Reed."

Family. It was a great word. He smiled and hurried on to Scott's room. He knocked but didn't wait for the "Come in."

Scott was sitting on the floor, his back against the wall. He had a book in his lap, but he closed it. "What's up?"

Reed shrugged and did his best to look like he didn't care. "Got a question for you."

"Sure."

Reed sat on the end of the bed. "Do you trust Mina?"

Scott looked surprised. "I guess so. I don't know her very well. Why?"

Reed got up and walked to the window and looked out. No moon. "I'm in jam." When wasn't he? But this was Scott. Scott wouldn't say that.

"What happened?"

"It's those fake doubloons. You told me they were trouble. You were right."

"Okay ..."

Reed went back to the bed and sat down. "You know I went up to see Mina yesterday when I took you to work."

"Yeah."

"They sort of fell out of my pack." Who was he kidding? He was so rattled being close to Mina that when Jackson came up, he knocked his pack over and dumped them.

"Did Mina see them?"

"That's why she wanted to meet me for coffee. I was dumb enough to believe her when she said she thought I was nice and she wanted to dump Jackson."

"Hold on. You weren't dumb to believe her. She'd be making a smart move. Jackson is trouble."

"And I'm not?"

"Come on, Reed. You know what I mean. I wouldn't put it past him to hit her if he got mad enough. You yell. But you don't hit."

Reed ran his hands through his hair. "That's not really what's got me worried."

"Okay ..."

"One of the doubloons is missing. When I was having coffee with Mina, she told me the same thing you did. She said I could wreck Dr. Jessie's whole research project. I don't want to do that. All I want is another job. After I talked to her, I thought about it. I can get another job somewhere else and still look for the real doubloons on my own. I decided to take the fake ones back."

Reed stopped. He couldn't remember when he'd talked so much about himself. And he wasn't through. Scott seemed to understand. He didn't say anything.

He took a deep breath and forced himself to finish the story. "When I took them back to Parnell, one was missing. Mina had two chances to take one. She's the only person who could have."

"Not so. I don't know Mina well, but I don't think she would do something like that. Unless she spotted one you missed when you were picking them and didn't tell you. You think that's what happened and she kept it?"

"Maybe. Or when we were at Starbucks, I left my pack at the table while I went for our coffees. She knew which pocket I kept them in because she saw where I put them back."

"You're being too suspicious. Who else was there when you knocked over your pack?"

"Dr. Jessie, Dr. Dexter, and Jackson, but they were arguing. None of them noticed."

"What were they arguing about?"

Reed got up and went to the window again. It was still dark, still nothing to see. "I was kind of distracted, but Jackson showed up while I was there. When he saw me, he started yelling that I didn't have any business talking to Mina. That's when I knocked over the pack. Dr. Dexter insisted Jackson didn't have any business there either, and Dr. Jessie said Mina had the right to talk to whoever she wanted." Reed paused. When Scott didn't comment, he said, "They were all furious. I'm sure none of them saw the doubloons I had." He ran his hands through his hair. "Just Mina."

"But why would she say she wanted to talk to you if she took it?"

Reed crossed the room and dropped down on the bed

again. "Maybe she didn't notice until I was picking them up. Maybe she just said she wanted to talk to me to get a chance to grab one."

"Why would Mina want the doubloon? She already told you it could wreck Dr. Jessie's project."

"Maybe to rat me out."

"She could have done that without talking to you. You're overthinking this."

"We were going to get a pizza tonight. Mina said she would text me when she was finished talking to Jackson. I should have heard from her over an hour ago."

"Call her and ask what's going on."

"I did! I've called three times. It goes to voicemail."

Scott stretched and got to his feet. "It's almost ten. Maybe she had a hard time convincing Jackson she wanted to break it off."

A flicker of hope stirred in Reed's chest. Maybe that was it. It would make sense. Jackson was probably used to her doing what he said. "You think she might be interested in me?"

"Of course! Jackson is a jerk. You don't have to spend much time around him to know that. It's one thing to be passionate about a cause. He's more than that. He's angry at the world. His cause is an explanation for his fury. If he wasn't mad about the dig, he'd find something else to yell about. Mina's a smart girl. She knows what makes Jackson tick. You're a nice guy without an ax to grind."

"I'm younger than she is."

"Not that much. You're a good guy, Reed. She'd be crazy to want to stay with Jackson, even if you weren't showing interest. Call her one more time."

That hope got a little stronger. Reed pulled his phone out of his pocket and dialed the number he had memorized. One ring ... two ... four. The recorded voice said, "This is—" Reed cut the connection.

"No answer?"

"Voicemail."

"Let it go for tonight," Scott said. "Maybe her phone is charging. I'll talk to her in the morning at the dig."

15

Friday

Scott climbed off the back of Reed's motorcycle and handed him his helmet. "Thanks for the ride."

"Thanks for offering to talk to Mina. She's here."

"Yeah. That's her faded blue pickup. She calls the color *denim*."

Reed snorted. "Maybe her sense of humor will get me over this rough spot. I really need to talk to her. Tell her the guy who picked her up at Starbucks wants to make an official date. Maybe that will make her laugh, and she'll agree to call me."

"Don't worry so much. She was probably too tired return your call you last night. I won't have to encourage her. She'll call you today."

Reed nodded, but Scott could tell he wasn't convinced. He decided to change the subject. "You're going to look for the real doubloons?"

"I close tonight, so I don't have to be at the hardware store until noon. I found a good place for a cave on the topo map. It looks like a stream bed goes in one side of the hill and comes out at another place a couple of miles on. The conquistadors must have always been on the lookout for fresh water."

"Good luck!"

Reed nodded and pushed his visor down and backed the motorcycle around.

Scott watched as his brother headed out of the parking lot and turned toward the hills. He hoped his read of Mina was right. Scott didn't want to see Reed disappointed. Mina was the first girl he'd shown any interest in since moving in with them. Madison had let everyone at youth group know she was interested in Reed, but Reed hadn't followed up. Scott got it. Reed wanted to start with someone who didn't know his history. Mina was perfect.

Shouldering his pack, Scott started up the paved path toward the Well. It was early. Not quite seven a.m., but he might see Mina. She liked coming here when no one was around. She said she could connect to the Ones Who Went Before when the place was deserted.

Scott walked past the trail down to Dr. Dexter's camp. He and Dr. Jessie always showed up about 8:30, so Scott knew he had plenty of time to talk to Mina without being interrupted. Scott followed the plank walkway enjoying the cool morning. He could see why Mina liked being here before everyone else. It was as if for a little while this special place belonged to him. When he reached Dr. Jessie's camp, he didn't see Mina at the sifter or under the canopy. "Mina?"

No answer.

Where else could she be? Her pickup was in the parking lot. He hadn't passed her coming across the mesa. The only place left to look was at the cliff dwelling. She'd shown him the dwelling the first day, so he knew the way. The aluminum ladder that provided access peeked up over the edge. Scott went to it and looked over. No sign of Mina.

Getting down on his knees, he leaned over and called. "Mina! You down there? It's Scott."

No response. Turning around, Scott started down the ladder. If she was working inside the dwelling, she might not hear him calling. But she wasn't in the low shallow room under the soot-stained rock overhang.

The only place he hadn't looked was at Dr. Dexter's camp. Because Mina was assigned to Dr. Jessie, Scott couldn't think of any reason for her to be there. But the camp was directly across the lake from the dwelling, so he went to look. It was as deserted as he'd expected.

As Scott turned to go back to the ladder he'd come down, a flash of light caught his attention. Not light, of course, it had to be a reflection of the morning sun. Scott scanned the area. It flashed again, eight or ten feet to his right. He spotted a tiny object balanced on the edge of the Well.

He told himself it was a bit of galena in a pebble, not worth the risk of getting that close to the edge. More, the dirt around it had been disturbed. By what? Scott gave in to his curiosity. Stepping cautiously, he went to see what had caught his eye. When he was within reach, he squatted for a closer look. Not galena, not even a pebble—a silver bead like the beads on Mina's necklace.

His stomach did a somersault. What was this bead doing here? A second bead caught the sun. As he reached for it, a splash of bright red at the foot of the cliff caught his eye. A cardinal? When it didn't move, Scott took a deep breath and leaned out for a better look. Too large for a bird, the swatch of red gradually took shape as a smock, a smock topped with a fan of black hair.

Mina. What was she doing down there, and at the edge of the pool?

"Mina ..." The name caught in his throat. He swallowed and tried again. "Mina!"

No response. She didn't sit up, didn't pull back from the pool, didn't even turn her head—as if she didn't hear him.

He tried again, shouting as loud as he could. "Mina!" Still no response.

Was she hurt? As best as he could without leaning out too far, Scott looked for the way Mina had gone down. The ladder would never reach, and it was still propped against the wall behind the dwelling. He didn't see any toeholds like archaeologists sometimes found, ancient ladders chipped into a cliff and worn smooth by the feet of men and women going up and down.

He shouted again. "Mina!"

Complete silence answered him from the edge of the water so far below. But this time he didn't expected her to hear him. She had to be hurt. Had she fallen?

Shoving the two silver beads in his pocket, Scott inched his way back from the edge. Then he turned and ran for the ladder. Taking the rungs two at a time, he made his way back to the top. When he reached the top, he scanned the area, hoping that for once Dr. Jessie had come in early. But he was out of luck.

He headed for the walkway and started running again. It hadn't been built to take the weight of someone moving as fast as he was. Halfway around, one of the planks shifted, threatening to pop up and hit him. Ignoring the warning not to walk on the fragile ground cover, Scott stepped off the walkway and kept running.

When he reached the trail that would take him down to Dr. Dexter's camp, he stopped. He had a stitch in his side from running. Too fast, he sucked in cool air. He was close to panicking, and he knew that wouldn't help Mina. He forced himself to slow his breaths. He counted. One, in. Two, out. Three, in. Four ... When he could breathe normally, he headed down the steep path, moving as quickly as he could without sliding and losing his footing.

When he reached the bottom, he moved around Dr. Dexter's camp to the edge of the pool. Running here was out of the question. Without a path, he was walking on mud or small rocks. But he kept going, hoping one of the Well's water scorpions wouldn't decide to go after his bare legs.

Scott lost all sense of time as he inched his way around the pool. Most of the time he had to stay focused on his feet to keep from falling, but whenever he could, he took a quick look at the figure lying unmoving on the side of lake. He kept telling himself it didn't have to be Mina. Other people had red shirts. Other people had black hair.

Not that he wouldn't feel terrible about anyone lying there hurt, but he knew Mina. Reed liked Mina. Whoever it was didn't move.

Feeling sick, he had to force himself to keep moving forward. Every instinct told him to run the other way. Whoever lay there so still was hurt, maybe even dead. He wouldn't know what to do. All the first aid he knew came from Boy Scouts, and somehow he knew the person there needed more help than he had to offer. Still, he had to try.

When he reached the bright red smock and black hair, he froze. It was Mina, and she wasn't moving. Her hair was moving ever so slightly as the water sloshed from the disturbance his feet made. Her face was in the water. She had to be dead.

"Mina?" The name came out choked and too soft for anyone to hear. But his instinct told him it didn't matter.

Still, he might be wrong. He knew he didn't dare take a

chance that she was still alive. Holding his breath, he leaned down and turned her over. Small brown leeches clung to her face and neck. Those endemic Well leeches that stayed on the bottom during the day. Scott pushed the irrelevant detail out of his mind and forced his attention back to the body at his feet.

Mina's dark eyes were open, staring up at him. He knew she didn't see him, but it was unnerving. Squatting, he forced himself to pick up her hand to check the pulse in her wrist. Her fist was so tightly closed, he knew he couldn't feel anything. Dropping her hand, he put his fingers on her cold neck. Nothing. He turned his head and threw up.

Shaking, Scott stood up and moved away. Staying far away from the leeches, he scooped cold water and splashed it on his face. Then he pulled his phone from his pocket and called his dad.

"Hey, bud! What—"

"Mina's dead! She's lying in the water all covered with leeches. Dad, it's awful. I've never seen anyone dead before ..." He trailed off, swallowing the tears that wanted to come.

"Where are you, Son?"

"At the Well. In the Well, actually. I came around to talk to her, and she wasn't there." Once the words started, they wouldn't stop. His dad let him talk. When he got to the leeches, he choked.

"Take a deep breath, Scott. In through your nose—*one, two, three*—out through your mouth."

Scott swallowed air, choked again.

"Try it again. Breathe in through your nose, slowly. Then breathe out through your mouth, slowly."

This time, Scott got a decent breath. He took another one. After the third breath, he said, "Okay, dad. I'm calmer. It's just that I've never seen anyone dead."

"You've never seen a dead *body*, Son. Mina is gone from

that body. She's in God's loving care. Remember that. It's important."

Scott nodded.

"I assume you checked for a pulse."

"At her neck. Nothing."

"All right. I'm getting in my car. I'll be at the Well in about twelve minutes. As soon as we hang up, I'll call the sheriff. You need to stay in the vicinity, but you don't need to stay right beside the body. Find a dry place where you can sit down with your back it."

Scott moved. His dad's instructions were calming him down.

"When you find a good spot, look up at the sky, study the clouds. Everyone's hoping for another monsoon storm this afternoon. See if you can spot a thunderhead or two. Then study the water. Watch for bugs. See if you can spot a water treader or two."

"I see a rock where I can sit. I'll be okay now, Dad."

"See you soon. Give me five minutes to call the sheriff. Call me back if no one else shows up. Jessie or Ken should be getting to work pretty soon."

Scott disconnected. But before he headed for the rock, he had to do one more thing. Taking a deep breath, he went back to Mina—to her *body*, he reminded himself. Trying not to think about what he was doing, he squatted beside the body and picked up the cold hand. Turning it over, he did his best to open the fist.

The fingers wouldn't budge. The little finger touched the palm, but something winked at him from between the index finger and the palm, something gold. Scott felt the pulse begin to pound in his neck. Gritting his teeth, he brought the heavy hand closer to his face. He saw symbols etched in the surface, symbols representing the sixteenth-century Spanish government. Mina had clutched a gold doubloon as she fell. He couldn't be sure, but his instinct told him this one was the real thing.

Scott placed the hand carefully back beside the body. Then he got to his feet and headed for the rock he'd chosen as the place to wait for help. It was on the shaded side of the Well, so the stone was cool to the touch. Before he looked for thunderheads or water-treaders, he had another call to make.

No answer. Reed must be inside the cave. Should he leave a message? What message? He couldn't say, "I found Mina's body."

Instead, he said, "Call me, Reed, ASAP. It's important!" The fact that he called his brother by his name should alert him that something was wrong. Scott hoped Reed would get his message and call back. Reed needed to know about Mina and about the doubloon before the sheriff arrived.

WHISTLING a new tune the worship band had played at church, Reed tossed his dirty jeans and shirt into the corner of his closet. The song, with its good beat and easy-to-remember lyrics, was stuck in his head. He still wasn't sure about the whole God-thing, but he liked the worship band. He couldn't remember when he'd whistled. That was more for Uncle Paul.

But as he visualized new cave he'd explored a couple of hours ago, he felt renewed confidence in his plan to find the gold doubloons that would take him to the University of Virginia. He still had three passages to explore, all of them high enough for a man to stand up in, particularly a man of the shorter stature of the conquistadors. He reached for the clean clothes he'd laid out for work.

A knock on his door interrupted his thoughts. "Son, we need to talk."

The door muffled the words, but Reed's heart stopped at the tone of Uncle Paul's voice. Something was wrong, very wrong. "Just a sec. I'm in my underwear."

"Finish getting dressed. Then come downstairs and have a cup of coffee with me."

That cinched it. Something terrible had happened. His foster father knew he drank coffee but discouraged it, suggesting he stick with milk or hot chocolate until he finished growing. One leg was already in the jeans. He jammed the other one in and hopped to the door. But before he could get it open, he heard Uncle Paul's feet on the stairs. Reed pulled his shirt over his head and grabbed his socks and athletic shoes. As he dashed toward the stairs, the doorbell rang.

"I'll get it!" he called. "I'm on my way down."

"Stay where you are!" Uncle Paul's tone was stern, almost harsh, so unlike the way he usually spoke that Reed stopped dead. Who was at the door?

"I need Lloyd Harper, Jr. to come with me."

The sheriff. Reed's stomach clenched. Now what was he supposed to have done? At least he was here at home. Uncle Paul would invite the sheriff in. The three of them would talk.

Instead, his foster father said in that same harsh voice, "No one by that name lives here."

"So that's the way you want to play it, is it? Then I need to see *Reed* Harper."

"He can't come to the door right now."

Uncle Paul didn't like the sheriff, but he always cooperated with him. What was happening?

"Then I'll help him come to the door."

"Do you have a warrant?"

"I'm not arresting anyone. I just want to ask *Reed* some questions—at the office." The sheriff sounded determined.

Reed's heart thumped against his ribcage. He hadn't done anything. No speeding ticket. No trouble at the dig. Mr. Parnell at Seven Cities—the missing doubloon?

"Reed is a minor—in my custody." Uncle Paul sounded just as determined as the sheriff. "He's not going anywhere unless you have a legal document that gives you the authority to remove him from my home."

A pause followed, such a long pause Reed started to hope the sheriff had given up and gone away. The next words told him how wrong he was. "I'll be back, Russell. And next time I'll have a warrant. That girl is dead, and Lloyd, Jr. is in it up to his neck."

Dead—what girl? The answer hit him like a kick to the gut. *Mina.* The sheriff had to be talking about Mina. The reason he couldn't get her on the phone, the reason she hadn't returned his calls. But *dead*?

Reed sat down hard on the top step. Mina couldn't be dead. The stairway beneath him started to spin, slowly at first, then faster and faster until he had to put his head between his knees to keep from getting sick. His ears roared. Through the din, he heard his shoes bounce down the stairs, slide through an opening, and land on the floor below.

Then Uncle Paul was on the step beside him. Strong hands under his elbows pulled him to his feet. "Come on, Son. Let's splash cold water on your face."

The voice came from a long way off. Reed stumbled getting to his feet, but Uncle Paul had him. The cold water helped, but he still felt sick. "Mina is *dead*?" The word stuck in his throat, gagging him. He looked at his foster father in the mirror. The glass melted and surged toward him like surf on the beach.

Uncle Paul turned the faucet back on and pushed his head down gently. "More."

As Reed splashed, Uncle Paul applied a wet washrag to the back of his neck. After a moment Reed pulled his head up, turned off the water, and stepped back from the sink. Taking the rag, he scrubbed his face with it. Then he looked at Scott's father, the man who had taken him in. At least he wasn't with Lloyd, Sr.

"What happened?" His voice broke. He cleared his throat and tried again. "What happened to Mina?"

"Come downstairs. I'll tell you what I know over coffee."

Reed sat down on the edge of the bathtub. He still felt like crying, but he had to stop. He wasn't a baby, and Uncle Paul wouldn't be able to tell him anything if he was sobbing. Taking a deep breath, he got to his feet and went to find his socks and shoes.

He found his socks on the step where he'd sat to listen, the step where he'd heard the sheriff say words he didn't even want to think, *Mina is dead.* Or maybe the sheriff hadn't said that. Maybe he'd said *that girl.* Whatever the words, Reed had known immediately who and what. He pulled one sock over his toes and worked to across his foot. Then the other one, automatically, because he had to.

But where were his shoes? He vaguely remembered a thump, as the shoes tumbled down the stairs. They had to be on the floor beneath the stairs. Pulling himself to his feet with the banister, he went down one step at a time. His head hurt, a dull ache that encased his head like a helmet.

The running shoes had bounced different directions. They sat several inches apart, one upright waiting to be put on, the other on its side, displaying the trademark. He stared at the shoes for a moment. He'd been so proud of trademark when he bought the shoes with the money Uncle Paul loaned him after he moved in with Scott. His account with his foster father was clear now, a fact he was proud of. His job didn't pay a lot, and the after-school hours had been sparse back then. That was why this summer job meant so much. For the first time in his life, he was saving money.

His job ... He was getting dressed to go work when the doorbell rang. Now he would be late. Picking up the shoes, he dragged himself on the way he used to after Lloyd, Sr. delivered a vicious pounding. Reed knew he should hurry, but he couldn't make his feet move faster. One foot at a time, he crossed the open expanse of the living room to the corner designated for the kitchen.

Carafe in hand, Uncle Paul poured black coffee into two blue pottery mugs. Two blue plates sat across from each other in the middle of the oversized picnic table they were using until the house was finished. A carton of milk, a plate of bagels, and the peanut butter jar told him he was expected to eat. *No way* ...

"I don't have time," Reed began.

"You have all day," Uncle Paul said. "I called Joe and explained that we have a family emergency. I promised him you'll be back at work in a couple of days."

"He'll fire me."

Uncle Paul shook his head. "He understood. I think he'd already heard the news. I know you and he have had a bit of a rough time, but he's actually a very understanding guy. You don't see him at church because he goes to the late service, but he's active in the men's group."

Reed started to explain that the trouble was with Denny, not with Mr. O'Riley, but he didn't have the energy. He sat down at the picnic table and dropped his head into his hands. "What happened? Did she wreck her truck?"

"Drink some coffee and have a bagel. I'll tell you when you have something in your system."

Reed started to refuse, but it was too much trouble. Picking up the mug, he took a gulp of coffee. It filled his mouth, scalded his tongue, and slid down his throat before he could spit it out and put down the mug.

The pain felt right. But when the tears that sprang to his eyes threatened to turn into a sob, he rubbed the back of his hand across his face.

"Here," Uncle Paul pushed a cold glass into his hand.

Reed gulped cold liquid, ice water. It gave him an instant headache, a second pain that shocked the tears away. Swallowing, he whispered, "Tell me what happened."

Uncle Paul nodded and sat down across from him.

"It's not totally clear. Scott found Mina's body at the edge of the pool directly beneath the dwelling Jessie has been excavating."

"This morning? After I dropped him off at the Well?"

Uncle Paul held up one hand. "Mina was already dead, Reed. You couldn't have done anything for her even if you'd been there."

"But why didn't Scott call me?"

"He did. You were out of range."

"Why does the sheriff think I had something to do with it? It was an accident, wasn't it?" It had to be an accident. No one hated Mina. *Jackson.* Mina was meeting Jackson the night before to tell him she was moving on. What if Jackson ...

"Scott told me he thought she struggled with someone before she went over."

"Somebody pushed her?"

"No one knows what happened."

"But why does the sheriff think I would push her? She was

my friend! I quit the job with Seven Cities because she convinced what they wanted me to do wasn't right."

"I know, Son. It seems Jackson told the sheriff he overheard an argument between you and Mina."

Reed shook his head. "He's lying. The argument was between Mina and *him*. Mina told me she was going to tell him he's stuck in the same place he's been in since high school. She was going to tell him she was moving on."

"When was this?"

"Last night. Mina and I were going to go get pizza. It was going to be our first date. She asked me to leave. She said after she settled things with Jackson, she would text me. Uncle Paul, she never did!"

16

Saturday

Scott opened his eyes to a shadowy bedroom and a queasy stomach. The green numbers of the clock on his bedside table read 4:52. Morning, then, but what had awakened him? Was he sick?

He took a deep breath the way his mother had taught him. Nothing changed. He tried again. After the third breath, he decided he wasn't sick. Sitting up, he swung his legs over the side of the bed. He wasn't sick, but something was wrong.

Scott listened. The house breathed around him with the even rhythm of Saturday morning sleep. Scott longed to crawl back in bed. Dr. Jessie had declared a free weekend, and he'd planned to spend it relaxing. But he knew it wouldn't happen. Something was bothering him, something that made his hands tingle.

Emergency!

But what? No smoke. No shouts. Rain didn't pound the

roof. Even the wind that usually slammed the side of the house this time of year was still.

Emergency!

Scott did a quick inventory of his fuzzy mind. *Mina.* She was dead. How could he have forgotten? But there was no emergency for Mina now. She was at peace.

Reed! His brother wasn't at peace. Mina was the first girl Reed had let himself like since he had moved in with the Russells. They'd had a lot in common—alcoholic fathers and being on their own for college. Now she was dead. Even though it was ridiculous, Reed blamed himself. He'd heard the reasons: Mina died clutching a gold doubloon. Reed was sure if he hadn't brought doubloons to the dig, hadn't spilled them, Mina would be alive.

It didn't matter to Reed that Mina's doubloon was the genuine article and his were reproductions. No one blamed him—no one except Sheriff Winston. And, for some unknown reason, Sheriff Winston hated Reed.

Emergency!

Scott shook his head to clear it. Sad as it was, Mina's death wasn't an emergency. As unfair as Sheriff Winston's accusations were, he hadn't been able to take Reed into custody, so that wasn't an emergency either.

Emergency!

Scott was in the bathroom washing his hands when the emergency hit him. *Reed!* How could he have missed it? If he couldn't sleep because of Mina's death, did he think Reed was in his room deep in pleasant dreams?

Mentally kicking himself for being so slow, Scott crossed to Reed's room. The door was closed, so he tapped on it. To his surprise it swung open.

"Reed?" In case his brother was sleeping, he said it softly.

But he didn't need to worry. Reed's bed was empty. Where was he?

The answer, when it hit him, was so obvious he didn't know why he'd wondered. Reed had wanted to be where Mina died. He was at the Well. Had he gone just now or last night? Scott hoped for just now. Didn't Reed know how crazy it was to go to the scene with Mina's killer still out there? Bad enough in the morning light, even more dangerous in the dark. Racing back into his room, Scott pulled on the jeans and T-shirt he'd dropped on the floor the night before. Grabbing his sneakers, he catapulted out of his room and down the stairs.

He wasn't surprised to see that Reed's motorcycle was gone. Still, the realization made him want to throw up.

Didn't his brother know how risky it was to go there alone? Mina's killer was still out there. His next thought scared him even more. What if Reed had guessed who the murderer was? What kind of crazy risk was that he taking?

Scott had to get to the Well—now. He should have bought the thousand-dollar Camry from Mrs. Friedman at church instead of saving up for an old Ford Ranger. Wishing was a waste of time. He needed transportation now. Marty's white pickup sat in its usual place.

He should ask permission. But instead of going back in the house, he crossed to the board where they kept all the vehicle keys. If he asked Marty, he was sure she would say it was okay, but she would want to go with him. Then his dad would want to come along. Marty would suggest they call Reed's friends, and his dad would insist on making a plan.

No time to argue. Scott knew where Reed was, even if he couldn't explain how he knew.

Yanking open the driver's side door, he flung himself into the seat and turned on the motor. He would apologize later. If

Reed was okay, he would be so grateful he would accept any consequence Marty set for him. If Reed wasn't okay ...

Scott pushed the thought away. Jabbing the garage door opener, he threw the pickup into reverse and backed out. As he swung around in the driveway, he pulled on the headlights. Taking a deep breath, he made himself slow down. He didn't plan to stick to the speed limit, but he knew better than to take the steep driveway too fast. It wouldn't do Reed any good if he slid the pickup into a ditch.

When Scott reached the road, he turned south. As he drove through the silent streets of Jerome, he considered which route to take out of Cottonwood—I-17 or the Cornville Road. The smaller road was more direct, and since he didn't know where repair work was underway on the freeway, he opted for Cornville.

Normally Scott would enjoy being on his own in the pickup. He would choose a playlist on his phone and enjoy some music. But now he drove in grim silence. As he left Cottonwood behind, the sun came up. He was grateful that the two-lane road was deserted this early. He didn't know what he might have done if he'd found himself following a horse trailer or a dump truck.

As he drove, he considered his next step. When he reached the Well, he would have a choice—go around the top or start at the bottom. Whichever way he went, had to be right because he wouldn't have time for a do-over.

Scott didn't know what he expected to be happening or how he would stop it, but that didn't matter. He knew he would think of something when he was faced with the need to save Reed. After driving through the early morning for seemed like hours, but was probably only about forty-five minutes, Scott pulled Marty's borrowed pickup into the parking lot at the Well.

Six a.m. was still too early for anyone to be around, so Scott drove the pickup as close as he could to where the trail took off. As he skidded to a stop, he turned off the engine and pulled the keys from the ignition. He wasn't in a parking place, but just like taking the pickup if Reed was okay, or not even here, he would gladly accept the consequences. If Reed was in trouble, it wouldn't matter.

Flinging his door open, Scott threw himself out. When he reached the metal arm that told visitors to keep out, he catapulted over it and kept running. He sped past the Hohokam pit houses and up the trail to the overlook. Until he found himself sliding toward Dr. Dexter's camp in what was little more than a controlled fall, Scott didn't realize he had decided on his route.

But as he reached the level of the water, he knew he'd chosen the best location. From the bottom, he could see across the pool, both the top where he imagined Reed meeting Mina's killer and the bottom where ...

Scott's mind shied away from the memory. He couldn't cope with seeing Reed where he'd found Mina.

Please, God!

Not so much a prayer as it was his next breath, Scott found the entreaty had replaced his sense of an emergency. Now that he was here, he knew he couldn't face whatever was coming alone. When he reached the water's edge, he looked across at the top. No figures struggled there. Forcing himself to look down, he searched for a human shape.

Please, God!

It didn't have to be Reed. If his brother found the killer and the two of them struggled, Reed might be stronger. He was definitely stronger than Mina.

As Scott scanned the opposite shore, he thought it was empty, at least of what he was afraid of seeing. He started to relax. Then he spotted something that didn't fit. He wasn't sure what it was, just something too large to be natural.

Please, God!

He closed his eyes. The anomaly could be anything—a ladder, a camp chair, even part of the ancient structure above. It didn't have to be a person, much less Reed. After a moment, he forced himself to open his eyes and study the shape. He couldn't be sure it wasn't a person.

Swallowing the bile that rose in his throat, he took a deep breath. He had to check it out. No matter how afraid he was. If he had a pair of binoculars, he wouldn't need to make the difficult trek around the side of the pool.

Scott considered searching Dr. Dexter's camp. Almost as soon as he thought it, he rejected the idea. He knew he wouldn't find a pair, and wishing for one was wasting time. If someone was lying there alive, he had to find out quickly and get help.

Please, God!

Scott gritted his teeth and started around the pool. Part of him wanted to jump in and swim, but that would be dangerous without diving gear. This body of water wasn't a lake. After fifteen minutes, it seemed like he wasn't any farther around than after five. The shape was definitely human, and from the size, probably male.

Scott didn't know whether the man had fallen or been pushed, but either way if he was alive, it would take too long to get there. Once he reached the person, he would still have to determine whether he was alive or dead before knowing who to call for help.

Please, God!

Unable to bear the idea that Reed was lying by the water dead, Scott stopped picking his way around the water. Pulling his cell phone from his pocket, he punched in 9-1-1. Then he resumed his slow progress.

"9-1-1. What's your emergency?"

"A man fell from the top of Montezuma Well. He needs help."

The operator didn't respond.

"Ma'am! Did you hear me? My friend fell. We need EMTs who know how to climb. Send them around the top until they're above the cliff dwelling. They'll need to rappel down. And send a helicopter to get him to the hospital!"

"Your friend is breathing?"

Scott didn't hesitate. He was close enough now to make out a windbreaker. Reed's was that same faded blue color, and it had a tear in the right sleeve above the elbow.

Please, God!

"Yes! Tell them to hurry."

17

Sunday

Marty opened the heavy umbrella that shaded the deck table. Angling her chair toward the Mountain, she looked out at the old mine shaft with its *Keep Out* sign. She didn't know why she'd chosen to come out here to wait for Paul and Scott. She could have sat on the front porch with its picturesque view of Jerome. From there she could have watched for them.

This desolate view of the bare mountainside evoked so many unhappy memories. She'd lost her entire family while living in the house that sat on this foundation. More than twenty years ago, it had been her parents and then her little sister. Not quite three years ago, her grandmother. Soon after that terrible loss, the house burned down to the foundation in a fire that almost took Paul from her.

Why had the back of the house drawn her as she waited for news of the foster son she'd almost rejected? Closing her eyes, Marty concentrated on her breathing. In ... trust, out ... fear, in

... trust, out ... fear. She sat in a comfortable chair on a new deck, surrounded by memories.

Hearing the screen door behind her, Marty opened her eyes.

"I thought I might find you here." Paul tipped up her chin and kissed her gently.

"Is Scott with you?"

"He'll be home later this afternoon. He's taking your pickup to wash it and fill it with gas."

"I'm grateful, of course, but he didn't have to do that."

"Yes, he did. His instinct about Reed was good, but he should have asked permission to borrow your pickup. Even if he didn't want to wake us, he should have left a note."

"You're right, of course. How is Reed?"

"Still alive. In a coma."

Paul pulled a chair around and sat beside her. "What else?"

"The specialist thinks Reed should have regained consciousness by now."

"Dr. Zimbelman is Reed's doctor. What does he think?"

"Glenn says Reed is young and strong. He advises patience."

"There's more, Paul. I hear it in your voice. What aren't you telling me?"

"The sheriff arrested Reed."

Marty sat up. "Reed is in a coma struggling for his life, and Larry arrested him. How did he manage that?"

"By putting a guard at the door and not allowing visitors."

"That's cruel! Reed needs our support. If he wakes up and thinks we've deserted him ..."

"I know. I'm working on it. I have the name of a lawyer in Flagstaff who should be able to handle it, but since it's Sunday I can't reach him until tomorrow."

"But why did Larry arrest him?"

Paul shook his head. "He says guilt made Reed try to commit suicide by jumping from the spot where he pushed Mina."

"He's wrong."

"There's more. Larry still insists Reed is responsible for Bernie's death. He says Mina's death makes two possible murders Reed is involved in. That's one too many for him."

"Have they got the results of the autopsy back?"

Paul nodded. "Glenn Zimbelman called in a favor and got Bernie's case bumped to the front of the line. A heart attack killed Bernie, not a blow to the head as would have happened if Reed pushed him against the wood stove."

"I don't understand," Marty said. "Reed can't have caused Bernie's heart attack."

"According to the Larry, that's exactly what happened. He insists Reed's theft of the journal upset Bernie so much he had a heart attack."

"But Reed took the journal several hours after Bernie died."

"The sheriff says we only have Reed's word for that. According to his theory, Reed took it before Bernie died. He's got his mind made up."

"I knew Reed didn't have enough time to wait for Larry to realize that his problem is with Reed's father. We're going to be visiting our son in prison before our sheriff gets that much self-knowledge. What are we going to do?"

"I have a couple of ideas," Paul said, "but first tell me about church."

"Pastor Ray announced about Reed's fall, so of course we prayed for him. He's now on the prayer chain. I know Ray will want to go see him as soon as he wakes up. Maybe he can get in."

"We'll get in, Marty. I promise you that."

Marty patted Paul's knee. "The sermon focused on the thirteenth chapter of First Corinthians."

"Did he talk about our family motto?"

"How could he not? *And now faith, hope, and love remain, these three. And the greatest of these is love.* Ray had us read it together. I heard people all around me saying words I repeat every day. Even more, I heard echoes of people saying the same words in many languages across the globe and down two thousand years. That company of believers gives me strength I can't find anywhere else."

Paul took her hand and threaded his fingers through hers. "That's one of the reasons I still go to church."

They sat for a moment in companionable silence. Then Marty said, "What are we going to do to keep Reed out of prison?"

"The first step is to make a list." Paul released her hand and got up. "I'm going to get paper. Do you want something to drink?"

"Cold water, please."

He wasn't gone long. When he returned, he had two glasses of water and the tablet and pencil they kept in the kitchen for leaving each other notes.

Marty accepted the glass he held out. "If it's a suspect list you have in mind, it won't be very long."

"I know, but we need to be organized. I don't want Scott to feel left out of our discussion."

"What discussion?" Scott came out of the house, letting the screen door slam behind him.

Paul turned toward his son. "We're making a list of suspects to interview."

Scott rolled his eyes. "Sheriff Winston needs help looking at someone other than Reed. I can't believe ..."

Paul held up his hand. "Neither can we. Sit down and help us with the list."

Scott dropped into a chair. "Three people. In order of closeness to Mina—Jackson, Dr. Jessie, and Dr. Dexter."

Paul jotted the names on the tablet. "Anyone else?"

"What about one of the men Reed worked for at Seven Cities?" Marty said. "It's a bit far-fetched, but that gold doubloon in her hand had to mean something. Seven Cities is interested in doubloons."

Paul added the name to his list. "Maybe. But I think they're unlikely. Mina's doubloon was authenticated as genuine. From what Reed said, Don Parnell at Seven Cities only has reproductions."

Scott looked frustrated. "I wish the sheriff would remember that!" "Reed never had any real doubloons. Why would Mina be holding a real one if Reed was the one who pushed her?"

"Larry isn't thinking straight right now," Paul said. "That's why we need to help him."

Marty nodded. "When we interview, we need to ask questions that identify clues the sheriff can follow up on." "Let's make a list of those." Paul handed her the tablet. She turned the page and started to write. "One thing we need to find out is why a doubloon would be important to each person."

"Right there, you've eliminated Dr. Dexter," Scott said.

Paul looked skeptical. "Maybe not. We need to ask all of our suspects and keep an open mind for interpretations to any answer we receive. And we need to remember a murderer will be quick to lie."

"Another thing to find out," Scott said, "is how that person felt about Mina."

"And if that feeling has changed," Marty added a note. "We'll need to be careful how we work our questions in. If we come across as grilling our suspect, the guilty person will spot it immediately and lie accordingly."

"Agreed," Paul said. "Which is why we need to assign suspects carefully. If at all possible, the interview needs to be woven into some other agenda."

Marty stuck the pencil behind her ear. "I've been wanting to take an in-depth look at Montezuma Castle. Jessie would be an ideal guide. I gather she's been studying this entire settlement for several years—not just the Well."

Paul nodded. "That will work."

"Dr. Dexter is the natural one for me," Scott said. "I'll see him at work tomorrow. I can ask questions one at a time as I get openings in other topics."

"Or you can make an opening." Marty retrieved the pencil to write the appropriate name beside each suspect.

"That leaves Jackson-Wassaja for you, Dad." Scott grinned. "Better you than me. But what's your excuse for talking to him?"

"Easy. He's George Henry's grandson. I can find a reason to talk to George again. I'm sure he'll be glad to put me in touch with Jackson. I think the elders are all worried about Jackson."

"Great!" Scott jumped to his feet, knocking over his chair. As he righted it, he said, "We've got a plan. Marty, may I use your pickup to go get Reed's motorcycle? It's still in the parking lot at the Well."

"You may. On one condition."

The look Scott gave her made Marty smile. "No. You don't have to take me or your dad with you. All I'm asking is that you keep thinking about questions that will help us gather clues. You can do that while you drive."

"Done! All of us can think up more questions and trade at supper this evening." He left as quickly as he had come, letting the screen door slam.

Paul looked at Marty. "Did we have that much energy at that age?"

"I'd have to ask my mother that question. I sure don't remember it if I did."

Paul pushed back his chair and got to his feet. "I need to make a few notes to get ready for the lawyer. It's important to give him enough of the picture so he'll want to help us convince the sheriff to do the right thing. Are you ready to come in?"

"In a few minutes."

He gave her a curious look but didn't comment.

Marty studied the charred swath the forest fire had cut on the mountain, the same blackened path she'd looked at for two years. For the first time she noticed a smudge of green and red around the edges. Wildflowers were starting to take root in the carbon-rich soil. Next year or perhaps the following year aspen saplings would appear. Later the ponderosa would begin to recover.

As Marty swallowed cool water, she knew why she'd chosen this view as she faced the consequences of Reed's disastrous fall. Looking at this injured mountain, she could believe God would get them through.

18

Monday

S cott's steps slowed as he went down the incline. Dr. Dexter sat on at campstool in front of his makeshift desk, intent on something that looked like a map. With a sinking feeling, Scott realized he'd rushed over here, half-convinced the geologist was a murderer without even thinking about how he was going to open the conversation.

Still, Reed wasn't the murderer. Why not Dr. Dexter? Now as he got closer, the man's familiar face and obvious concentration on his work gave Scott a moment of doubt. What motive would the man have for pushing a teenage girl to her death—and how was he going to bring up the topic without sounding like he was accusing the geologist?

He soon found he didn't have to worry. As soon as Dr. Dexter saw him, the geologist said, "What on earth are you doing here, Scott? I thought you would be at the hospital with your brother. I certainly didn't expect you to turn up for work."

"They wouldn't let us in to see Reed. They have a guard on

the door. We explained that we were just there to talk to him and let him know we loved him. None of us would try to get him out of the hospital! That's where he needs to be." Scott cut off the flow of his words, afraid he might burst into angry tears. He was here to interrogate a murder suspect, not let his emotions run away with him.

"I heard the sheriff accused Reed of pushing Mina and then trying to commit suicide because of his guilt."

"That's not true! Reed would never do anything like that. He was in love with Mina!"

"Simmer down, son. I didn't say I believed that. All I said was I heard that's what the sheriff thought. He seems to have a chip on his shoulder about your brother. There must be some history there."

Scott sighed and dropped cross-legged to the ground. "You can say that again. But it isn't with Reed." Except maybe since Bernie died, but Scott didn't want to go down that rabbit trail. "The sheriff carries a grudge against Reed's dad. I don't know why. But whatever the reason, the sheriff takes it out on Reed every chance he gets."

Dr. Dexter looked confused. "But I understood Reed was your brother. Marty is much too young to be his mother. Isn't Paul Reed's father?"

"Reed is my foster brother. His name is Reed Harper."

"I guess I never heard his full name. He looks more like Paul ..."

Scott nodded. "... than I do. I take after my mother. When Dad and Marty got married, we all decided to become a family."

"From what I see, the four of you have succeeded in doing just that. I'm curious. How did Reed come into your family?"

Scott picked up a rock. Just in time, he stopped himself from throwing it. To ease his impatience, he started tossing it from one hand to the other. "It's a long story, but the short version is that Reed was a friend of mine who ran away from home. My dad took him in."

Scott got to his feet. It was time to get to his reason for coming. Even though it hadn't been hard to start a conversation, they were a long way from what he had come to talk about. How could he steer the conversation back to Mina without seeming too obvious?

First, he had to get the conversation out of the past into the present. Walking around behind Dr. Dexter, he looked over the older man's shoulder. "What are you working on today, sir?"

"I'm sick about what happened to Mina, of course, but you realize the find of a genuine gold doubloon here will go a long way to helping Jessie prove her theory, don't you?" He pointed at the map, to a place Scott thought was about where the cliff dwelling Dr. Jessie was excavating would be. "I'm studying the geological layers I've mapped to see if I can match the time period of the stratum where Mina found the coin with the stratum archaeologists identify with the time of the builders of Montezuma Castle. If the time periods line up, that will support Jessie's theory. If they don't, we'll have to look for another explanation for how Mina's doubloon got into the dwelling. You can see why I need to back up Mina's find with scientific data. It's the only way that doubloon will help Jessie with the paper she needs to write."

"You know where Mina found the doubloon?"

"Hmm. I went into the dwelling this morning and found evidence of new digging. Mina had cleared an area approximately four inches square and six inches deep. She kept the dirt to be sifted just as Jessie taught her. But what she was doing there in the middle of the night, and what she used for light, I have no idea. What I do know is what this find is going to mean to Jessie."

Scott went back to where he'd been sitting. As he dropped to the ground, he studied the geologist, doing his best to keep the man from realizing what his was doing. Dr. Dexter's expression reminded Scott of the look he'd seen on Reed's face every time he talked about Mina. Or the look on any of his friends' faces when they talked about their girlfriends. But he was sure nothing like that existed between Dr. Dexter and Dr. Jessie. Dr. Jessie treated him like a friend, an older friend she respected, not like someone she was interested in. Didn't Dr. Dexter realize how much older than Dr. Jessie he was? The guy had gray hair! And Dr. Jessie was the same age his mother would have been had she lived.

Sorrow stabbed Scott every time he thought of his mother. This time it caught him by surprise. It hurt so much, he had to struggle to keep from doubling over. Dr. Jessie looked so much like his mother. Sometimes when he watched her from a distance, he thought he was seeing Mom.

Of course, she didn't act like Mom or sound like her. And she wore some kind of heavy perfume. His mother had always smelled like vanilla. Sometimes when he really missed her, he would sneak into the kitchen and open the little bottle of vanilla flavoring. *If only Mom hadn't died after that terrible car wreck.*

The thought came back like a toothache in a tooth the dentist had pulled. An old refrain he struggled to never think again. Every time he gave in, it put him on a path that led into darkness. With Pastor Ray's help, he'd learned to push the treacherous thought away by thinking of things he was grateful for. Like that his father hadn't died in that same wreck. Like that they had Marty in their lives.

For the first time, he realized his dad was probably as much older than Marty as Dr. Dexter was to Dr. Jessie. He'd never thought of age when he thought of Marty. Now that he did, he knew it didn't matter. Without trying to replace Mom, she somehow soothed the ache that was always in his heart. Marty fit with their family. It wasn't at all the same thing as Dr. Dexter and Dr. Jessie.

"What on earth are you thinking about, Scott?"

Dr. Dexter's voice brought Scott brought back to the dig." I ... I just keep wondering what happened to Mina."

"Jessie thinks she was climbing back to the top using the hand and footholds the builders carved for themselves. Those indentations are so shallow it would be easy to miss your footing, especially at night."

"But what about all the footprints at the top? It's those footprints the sheriff claims prove Reed pushed Mina to her death."

Dr. Dexter shrugged. "Maybe Mina made it to the top and turned around to look back down. She might have stepped too close to the edge. It's hard to know. She must've been excited. She would have understood the archaeological importance of what she'd just found—and what it would mean to Jessie. She practically worshiped Jessie, told me more than once that she wanted to pattern her career after her mentor. And remember, it was dark. I don't think there was much of a moon that night."

The older man frowned. "What do you think happened, Scott? After all, you're the one who found her body."

The image of Mina's body flashed into Scott's mind—first as he looked over the edge and saw the crumpled figure below and then in vivid detail as he knelt beside her body trying to lift her head out of the water. Spots danced in front of his eyes, and his stomach knotted. He put a blind hand out, felt the solid ground, and got to his feet. "I'm not feeling well, sir. Maybe it was a mistake for me to come to work after all."

Through a haze, Scott watched the geologist stand and move to his side. As an arm went around his shoulders, he heard the older man say, "Are you all right, son? You look a little green. Let me help you get home."

All Scott wanted was to be alone. He needed to walk. After the spots faded and his stomach settled down, he needed to run, run until he had a stitch in his side and couldn't catch his breath. How he needed to talk to Reed. The memory of his brother lying where he'd seen Mina punched him in the gut. He had to get away, not from Dr. Dexter, but from this place, from his memories. He had to move, remember he was alive.

Taking a deep breath, Scott said, "I'll be all right. Thanks for your offer, but I can get home by myself." He took a step toward the path, careful not to step between the spots that looked like a swirling snowstorm.

"If you're sure ..."

"I'm sure." Scott took a second step and then a third. Walking away was helping.

As he started up the incline, Dr. Dexter's voice followed him. "Whatever happened to that lovely young woman was a tragedy. She had the makings of a first-class researcher. Jessie liked her, and Mina had her whole life ahead of her. Personally, I'm sure it was an accident. I don't know how your brother fell, but reassure your family that I don't think for one minute he harmed that young woman, no matter what the sheriff says."

PAUL BACKTRACKED from the Yavapai-Apache reservation into Clarkdale, turning onto Park Road. He hoped this visit to Tuzigoot didn't turn out to be a wild goose chase. But Jackson's grandfather had assured him this was the most likely place to find the young man. Whenever Jackson and Mina disappeared in high school, any searcher was sure to find them at the Tuzigoot ruins. As Paul passed along the western end of Pecks

Lake, he could see why it had been their special place. The water glistened blue in the sunlight, forming a stark contrast to the brown baked earth around the monument. He parked and walked up the path toward the ruins.

"Go up to the very top," the old man had said. "Jackson told me they liked to climb up there and look out over the whole area. With the interlocking walls of the dwelling below them, they would imagine what life must've been like for the Ones Who Went Before." Mr. Henry shook his head. "Even then the two were starting to look at the past from different perspectives. But my grandson has always had the idea that people agree with what he wants them to think. Even while those two kids were in high school, Mina talked about digging through the layers below to find out more about how the old ones lived." He paused, a mixture of shame and dismay clouding his face.

"Jackson wasn't interested in archaeology," Paul prompted. "What did he talk about back then?"

The old man sighed. "Jackson was already showing signs of this fanaticism that drives him. He wants to keep people away from the ruins—tourists and researchers. He says we must protect the past, preserve as it has come down to us."

Grandfather Henry hesitated again. This time Paul waited.

"Now, with Mina gone, he's taking refuge in the past," Mr. Henry said softly. "He wants things to be like they were when those two were young. He tells himself Mina had changed her mind and was coming back to him. But me—I don't think so. I saw a young woman moving on with her life, exploring an exciting career possibility. Like her grandmother, she had big ideas. But my grandson is standing still, becoming more of what he's always been."

A long speech for the old man, but Paul wanted to be sure he understood before he got back in his SUV and drove to the national monument. "Jackson has been spending a lot of time at Tuzigoot since Mina died?"

Grandfather nodded. "Tells me that's the only place he can be quiet. He says Mina's spirit lingers there to comfort him."

Paul waited, but the old man didn't say anything more. "You're not sure." Not a question, an observation. Something he saw in the set of Grandfather Henry's chin.

"Maybe Mina's spirit lingers at Tuzigoot with the old ones, or maybe it lingers on the rim of the sacred well, where someone took her life from her. But my grandson swears he won't go back to that place until he sees Mina's murderer in jail —or dead."

At first Paul wasn't sure he'd heard the last two words, but they hung in the air, refusing to evaporate. According to the sheriff, Jackson was convinced Reed had killed Mina. In a breath his interview with the young man escalated from necessary to urgent. "Jackson is convinced Mina's death was deliberate? He discounts the possibility of an accident."

Grandfather Henry sighed. "Jackson gets an idea in his head, and he thinks everyone should agree with him."

"And you, sir—what do you think?"

He looked over Paul's shoulder, seeming to study the gray-green mesquite tree that provided the welcome shade the two men sheltered in. He was silent for so long Paul decided he wasn't going to answer. "Thank you ..." he began.

"I must wait for more before I decide what to think," he said to the branch over Paul's head. Dropping his gaze, he added, "More that you will uncover, Dr. Paul."

Realizing he'd been dismissed, Paul got to his feet and made his way back to the SUV. The old man's pronouncement, rather than reassuring him that he would get to the bottom of the mystery, disturbed him. It was as if Grandfather Henry knew the answer would not be happy. What else could it be?

Whether accident or murder, Mina's death was devastating to everyone who knew her. Still, he knew one thing for certain—Reed had had nothing to do with it.

Now as Paul walked up the steep path that wound around the hundred-room pueblo of Tuzigoot, he caught sight of Jackson sitting cross-legged in the shade of the single tower at the top. Speculation about the use of the tower ranged from a storage place for corn to a lookout for enemies. Paul leaned toward the storage theory, himself. From what he'd read, the years Tuzigoot was inhabited had been calm ones, so the likelihood of the need for a lookout was slim.

As Paul rounded the last bend in the paved trail, Jackson caught sight of him and got to his feet. "If you're here to argue with me that Reed is a killer," he shouted, "turn around right there!"

Paul shook his head and held up a hand to stop the flow of angry words. "If you've got room in the shade for me, I want to sit down and tell you why I'm here."

The young man looked uncertain, and Paul wondered if Jackson would maintain his belligerent stance, or if curiosity would win out. Finally, he relaxed. "Ten minutes. If I find you're here to argue, I'll call Ranger Samuels down there and tell him you were trying to pry one of the bricks loose."

Surprised, not only by the actual words, but also by the venomous tone, Paul studied Jackson, feeling as though he were seeing him for the first time. If Jackson would lie to chase off someone who disagreed with him, what would he do to a woman he saw as unfaithful? Keeping his voice neutral, Paul said, "Let's sit down. I won't keep you long."

"How did you find me? No one knows I'm here!"

Ignoring the question, Paul sat cross-legged on the ground at the edge of the shadow cast by the wide, tall tower.

"I asked you a question!"

"I'll answer it after you sit down. I want to have a conversation, not a shouting match."

Jackson frowned, but after a moment, he sat across from Paul.

"All right. I'm sitting. Answer my question!"

"Your grandfather suggested I look here."

"He knew you wanted to question me?"

"Have a conversation with you. You knew Mina best. I need to know why you're so sure my son killed her."

"He was stalking her!"

Paul knew when he was being baited. Scott had told him how hesitant Reed had been to even talk to Mina. Even though he was a bit older than Scott, Paul was sure Reed had never had the nerve to ask a girl on a date. The idea of Reed stalking Mina was absurd. If Mina had told him to leave her alone, he would have—and beaten himself up for approaching her at all. Paul swallowed, reminding himself he wasn't here to defend Reed. He was here to find out what this angry young man was thinking.

"So, you think Reed followed Mina that night when she went to the dig?"

"That's the only explanation. Mina would never have fallen from there—and I mean never. When we were growing up, Mina and I used to sneak into the park after hours and climb up and down the walls of the Well using those exact hand and foot holds. She knew without looking where every single one of them was."

"You never got caught?"

Jackson snorted. "What would anyone have done to us? We had more right to be there than any of the tourists or even the government people who think they own our ancestral home."

"Okay. So ,Mina wouldn't have fallen, and Reed was

stalking her. Even if I grant you those two points, they don't add up to a push from Reed."

"Sure they do. Mina saw him out there. She laughed at him. Told him he didn't have a chance with her. She was my girl. She wouldn't have had anything to do with a loser like Reed. He was already a killer. It was probably easy for him to kill again."

Paul took a deep breath. He'd heard Reed's side of this particularly nasty accusation, and he believed his son. But if the sheriff had this piece of speculation, it explained a lot. Had Jackson gotten it from the sheriff or vice-versa?

"You don't know what I'm talking about, do you? It was before your son came to the Verde Valley."

Paul held up a hand. "I know all about the Bats. Reed left L.A. long before that particular gang got old enough to become fascinated with murder."

"So says B.T.!"

So, Jackson had heard about the Bats from the sheriff. Only Larry Winston would refer to Reed as *B.T.* It was time to ask the question he'd come to ask. "What if it was the other way around?"

"What do you mean?"

"What if Mina told you she was moving on—either with Reed or on her own? Were you there with her that night? You spend a lot more time around the dig than Reed does. You might even know something about the gold doubloon."

Jackson jumped to his feet. "I've answered all the questions I plan to. Are you leaving, or shall I call the Ranger Samuels over? He's my friend, and he'll believe what I tell him. "

Paul was tempted to say, "Don't be so sure." He knew Samuels. The Verde Valley was a small professional world. But he held his tongue. He'd found out what he needed to know. Jackson was as unscrupulous as he was angry. In love with

Mina or not, it was possible he'd turned that anger on her. If she told him they were through, that she was interested in Reed, even that she was tired of his rabid preservationism, he might have pushed her in a moment of uncontrollable fury. Remorse could easily have driven him back again and again to this place where the two had been a happy couple when they were in high school.

With deliberate motions Paul got to his feet. No reason to stay, but no reason to give Jackson the idea that he was afraid of his threats either.

19

Marty parked and headed for the Montezuma Castle Visitor Center. And her suspect interview with Dr. Jessie Jensen. Marty had no idea how she was going to find out what she needed to know without immediately putting the other woman on guard.

"Think of it as research," Paul told her as they cleared up the breakfast dishes. "You're good at that."

"I'm good at research in books on antiques—not people, not oral history, not like what you do."

"Yes, like what I do. A couple of weeks ago I watched you draw facts about that table you're working on out of Lou Springer, enough that you were able to authenticate it as a genuine Duncan Phyfe. And Lou wasn't particularly interested in talking to you. She was getting rid of the table—a piece of junk cluttering up her garage. But once you got her going, she knew more about the table than she thought she did."

"That was a table, Paul. Not a murder."

He closed the dishwasher and pulled her to him. "Trust

me. You'll do fine. Jessie loves to talk. Ask her what brought her here."

Marty thought the answer to that question was *Paul.*

As if he'd read her mind, Paul tipped up her chin and gave her a kiss that reminded her he wasn't interested in Jessie.

Marty came back to the present. She'd been determined not to be nervous, but in spite of Paul's coaching, her stomach knotted as she moved from the July sun of the sidewalk into the shade of the covered walkway that led to the Visitor Center door. Before she could open the door, Jessie came out.

"Good morning, Marty. I took care of your park fee." The other woman's tone was cool, not hostile, but not friendly either.

Marty forced herself to relax. Just like Lou Springer, she told herself. *Paul's right. I can do this.* Using the tone she'd used when Lou handed her a mug of coffee, Marty said, "Thanks for your thoughtfulness. I could come here any time. I know the rangers give talks, and I understand there's an excellent self-guided tour. I asked you because I thought it would be fun to see this site through your eyes."

Jessie smiled. "Let's start around the trail. We can talk while we walk."

A pleasant reply, but not a response. Not surprising. Jessie Jensen was a smart woman. She had to realize Marty had more on her agenda than sight-seeing. Marty decided to answer the unspoken assumption, at least partly. "More important than seeing Montezuma Castle again, visiting it with you gives us a chance to get to know each other."

When Jessie still didn't respond, Marty added, "You're Paul's friend, and you were Linda's friend. Scott likes you. I want to get to know you, partly for myself, and partly because I hope you'll continue to visit our family."

Her own words surprised Marty. She'd set up this meeting

to try to discover if Jessie might have pushed Mina to her death, but now she realized if Jessie wasn't a murderer, she did hope the other woman would continue to visit their family. She was grateful for their last conversation. He'd acknowledged that when Jessie first arrived, he had been hypnotized by the past he and Jessie shared with Linda. Sofia had been right. Paul, had realized on his own that he wanted to stay in the present, not return to the past.

Jessie stopped at a place on the trail that was directly in front of the "castle." Marty looked up at the ancient apartment that had been built almost a hundred feet above the canyon floor where they stood. Jessie said quietly, "Your invitation must mean you think you've won."

Marty blinked. "I didn't realize we were in a contest."

"Of course, you did. If you really mean it when you say you want me to be your friend, you must know we have to be honest with each other."

Marty studied Jessie. She hadn't wanted the conversation to go this way, but if this was what Jessie wanted, she could meet her halfway. "Paul made his decision. You and I were never in competition. Paul had decided what he wanted—to try to recapture a wonderful past or take a chance on an equally wonderful future. He's decided on the future."

She moved back to the loop trail and began walking. Because the trail was paved, they didn't have to pay attention to their feet.

Jessie laughed suddenly. "You're right! Paul has always been his own man. Linda and I were never really in a contest any more than you and I have been. Paul knew he had a choice in college, and he knows he has a choice now."

Marty smiled. "Then let's see if you and I can be friends. I meant what I said. You're important to Paul and to Scott. I'd like to see if we can do more than just tolerate each other."

Jessie gave in suddenly. "Okay. I'll give you a brief tour of my world now. If this morning goes well, one of these days you can give me a tour of your world. I don't know a thing about restoring old furniture."

Marty was sure Jessie knew the difference between old furniture and antiques, but she decided to let the dig pass. If Jessie saw herself as a loser and Marty as a winner, she would probably continue to poke at anything Marty did—at least for a while.

Marty decided to change the subject. Time to see how Jessie would explain her interest in this area. "Since you went to high school with Linda," Marty said, "I assume you grew up in Virginia."

"Richmond."

A tow-headed boy who looked about ten raced around them. "I want to go inside!" he shouted.

"Slow down, Jason! If you want ice cream with your lunch, come back here right now!" A man with graying hair came up behind them breathing hard. "Excuse me, ladies. If I don't catch my grandson, my daughter will never forgive me." He stopped and grinned at them. "Or my daughter might actually thank me. It's my wife, I need to worry about. Got to go!"

Jessie looked at Marty. "You missed Scott at that stage. He was every bit as much a handful as Jason evidently is."

Marty decided to take the comment as a statement of fact rather than the dig she suspected the other woman meant. She said simply, "I did. Scott was fourteen when I first met him."

Instead of waiting for whatever Jessie might say next, Marty nodded at the apartment complex so high above them. "I know no one is allowed in these ruins. I think Tuzigoot is about the same age, but it's open to walk through."

"The Castle is unstable because so many people climbed all over it before 1906 when, thanks to Teddy Roosevelt, it was designated a national park. The looting and damage done here is heartbreaking. Sometimes I try to imagine what the first visitors in the 1890s saw.

They carried off most of the artifacts, so we know less about these people than we might have. A few artifacts have surfaced in private collections and made their way to museums, but the vast majority disappeared into garages, attics, and probably trash bins." She looked longingly up at the cliff dwelling. "When I first had the idea for the research I'm doing, I wanted to do it here at the Castle. When I finally faced the impossibility of that plan, I asked for, and got, permission to work in the much more modest dwellings at the Well. They were inhabited at the same time, but I suspect by people much lower in whatever class system the Sinagua, now more properly called the Ancestral Puebloan culture, embraced."

Marty heard the disappointment in Jessie's voice at not being able to work here. She wanted to keep the archaeologist talking. The more she talked, the more clues Marty had a chance of picking up. "Scott told me the Castle was built about eleven-hundred CE. How many people lived in this dwelling?"

"The total number over the three hundred years it was occupied would be difficult to estimate. From what we know, people moved in and out of here. At its peak, however, we estimate about two hundred occupants, including men, women, and children. If you're interested, we can walk a little bit farther to a diorama the park service installed. It shows what it looked like inside when the Ancestral Puebloans lived in this canyon."

"I'm definitely interested."

As they resumed walking, Marty decided to do her best to turn the conversation in a personal direction. "Montezuma Castle near Camp Verde, Arizona, is a long way from

Richmond, Virginia. How did you get interested in the ancient Native American cultures of the Southwest?"

Jessie gave her a sideways glance. "The first time I came to this part of the country was when Paul and Linda moved to Arizona. Because I was studying archaeology, they brought me to Montezuma Castle for a visit."

They had just about reached the diorama. Marty stopped. "Tell me what I'm looking at."

Jessie laughed. "You really don't want to talk about my history with Paul and Linda, do you?"

Marty ignored the challenge. "I want to find out about your world now. Tell me how these people built this amazing structure."

Jessie grinned. "All right. This cliff is limestone. Unlike traditional cliff dwelling builders that used ledges as floors and overhangs as roofs, these builders constructed a three-story apartment complex in a large alcove. They made the face of their building curved to match the cliff face. Occupants accessed the top, or third, level from a walkway. They reached the bottom level by ladders from the ground and the center level by ladders, either from the first level or the third level.

What the diorama doesn't really show is the way they constructed the roof from ten-foot long timbers, reeds, and grasses. They leveled the floors by bringing in dirt. It was quite an engineering feat, particularly when you remember they constructed the entire building with stone tools and muscle power."

"What a lot of work!"

"That's just the building. I'll show you where the farms were."

They continued walking along the path, passing under large cottonwood trees. When they reached picnic tables that overlooked the river, Jessie stopped. "We can sit here for a while. I'm sure this spot is one of the things that drew the people here. Remember, this canyon is one of the few riparian areas in what was high desert all around, much like what's there today, in fact."

Glad she'd chosen jeans and a sleeveless shirt to wear, Marty perched on the tabletop and let her legs swing free. "What crops did they raise?"

"Nothing exotic. Beans and vegetables. They hunted small game and gathered seeds to round out their diet."

"I think Scott said something about cotton."

"They were quite advanced weavers. The few scraps of fabric that survived the looters show intricate designs. Their pottery, on the other hand, was plain and serviceable.

Marty studied Jessie. She obviously loved her work if she had the patience to explain such basic information to a lay person, particularly a woman she didn't particularly want to like. Had Mina somehow threatened Jessie's work? Somehow she had to get Jessie talking about Mina.

After they'd sat in comfortable silence for a few minutes, Marty decided there wasn't an easy transition into the topic. So, she jumped in. "You know, Jessie, I'm afraid we've all been so focused on Reed's feelings about Mina's death that we haven't thought about what her loss must mean to you." She waited, hoping Jessie would take the opening and talk about her relationship with her young assistant. She could learn a lot more if the other woman would talk freely instead of answering questions.

Jessie didn't cooperate but remained silent.

Marty tried again. "From what Reed and Scott told me she seemed more knowledgeable about your project than anyone would expect from a second-year college student. How did you find her?"

Jessie moved restlessly. After a moment she got to her feet

and moved toward the riverbank. Marty wondered what her obvious agitation meant.

With her back still to Marty, Jessie said, "I didn't find her. She found me." Jessie walked closer to the water. Picking up a stick, she tossed it in. The current caught it and swirled away.

When it was out of sight, Jessie turned and headed back to the picnic table. "Dr. Colton, one of the history professors at Yavapai College, has an interest in archaeology. She heard about my project and asked me to come and talk to her class about how archaeologists make observations, collect data, and develop a theory."

Jessie sat back down at the table. Tracing a design in the dust with her finger. "I used my own project as an example. I began by observing and being curious about the traditional name of this place." She stopped drawing and looked up. "Since it's long been accepted among historians in general and archaeologists in particular that Montezuma was never in Arizona, I wondered where the name had originated and why it had stuck. Coronado's expedition struck me as a possibility."

"The Spanish conquered Montezuma just a few years before Coronado and his men came to the Southwest, didn't they?"

"The men with Coronado would have been familiar with the name *Montezuma* and the stories of that culture. I'm sure they never thought Montezuma had come here, but it made a fitting title for this sophisticated complex. I started to wonder if the Castle was inhabited when Coronado came through. That was when I made a hypothesis that flies in the face of archaeological tradition. The next step of course was to start collecting data." She paused and looked at Marty, almost as if she waited for a student to raise her hand and ask a question.

Marty had lots of questions, but none about what Jessie had

just said. Feeling the pressure to speak, she said, "I guess Mina was in Dr. Colton's class."

"She came up to me after the presentation and asked some very thoughtful questions. When she showed up at Montezuma Well two days later with the paperwork for an independent study filled out, I was impressed enough to agree to take her on for two weeks. I told her if during that time she proved to me she was actually some help, I would direct her independent study."

"From what Reed said she became a big help to you."

"I'm going to miss her. "

Marty decided to take a chance. "It sounds like your working relationship developed into friendship."

"I'm not sure I would say we were *friends*. Mina wasn't my peer. I was her mentor. She was an apt pupil."

Marty wondered if the pupil had surpassed the teacher. She decided to ask the question they were all curious about. "Where did Mina get the gold doubloon she had in her hand when she died?"

Marty thought Jessie was going to speak. Instead, she looked away. Something was bothering her. Marty decided to probe a little more. "What do you think happened to Mina?"

Jessie shrugged. "It had to be an accident. Mina was comfortable along the cliff like none of the rest of us were. I guess she and Jackson played there as children. I can't imagine how she lost her balance, but there's really no other explanation."

"What was she doing up there at night?"

"No idea." Jessie got to her feet. "I've got to go back now, Marty. I have an appointment."

Marty watched her retrace their steps, except now Jessie was walking fast, almost as if she needed to escape. From more questions? Or from a memory?

20

Scott looked around the table of adults. They had all picked up their spoons and were eating the gazpacho. It looked delicious, and he was hungry, but impatience won out over hunger. They were running out of time. He could feel it. Reed was still in danger from Mina's killer. Instead of picking up his spoon, he put both hands on the table, one on each side of his bowl. To keep himself from jumping to his feet, he took a deep breath. "I know it sounds silly, but I guess you're all wondering why I called this meeting."

Dad winked, and M2 smiled. Granny Sofia said, "It looks like your folks know, but I'm wondering. I know it's about Reed. He's the only thing that matters to us right now. What do we need to decide?"

Scott nodded in the direction of his parents. "The three of us interviewed the most likely suspects for Mina's murderer—and Reed's attacker. We need to compare notes and decide who we think the killer is."

"Proactive as always," Granny Sofia said. "That's one of the things I love about this family. But I haven't interviewed anyone. I don't even know who is on your suspect list. So why include me?"

Dad looked at him. "It's your meeting, Son. Do you mind if I answer?"

Unable to resist the cold soup anymore, Scott shook his head and picked up his spoon. Relieved his dad had taken the lead, he, took a bite. He swallowed the spicy tomato broth and scooped up another spoonful. One bite demanded another.

"I'll do my best to answer, Sofia. I'm not sure completely sure why Marty or Scott wanted you to this meeting, but I wanted you here because I think we need a neutral sounding board."

M2 looked at Scott. "When Scott's debate team is practicing to get the argument right, it helps to have an audience. We're not exactly debating, but we need an audience to help us focus on the right suspect."

Granny Sofia picked up the casserole dish she'd brought and transferred a taco wrap to her plate. She handed the dish to Scott. "I'll listen as neutrally as I can."

"Scott," Dad said, "why don't you go first?"

Scott took two wraps and handed the dish to Marty. "I interviewed Dr. Dexter. He talked a lot about his reasons for coming this summer, but they all seemed to revolve around Dr. Jessie's research rather than anything directly related to geoarchaeology. The dating of this settlement has already been done, and the times are too recent, geologically, to warrant his expertise."

M2 reached for her glass of ice water. "So, what's he doing here?"

Scott hesitated. "This may sound crazy, but I think he's in love with Dr. Jessie. I think he came to spend time with her and try to get her to notice him. Is that too junior high? He seems a little old to be chasing a crush, but I swear that's what it sounded like to me."

M2 smiled and looked at Dad. "No, he isn't too old. Sometimes even mature adults chase crushes."

Dad returned M2's look. "It's not just grown men who get crushes that aren't reciprocated."

Scott considered teasing his father about using a big word like *reciprocated* when a little one like *returned* would've done just as well, but the topic of the conversation was too serious for teasing. Still, something was going on between his parents. He started to ask, but he knew his dad would shake his head and say, "Private joke." Which meant, "None of your business." So, he didn't ask.

Granny Sofia turned her attention to Scott. "Do you think Jessie noticed?"

"No. But if that's his reason for being here this summer, I don't see why he would have anything against Mina. She sure wasn't a rival for Dr. Jessie's affection."

M2 gave Dad another one of those looks, but this time it didn't feel like a joke. Interesting, but still none of his business.

Granny Sofia took the lead. "Paul, who did you interview?"

Dad held out his hand to M2, who took it. "I talked to Jackson."

When he didn't continue, M2 gave him a little smile and pulled her hand back. "Tell us what you found out."

"Jackson has a terrible temper, and he's willing to lie to get his way. That's a new bit of information about the young man, but it's a long jump from lying to murder. I do think he really cared about Mina.

"I can imagine a quarrel with her over Reed, even a quarrel that got physical. But if the two of them knew the place where Mina died so well, I can't visualize an accident that would end in her falling over the edge there. I don't think Jackson is our murderer. He didn't have anything to gain and everything to lose with Mina's death. I can see him pushing Reed over while Mina was still alive, but not after her death."

All three of them looked at M2. She spread out her hands. "I hate to disappoint you, but I don't think Jessie had anything to do with Mina's death either. She genuinely liked the girl and is grieving her loss, both personally and professionally. Like Jackson and Dr. Dexter, she had nothing to gain from Mina's death."

Granny Sofia looked at Dad. "Did you tell me you have ice cream? Maybe it's time to shift our focus."

Scott's frustration had been growing as he listened. It was a relief to have something physical to do. "I'll get it." Pushing away from the picnic table, he went to the refrigerator and opened the freezer. Inside he found their two favorites, mint chocolate chip and butterscotch swirl. By the time he had the large round tubs and the ice cream scooper on the table, M2 had put out bowls and spoons.

As Dad scooped, Granny Sofia said, "When you can't make sense of a story, it's because a piece of the puzzle is missing. We're overlooking something."

Scott took a bite of his ice cream. The mint made it seem even colder, and he had two big chunks of chocolate. As it melted on his tongue, he considered Granny Sofia's comment. In a moment he had it. The gold doubloon in Mina's hand. Seven Cities might not want a genuine doubloon found."

Dad put the lids on the ice cream tubs. "True. A genuine doubloon would mean this site goes from a quiet, unimportant dig to a place of intense scrutiny and interest. No more salting of fakes and no more access for their clients."

M2 frowned. "Even if I could believe the two men Reed described to us would commit murder when they could simply pull up stakes and move, why would they leave the doubloon behind?"

"True enough," Dad said. "Murder for profit would be premeditated. The killer would be sure to get the evidence either before Mina died or soon after. Maybe Reed was right. Maybe Mina's death was an accident."

Scott scraped up the last bite of his mint chocolate chip and reached for the tub. Lid or no lid, he wanted another helping. "We're getting off the subject, guys. What happened to Reed? He did not try to kill himself!"

Dad held out his hands in a helpless gesture. "Maybe he went to see where Mina fell, got too close to the edge, and slipped. Whatever happened, we have to convince the sheriff he's making a huge mistake. We all know Reed, and we know he would never hurt Mina. We've interviewed everyone and considered all the possibilities. All that's left is two tragic accidents."

Scott put down his spoon. Dad was wrong. He hadn't seen two bodies in the same place. He, Scott had, and he was sure accident had nothing to do with what had happened at the top of that cliff, either time.

He looked around the table at the adults, calm because they didn't have a suspect. But Scott knew nothing was over. Just because their interviews hadn't turned up the killer didn't mean there wasn't one. He was convinced Reed was in more danger now than he'd ever been. The faceless murderer had failed once with Reed. He—or she—couldn't afford to fail again. Since the adults didn't agree, it was up to him to protect his brother.

SCOTT LOOKED OVER HIS SHOULDER. No one stood under the porch light of the house or looked out an upstairs window. He should have asked permission, at least told them where he was going. But he knew his folks. They would have tried to argue him out of it. When that failed, Dad would have forbidden him to go or insisted on coming along.

Once they got to the hospital, Dad would follow the policeman's orders, and they wouldn't get into Reed's room. Scott knew that for certain. It was past visiting hours, and even family wouldn't be allowed in now. He had better chance of success by himself. He wasn't sure how he was going to get in. He only knew he would.

He rolled Reed's motorcycle to the end of the steep driveway and onto the road. The ground was damp from today's monsoon, but it hadn't dropped enough rain this afternoon to create mud. Shoving the helmet on his head, he climbed aboard and started the motor. No one in the house would hear, not unless Sofia was leaving. But he didn't think that was going to happen anytime soon. M2 had put on the coffee pot, and the three of them were settled in to talk over the situation. But Scott was done talking.

Something had to be done—now. The killer would try again tonight, police guard at Reed's room or not. He could feel it in the pit of his stomach, and he could always trust that feeling. Intuition didn't belong only to women or girls. He hadn't been able to convince the three adults. He had no choice but to take matters into his own hands.

Scott couldn't bear the thought of losing Reed. No one else in the family could bear it either, but they didn't feel the urgency he did.

At the bottom of the hill Scott turned onto the highway and made his way through the now quiet streets of Jerome. The shops were closed, and with so few places to spend the night, the only tourists left were in restaurants. Traffic was light, and he made good time. Soon he was at the top of the switchbacks. No one was coming up, and very few cars were going down.

On the third switchback he got caught behind a slow Dodge Ram hauling a fifth wheel. He couldn't see any lights coming up the hill, and he was tempted to pass. But he knew better. It would be just his luck to meet a careless driver who hadn't bothered to turn on his headlights. Gritting his teeth, he told himself it wasn't that far to the bottom. Then there would be lots of places to pass.

He got around the pickup with its trailer just before the stop sign at the bottom of the hill. With the switchbacks behind him, he could focus on a plan for getting into Reed's room. He knew the guard wouldn't let him in, no matter what argument he used. He was going to have to find a way to sneak in.

The only idea he had came from TV shows—to find a laundry room, an orderly's uniform, and a laundry basket to disguise his intent. But he wasn't sure how realistic that would be. Did they have orderlies his age? He didn't know anybody at school who worked at the hospital, and on TV the orderlies always looked older. What else? Maybe wait for the guard to take a break. But he didn't think the guard would just leave his post. Someone would take over for him. If he could find a way to lure the guard from the door ...

It took about twenty minutes to get to the medical center, but by the time Scott made the turn into the parking lot, he still hadn't settled on a plan. He parked on the line between a beaten-up Toyota Highlander and a late model Cadillac Escalade, not a way a teacher of a motorcycle safety class would approve, but he wanted to avoid immediate detection if someone came looking for him.

As he expected, the lobby was deserted. A nurse sat at the reception desk busy at a computer. Hurrying to the stairs, he ducked into the stairwell and made his way to the second floor. Heart pounding, he leaned against the metal door to catch his breath. He wasn't used to sneaking around. When his breathing slowed and his heart settled back into its normal rhythm, he opened the door to the hallway a crack and peeked out.

The hallway was empty, and everything quiet. Evidently all the patients were settled for the night. Maybe the guard would think it was safe enough to take a quick break. Moving as quietly as he could, Scott closed the door behind him and inched down the open expanse between the stairwell and the corner. When he got there, he peeked around. As he'd expected, he could see Reed's room with the guard standing in front of it. What he hadn't expected was to see Granny Sofia talking to the uniformed cop and gesturing insistently toward a window on the back of the building.

"A young man," she said. "Reed's brother, Scott. I'm glad you haven't seen him. That means I got here in time."

The guard looked puzzled. "What are you worried about, ma'am?"

Granny Sofia laughed, a nervous titter Scott hadn't heard from her before. What on earth was going on?

"It's probably nothing. But he's at that impulsive age. And he's so worried about his brother. I thought he might have come here and tried to force his way into Reed's room. His parents and I know Reed is perfectly safe with you on watch. But at supper, Scott seemed so agitated. Then when I came out to go home, I realized he had taken Reed's motorcycle."

"No one has been by here all evening. I'm sure a teenage boy wouldn't get past me."

"Oh, I'm sure of that. In fact, that's what I was worried about. I didn't want him to get in trouble with the police. In case he's still on his way here, I'd like to show you where I'm sure he'll park."

"There's only one parking lot, ma'am."

"That's just it. I'm sure he'll park behind the hospital. If you have a minute, it would make me feel better to see that he's not already here."

The guard looked uncertain. "I'm not supposed to leave my post, ma'am." He looked over his shoulder, almost as if he expected to see his supervisor watching him.

Worried that the guard would look his way, Scott ducked back around the corner.

"I don't want you to leave your post, Officer. Just come over to the window for a second or two."

Scott held his breath. What was going on? Whatever it was, if Granny Sofia could get the guard to step away, even for a minute, he could slip into Reed's room.

Over the loud beating of his heart, Scott heard to guard say, "I guess it won't hurt to walk over to that window with you. You don't want me to go outside or anything like that do you?"

"Of course not! I know you can't leave your post."

Scott forced himself to breath. It was going to work. Without knowing it, Granny Sofia was creating the opportunity he needed.

"You can see it out the window. "The motorcycle is parked between a brand-new black car and a red one that's seen better days."

"Yes, ma'am."

The voices receded just enough.

Scott dove round the corner toward Reed's room. When he was at the door, he slipped inside. That had been a close call. He'd gotten away just ahead of Granny Sofia. He'd sure misjudged the signals. He'd thought the adults were sure to sit over coffee for a couple of hours. More than that, he hadn't expected Granny Sofia to read his mind. Thank goodness she hadn't brought his parents with her. Dad would have been more thorough, insisting on checking the stairwell and around the corner.

Scott glanced around the tiny antiseptic room looking for a place to hide. Not enough room under the bed. Even if he could have squeezed under, nothing would shield him from a casual glance.

The only hiding place was the bathroom. He would just have to hope no one came in. Reed was in a coma. He wouldn't wake up and ask to be taken to the bathroom. And if he did, so much the better. The reason he was here was because his brother couldn't be on guard himself.

The tiny bathroom barely had enough space to allow him to stand between the sink and the door, but he finally positioned himself where he could open the door a crack and see Reed's bed. At first he thought he could listen and open the door whenever he heard someone come in. But after a few minutes, he realized the bathroom door was so thick he couldn't hear anything that was going on in the room.

Pushing open the door as quietly as he could, he held his breath and listened. Silence. Just the faint beeping of the monitor that reassured him Reed's heart beat steadily. He needed something to prop the door open with. He tried an extra roll of toilet paper he found in a tiny cupboard. But it was so soft the heavy door pushed it out of the way. Next he tried the toilet brush, with the same result.

Finally he decided he would have to hold the door open with his foot. That meant standing with his leg at an awkward angle, but he couldn't see any other choice. He had to know what was going on in that room. He'd made it this far. He wouldn't let something like a heavy door keep him from watching over his brother.

With his cell phone tucked in his pocket, Scott lost track of time. But when his foot began to go numb, he knew more than a few minutes had passed. He was about to change legs when he heard the door to Reed's room open. A man's voice said, "I'm just going to check on our patient here, and then we'll be done for the night."

The guard's voice responded with something Scott couldn't quite hear. He had to look, find out who was coming into the room. When he peeked through the tiny opening in the door, he saw a doctor moving toward Reed's bed. Scott didn't recognize the man. A specialist or the murderer in disguise?

21

Reed struggled to open his eyes. He had to see the danger that loomed over him. But his eyelids were glued shut. He tried to reach up and pry them open, but his hands had turned to wood. He was caught in a nightmare, and he couldn't wake up. Someone bad hovered over him, someone intent on killing him.

He wanted to live, but he was sinking into a sea of fear, sinking so deep he couldn't breathe. Finally, his eyelids opened, not all the way, but far enough so he saw the syringe. It hovered over him. He knew a hand had to be holding it, but all he saw was the needle. He fought his way out to the surface of the fear where he could catch a breath. But the air didn't help. They syringe still hovered over him. Somehow he knew it held death.

Reed told his right hand to move, demanded that it move. He had to grab that syringe and throw it on the floor where it would break. His life depended on it. Nothing happened. He kept at it, demanding, persuading, begging his hand to move. Finally, his thumb wiggled. He wasn't paralyzed, but his thumb couldn't save him. He was going to die.

He went down into fear a second time, so deep he was sure he would never come up. He closed his eyes. He was helpless, but he didn't have to watch the needle plunge into his arm. He'd been afraid of needles since he was a little kid and a nurse plunged a needle in his arm at the wrong angle and tore a blood vessel getting it out. The bright red stain on his favorite T-shirt scared him so bad he thought he was going to die. But that childish fear was nothing compared to the terror drowning him now. He wasn't a little kid anymore, and he knew this time he really was going to die.

Words he'd heard at Scott's church whispered in his ear. *Though I walk through the valley of the shadow of death ...* That's where he was. What was the rest of it? He struggled to the surface of the fear, trying to remember.

He caught a breath. Instead of just the syringe he saw the hand holding it. A doctor in white scrubs and a surgical mask leaned over him. Cold eyes reflected evil, evil intent on using that syringe to deliver death. Reed tried to sit up. Ice picks of pain stabbed his eyes, the room spun, and a ruthless hand shoved him hard against the pillows. What was the rest of that psalm? Something about evil. *I will fear no evil ...*

How could he not fear this evil? Death was coming for him. He recognized it, just like he'd recognized it on the edge of the Well. Then he had wrenched free of the hands that grasped his shoulders—these hands that now held the syringe. Then he had gone over the cliff, sure he was falling to his death.

Everything had gone black and stayed black. But here he was in a hospital bed. He must have survived the fall into the Well. Because here he was walking into the shadow of death again.

This time he couldn't fight those hands, not even enough to turn away from the needle. As he started to go down into the fear a third time, he felt a loving Presence. He remembered the rest of that puzzling promise. *I will fear no evil ... for You are with me.* The Presence must be God. God loved him. That was why he didn't have to be afraid to die.

He closed his eyes and leaned into that Love. Then another presence came close, a pale reflection of God's Love, but love just as real. He opened his eyes to see Scott. Was his brother really there, or was he remembering his brother's love just before he slipped into death?

Then the doctor jerked sideways. Reed knew it wasn't a memory.

"No!" The shout was Scott's voice. His brother was really here.

But the hand still gripped the syringe. The doctor lunged for Scott. Reed struggled to move. He knew he had to grab the doctor's coat, divide his attention, force him to turn away from Scott, even for a split second.

Nothing happened. A lead blanket covered Reed from his neck to his feet. As he struggled to move, he remembered the youth leader at church saying, "When life gets too strong for you, remember—God has your back. Pray. Ask God for help."

But Reed didn't know how to pray. He listened when other people prayed, sometimes repeated the words they said. But that wasn't the same thing. What would he say to God? The Love he'd felt still held him. He squeezed his eyes shut and cried out to that Love. "Help! I can't do this. Help Scott!" That was all the prayer Reed knew. But he felt another loving presence.

He opened his eyes. Uncle Paul's face appeared above Scott's head. Scott lost his balance and fell against his dad. The doctor reached for something above Reed's head. Something changed in Reed's world. He couldn't breathe. The doctor was watching him. Reed couldn't see the face behind the mask, but he saw satisfaction in those cold eyes.

He struggled to take a breath. But his lungs wouldn't work. The lead that held him to the bed was in his lungs now. Colors turned from bright to gray. Reed's vision, now in black and white, narrowed. All he could see was the doctor's eyes. He was about to die. He closed his eyes and looked for the Face of the Love that still held him.

"Come back!" Scott's voice cut into his quiet world. "Open your eyes, Reed! Please, brother. You can't die now."

Reed didn't want to disappoint Scott. But he had to breathe to live. His lungs couldn't work full of lead. He prayed again. Weaker this time, but the same prayer. "Help." Air started pushing the lead out of his lungs. Reed took a breath, then another.

"Open your eyes. Please!"

Reed tried to obey. His eyelids felt like before, glued shut. They had opened once before. Maybe they would open again. He struggled harder. Scott's face appeared, fuzzy at first, then clearer. Reed saw tears running down his brother's face. He wanted to reach out and grab Scott's arm, shout that he was okay. He took a deep breath, then another. He tried to speak, failed, and tried again. Still nothing happened.

Scott smiled. "No worries, bro. Your eyes are open. That's all I need."

Reed felt the head of his bed move up. It jerked to a stop at the same time Scott shouted, "Watch out, Dad! The doctor's behind you. He's going to stab your shoulder with the syringe he's holding."

Reed blinked. Something had happened while he struggled to open his eyes. Aunt Marty had joined the struggle. As he watched, she reached around the doctor, grabbed the hand that held the syringe, and pulled the fingers back. With a reassuring clatter, the syringe fell to the floor. Uncle Paul pulled the doctor's arms back, and Scott jerked the surgical mask off.

"It's Dr. Dexter!" Scott shouted. A policeman appeared beside Uncle Paul. Granny Sofia, close behind the policeman, came to stand beside his bed. "I'm so glad to see you awake, Reed," she murmured.

Reed thought he must be dreaming. Was the whole family really here? Their love buoyed him up. He knew no matter what happened now, he wouldn't sink into that ocean of fear.

"What do you think you're doing?" barked the policeman. "Let the doctor go!"

Scott grabbed the policeman's arm. "You don't understand."

As the policeman shook Scott off, Dr. Dexter tried to twist free of Uncle Paul's grasp.

His foster father hung on. "He's an archaeologist, not a medical doctor."

Aunt Marty picked up the syringe and held it out. "And a killer."

Dr. Dexter stopped struggling, took a deep breath. "I'm sure you've heard of slander," You've got no proof."

"Whatever was in that syringe will prove attempted murder," Uncle Paul said.

Dr. Dexter shook his head.

"I came to check on Reed. We're worried about him—I knew I couldn't get in, so I borrowed this getup from a physician friend. He gave me the syringe. He promised it would help the boy."

"I saw you!" Scott said. "You were trying to mess with that line. When you dropped the syringe, you pulled it out at the connection."

Dr. Dexter frowned. "I did nothing of the sort. You disconnected the line when you attacked me. I can charge you with assault. The worst I can be charged with is entering a patient's room after visiting hours."

"And administering a drug. You're not a medical doctor!"

"I didn't administer anything, did I? I threw the syringe on the floor."

Scott's hands clenched in fists. "You did not! M2 forced you to drop it."

"A judge is going to have to make sense of this," the policeman said. "Let Dr. Dexter go."

Reed tried to make his vocal cords work. He had to tell them. "No! He's the murderer." It came out like a croak, not like words.

But Scott heard. "Be quiet, everyone! Reed is trying to tell us something."

Reed breathed the only prayer he knew. "*Help!*" He took a deep breath, tried again. His voice was soft, but most of his words came out. "He pushed me ... killed Mina."

Free from Uncle Paul's grip, Dr. Dexter crossed his arms. "The boy is delirious. I didn't push him—or the girl."

Reed gathered his energy to speak again. Taking a deep breath, he managed the most important words. "... put gold doubloon in the dwelling. Mina saw ..."

Dr. Dexter stared at him, shock draining the color from his face.

With a sick feeling, Reed realized how accurate his guess had been. Mina must have seen Dr. Dexter after Jackson left. Reed held his breath, hoping the man would break own and admit the truth. Then Scott's boss snorted. "The boy is delirious. Why would I plant a doubloon?"

"I know the answer to that," Scott said. "You're in love with Dr. Jessie, I bet you were going to help her find it. You thought she would be grateful and give you a chance."

"You make me sound like a love-sick teenager."

Uncle Paul took up where Scott left off. "Maybe that's what you are. You knew Jessie was still getting over her divorce. You followed her this summer thinking you could walk right into her life."

Dr. Dexter stared at Uncle Paul but didn't reply.

"When she didn't, you got desperate."

"Mina caught you," Reed whispered. "You didn't have to kill her."

Dr. Dexter looked sick but still didn't admit to anything.

Scott moved to stand directly in front of the geoarchaeologist. "You knew Mina would tell Dr. Jessie. You couldn't risk that, so you pushed her off the side of the Well." He took a deep breath. "I can prove it."

"You can't prove something that didn't happen."

"It did happen. I found the beads from Mina's necklace scattered at the edge. I was careful when I picked them up. How are you going to explain your fingerprints?"

Mina's beautiful turquoise and silver necklace. Remembering how it sparkled in the sunlight made Reed want to jump up from his bed and shake the man. Or slam him into the wall. Or at least give him a bloody nose. But he couldn't escape the lead blanket. He tried to shout, but no words came. Even his whisper was gone. A sound like a growl came from somewhere deep inside.

Uncle Paul put a warm hand on Reed's head. "I think that's enough, Officer Sanchez. Don't you?"

"Enough to give me grounds to take you all to the station until someone with more authority than I have can make sense of this."

Before Uncle Paul could object, the door to the room swung open and a doctor marched in. "What's going on? This young man was badly injured. No one should be in here besides medical personnel."

Aunt Marty detached herself from the knot of men. "We're glad to see you, Dr. Schmidt. We've had a near tragedy this evening. But it's all come right. Reed has come out of the coma!"

As Dr. Schmidt headed for the bed, Officer Sanchez made a sweeping gesture that took in everyone. "I'm taking these folks to the station,"

Granny Sofia cleared her throat.

Officer Sanchez gave her an apologetic look. "Not you, ma'am. I met you outside. You're free to go."

She smiled and beckoned to Scott. "May I take my grandson home? Surely his parents can speak for him."

Reed recognized the stubborn look on Scott's face. He hoped his brother would take one of those deep breaths he was always talking about and follow the escape route Granny Sofia was offering.

Reed saw he didn't need to worry. The old lady knew Scott as well as he did. Moving to stand beside him, she linked her arm in his. Then she smiled sweetly at the policeman. "You've got enough to do tonight. You can always talk to him tomorrow."

Officer Sanchez grimaced. "You're right about that, ma'am. All right, you two can go. The rest of you come with me." Placing one hand on Dr. Dexter's arm and the other on Uncle Paul's arm, he started toward the door.

As Granny Sofia followed, Scott looked over her head at Reed and mouthed, "See you at home."

Reed knew Dr. Schmidt had seen Scott's message because the doctor shook his head. "This young man won't be going home anytime soon. This is the first time we've seen Reed conscious. He's got a long recovery ahead."

Aunt Marty moved away from Officer Sanchez. Coming to the bed, she dropped a light kiss, the brush of a butterfly's wing, on Reed's forehead. "We understand, doctor. His family will be waiting."

Reed let her words soak in. It didn't matter how long it took him to get well. His family was there, ready to welcome him home.

22

Tuesday

Marty put down her coffee feeling as surprised as Scott looked. Sheriff Winston followed close behind Paul as he crossed the living area, heading for the kitchen. Why would the sheriff ring their doorbell before 8:00 a.m.? Especially this morning. Surely they had answered all the official questions last night.

Paul picked up his abandoned mug and headed for the microwave. "Larry needs a few minutes with us."

He didn't know what the sheriff wanted. If he had, he'd have worked it into that bold introduction. He knew about the panic that had been Marty's constant companion since the evening before when Sofia announced that Scott and Reed's motorcycle were gone. He would have warned her what was coming.

"I know it's early to be ringing your doorbell," the sheriff said, "but what I have to say can't wait."

Marty looked at Paul. Was something wrong with Reed?

Had he taken a turn for the worse after the excitement of the night before. Paul gave a tiny shrug. He had to be as worried as she was. The sheriff cleared his throat. "Mind if I sit down?"

She tried to speak. When no words came, she waved a hand in what she hoped was a good imitation of permission.

The microwave dinged, and Paul took out his coffee mug. "Larry, can I get you some coffee?

"No, thanks."

"Scott, can I get you more juice or milk?"

Scott jumped as if his dad had thrown cold water in his face. "Thanks, I'll get it myself."

"I might as well get straight to the point," the sheriff said. "I'm here to apologize for the way I've treated Reed and, by extension, your whole family."

Marty was glad her mug was halfway to her mouth. Otherwise, shock would have choked.

Paul raised his eyebrows. It was a moment before he spoke, but when he did, his voice was steady. "As you can imagine, Larry, we're all surprised. What's happened?"

With a flash of horror, Marty wondered if Reed had died. She searched her mind desperately for something, anything else that would make Larry Winston feel guilty enough to apologize.

"Dexter made a full confession last night. As Reed guessed, Mina caught him salting the cliff dwelling with a couple of gold doubloons. He was in love with Dr. Jensen, and he thought if he showed up the next morning and helped her find them, she would want to celebrate with him. He thought that's all it would take for her to fall in love with him."

Larry turned to Scott. "He got the idea when you told him what Reed was doing for that adventures tour outfit."

"I never told him anything about Reed!"

"Dexter insisted you told him Reed was salting fake doubloons."

"I never even talked to Dr. Dexter about Reed ..." His voice trailed off. A dull red splotch showed just above the neck of his T-shirt and spread up the left side of his neck. When he spoke, horror replaced outrage in his voice. "Except for once." He swallowed, took a deep breath. "After Dr. Dexter met Reed, he asked me about my foster brother. I thought it would make Reed look good if I told Dr Dexter how Reed was working two jobs to make enough money to go to college." Scott swallowed again. "He asked me where Reed worked. I told him at the hardware store and for Seven Cities. I never said anything about salting fake doubloons. I'm positive!"

Sheriff Winston squinted and looked at the ceiling as if searching his memory. "That's right. Now that I think of it, Dexter called Seven Cities and talked to that promoter, Parnell. Dexter got the information about the salting from him."

"Okay," Paul said. "But where did Ken get genuine doubloons on such short notice? It's not like someone can walk into an antique shop and buy them."

"Dexter has connections to a rare coin dealer in Phoenix. The guy sent him two by overnight mail."

Marty felt sick. Luck. It was good luck for Dexter that he happened to know a coin dealer so close to where he was working. But that good luck spelled disaster for poor Mina. If Dexter hadn't been able to get doubloons so easily, he couldn't have carried out his plan to fool Jessie. Mina wouldn't have seen anything illegal going on that night, and she would still be alive. If only ...

Marty brought herself back to the present. "Did Ken intend to kill Mina? Or was it an accident?"

"Dexter says it was an accident, but the evidence of that

broken necklace tells a different story. It shows intent. He was trying to strangle her when she fell."

Marty bit back what she wanted to say—*You should have collected your evidence before you accused an innocent young man.*

Scott must have been thinking the same thing because he made an angry noise.

Before the boy could speak, Paul reached across the table and touched his son's hand.

Scott looked rebellious, but he kept quiet.

Paul looked directly at the sheriff. "Larry, I hope next time you'll collect your evidence before you start accusing innocent people."

Marty wanted to cheer. Paul had spoken for all three of them, actually for all four of them.

Scott pulled his hand from under his father's. "What about Reed? We all know he didn't jump off that cliff. Did Dr. Dexter admit to pushing him?"

"He did. He said he was in the cliff dwelling making sure the other doubloon he'd hidden was still there when Reed showed up. He tried to tell Reed he was just working late, but your brother didn't buy it. Dexter thought he could take care of Reed the same way he took care of Mina, but he hadn't counted on your brother being so much stronger. Besides that, Dexter caught Mina off guard. Reed knew he was in danger."

When no one spoke, the sheriff hurried on. "Thank you all for listening to me."

As he started to get to his feet, Marty said, "One more thing, Larry. Why are you so hard on Reed? And I'm not just talking about everything that happened at the Well. Your attitude toward him started long before Mina's death."

For the first time, the sheriff looked like he wished he could be somewhere else. He cleared his throat.

"It's an important question," Paul said. "Reed isn't going anywhere, and neither are you. We need to make sure your accusations of our son stop here."

Larry wiped his forehead with the back of his hand. "You have my word."

Marty wasn't going to let him off the hook that easily. "We appreciate that, but why have you been so hard on him?"

The sheriff looked down at his hands.

Marty could tell he didn't want to answer, but she was determined to get an explanation. "We have a right to an answer to that question, Larry. You've made life in our family difficult almost from the moment Reed moved in here."

"I know. I know." The sheriff took a deep breath and looked at Paul. "You remember my sister, Stephanie."

Paul frowned. "Of course. What can Reed have done to her?"

The sheriff didn't answer, turned his attention to Marty. "You never knew her. She was really my half-sister, fifteen years younger. That never mattered, though. We were close from the time she was born. I was a lonely kid who could never do anything right. But to Steph, I was a powerful grown-up who could fix anything from a broken doll to a bloody nose."

"The receptionist at the jail, Kate, told me Reed's father, Lloyd Harper, Sr., dated Stephanie for a while."

The sheriff looked at Paul. "Could I trouble you for a glass of water?"

Scott jumped up. "I'll get it."

The sheriff cleared his throat. "I did everything I could to convince Steph that Lloyd was trouble, but that didn't matter to her. In fact, I think that was part of the attraction. Some good girls are attracted to bad guys." He shook his head. "I guess they think they can make those men over. Besides that, I guess Lloyd was attractive to women."

Scott handed the sheriff a large glass of ice water. Larry took a long gulp. When he put the glass down, he said, "Reed looks a lot like his dad. I guess every time I look at him, I see Lloyd, Sr. I've blamed Lloyd for Steph's suicide. That may or may not be true. But either way, it had nothing to do with Reed." He sighed. "I don't know how I can make it up to the boy."

"The first step," Paul said, "would be to tell Reed what you just told us."

Larry got to his feet. "I plan to go to the hospital first thing this afternoon and do just that. I don't want to go now because I thought you folks would want to have some time with Reed."

Scott looked up. "You mean we don't need the lawyer? We can go see Reed?"

Larry smiled, the first smile Marty had seen since he walked in.

"It sure does, buddy. You can see him as quick as you can get to the hospital."

Scott pumped the air. "All right!"

Marty and Paul got to their feet almost at the same time.

Larry waved them back to their seats. "Don't trouble yourselves, folks. I can see myself out. You enjoy your family time."

As soon as they heard the front door close, Scott shouted, "Let's go! What are we waiting for?"

Paul caught his son in a friendly neck lock. "A clean shirt for you, for one thing."

Scott grinned and pushed free. "Oh, right. I didn't think we were going anywhere today. Back in a flash. Can I drive?"

"You can and you may," Paul said over the sound of Scott's feet pounding up the stairs.

Marty put a hand on Paul's arm. "There's one thing you need to do before we go."

Paul studied his shirt. "Fresh today. It might be almost ready for the rag bag, but ..."

"Not your shirt. A phone call."

Paul looked puzzled.

"Jessie. Her entire world has collapsed. Her assistant is dead, her colleague is in jail and likely to stay there. On top of that, my guess is that her research project has been compromised beyond repair."

"True enough."

"She needs a friend, and I'm pretty sure you're it, at least in Arizona. Invite her over for dinner."

Paul studied her for a moment. Then he took her in his arms and kissed her. When they came up for air, he said, "You keep surprising me, Mart!"

Marty leaned back in his arms and laughed up at him. "I think that's a good thing."

Scott came back into the kitchen twirling the car keys around one finger, "You guys can do that anytime Let's go see Reed. We need to celebrate!"

EPILOGUE

M id-October

REED LOOKED DOWN on the path he'd traveled to reach the cave. Paranoid or not, he wanted to be sure no one was following him. The road that connected to the highway was deserted, and any vehicle larger than his motorcycle couldn't make it down the trail that led to the cave. Deliberately ignoring his aching legs, he scrambled down from his perch.

When physical therapy was the most painful, he imagined this day. He'd known he had to get back the strength in his arms and legs if he was ever going to explore this cave again. He didn't know how he knew, but he was certain the gold doubloons were here. Grabbing his backpack, he ducked into the cave's entrance.

Hands trembling, he settled his headgear and switched on the light. His heart rate kicked up as he crossed the room he'd explored on that day three months ago, the day he learned

Mina was dead, the day his world collapsed. Light danced across the floor and up the walls of the cave, but Reed ignored the occasional sparks of light that beckoned him. Another day he might bring Scott here to examine the minerals—after he found the doubloons.

He kept going. It only took a few minutes to reach the place where the main passage split. That morning he'd run out of time for exploring. Certain he could come back the next day, he went to the Russells' to get ready for work. Reed pushed away the memories that threatened to paralyze him.

He was here now. The same way he knew the doubloons were here, and he knew he would find them today. The ghost of that long-dead conquistador had promised him. The dream he'd had in the hospital was so real, he knew it would come true.

He'd kept the dream to himself, knowing even Scott wouldn't believe in his conquistador. But the short, slight man with the tattered clothes and the scraggly beard had promised him. Reed intended to hold him to his promise. Reed owed it to Mina. He promised her he would go to college. The doubloons, added to his savings, would pay his way to the University of Virginia. Once he got there, he'd figure out how to stay. Without the cash the coins represented, his only choice would be to live with the Russells and go to Yavapai Community College. That was the future.

Now he had to decide which branch of the cave to follow. He didn't have time for both. He closed his eyes and imagined the conquistador. Reed's instinct told him to go right, even though the roof was lower and the walls closer together. In the 1500s people had been shorter and slighter. What might be a squeeze for him would have presented no challenge to his conquistador.

Settling his backpack more firmly on his shoulders, Reed

ducked his head and started down the new path. He went slowly, watching the walls and the floor for any reflection from his light. Coronado's gold doubloons contained a high concentration of gold. Even after five centuries they would still glitter.

Nothing caught the light. Reed pushed on, sure he was headed in the right direction. He just hadn't gone far enough. In another fifty yards the passage divided again. This time he didn't hesitate. He went left.

The roof lowered suddenly. As he ducked, his headlamp dimmed. "Not now," he muttered. "Don't go out on me." He was too close to success to turn around. He could almost see his conquistador beckoning him on.

Reaching up, he gave the headlamp a little shake. Instead of giving him more light, it flickered and went out. Reed felt like letting loose with a string of curses. Scott wasn't here to look shocked or Uncle Paul to frown. But that wasn't why he restricted himself to milder language.

Whenever he was tempted to drink, hit someone, or curse, he told himself he wasn't like his father. When he changed his name from *Lloyd, Jr.* to *Reed*, he vowed to find a different way to live. That vow had nothing to do with what anyone else thought. It was a promise to himself, a promise he was determined to keep.

Now he had to decide what to do. Go on in the dark or go back. Everything in him wanted to go forward. But he'd be lucky to find his way back to the entrance without a light, and finding the doubloons would be impossible.

He thought about his options. No replacement bulb because he'd thought this one had hours of use left in it. No matches since he'd quit smoking. He didn't want to run the battery down on his cell phone unless it was absolutely necessary. The tiny penlight attached to his keychain!

It wasn't exactly suited to sweeping the cave passage, but it was enough. It had to be. Taking off his backpack, he fumbled in the dark until he found his keys. He switched on the tiny light and swept the floor of the narrow passage.

No one had been this way for a long time, maybe not since his conquistador. Rocks of all sizes littered the floor. He switched off the light. He should go back. He didn't know what time it was, but it was probably getting close to the time he needed to turn around and go home for dinner anyway. This was an important dinner, a celebration of his homecoming. Granny Sofia was coming, and Uncle Paul had promised several large pizzas loaded with everything from anchovies to double cheese and double pepperoni.

But the conviction that today was the day he would find the doubloons wouldn't go away. Reed closed his eyes and tried to decide what to do. He wanted to go on. He knew he should go home. As he hesitated, he heard a sound, faint but identifiable.

Somewhere just ahead water dripped. Most of the caves in this area, like the desert above, were dry and thirsty. But every now and then, a stubborn spring would find its way up from the mysterious source that fed Montezuma Well. Caves with springs, rare as they were, attracted wildlife and people alike.

So why hadn't he seen any signs of life in this cave? Maybe he had and not paid attention to what they might mean. He remembered the dark shapes clinging to the roof near the entrance and the scat he stepped over at the first branch. He wondered briefly about bears. But they were rare in these mountains now. Besides, it was the middle of the summer, long past the time when mamas would be raising babies.

The conviction he was in the right cave grew stronger. He would just have to be late for dinner. When he showed up with the doubloons, they would understand. Watching closely for any sign of animal, man, or doubloon, he started forward.

When the ceiling dropped again, he knew he'd have to crawl to keep going. Even a conquistador couldn't walk upright here. Maybe he was in the right cave but in the wrong passage. He turned off the light and listened again. Just ahead drops splashed rhythmically. A thirsty conquistador would have crawled for water.

Taking off his backpack, Reed got down on his hands and knees, switched the light back on, and directed the beam straight ahead. It caught the sheen of water, not so much a pool as a bowl hollowed out in the stone. Holding his breath, he swept the area around the bowl. Nothing but rock.

A noise he couldn't identify bounced off the roof, overpowering the sound of the water. Reed jumped. His light reflected against the wall, and a tiny light winked at him. For a moment he was disoriented, unable to process the sound or the light on the wall. Then he knew what both of them were: the alarm on his cell phone and the reflection of a bright object nestled between two rocks.

Reaching behind him, he found the outside pocket of his backpack. Grabbing his cell, he turned off the alarm. The clock told him it was 5 p.m., past time to turn around and go back. But he couldn't go back, not until he found out what his light had caught, either a bit of shiny mineral like galena—or a gold doubloon.

He punched snooze on the alarm and switched on the flashlight of his phone. Now was that absolutely necessary time he'd waited for. Taking a deep breath, he crawled a few more feet. When he reached the tiny light sparkling against the dark rock, he could see the edge of a clearly identifiable coin. It had to be a doubloon.

His pulse pounded in his ears as he plucked the coin from the tiny crevice where it had caught five hundred years before. Rolling onto his back, Reed held the doubloon with one hand

and his cell phone with the other. It was very like the fake coins he'd salted in his short-lived job with Seven Cities.

One side showed a cross, the other a collection of symbols. Unlike the reproductions, this coin wasn't actually round. Scott had showed him a photo of an antique doubloon in *The History of Spanish Coins*. Made by hand instead of by a machine, genuine doubloons were more like clumsy octagons.

The snooze alarm jolted Reed back into the present. Closing his hand around the doubloon, he hit snooze again. Then he switched off the light and stared up into the darkness. He had to make a decision, quickly. He'd found the first doubloon, but not the last.

One meant dozens more to pick up. He'd imagined them all together in a bag, but it wasn't going to be that easy. If he stayed to hunt them down, he wouldn't just be late. He would miss the party and disappoint the family that had taken him in, stood by him when everyone else thought he was a murderer, and rescued him when Dr. Dexter tried to kill him.

He was standing at a decision in his life as real as the two branches he'd come to in the cave. Left would take him to the doubloons, right to his family. He remembered Uncle Paul telling him that family was more important than any school he went to. Maybe he was right. A degree from UVA couldn't have saved him when he was lying at the bottom of that cliff or when Dr. Dexter pulled the plug on his oxygen. He needed to go home.

He switched on the light and looked at the doubloon again. Should he take it with him or leave it here in the place where it had been hidden for so many years?

If he took it with him, he could show it to Scott. Scott would help him find the rest of the doubloons. If they found the rest of them and he sold them to raise the cash he needed for tuition, Dr. Jessie would hear about it for sure. She would come back and start up the dig again.

Reed's stomach knotted. Other people would come looking for doubloons, and some of them would be as desperate to reach their goal as Dr. Dexter had been.

He could always go to Yavapai Community College. After all, it had been the school Mina chose to go to. Like Uncle Paul said, he could keep working and save up his money. If he got good grades, he could get an academic scholarship to go wherever he wanted to.

Reed couldn't believe it. Was he seriously considering leaving the doubloon here in the mountain? He could keep this one. He wouldn't sell it, just keep it as a souvenir. After all, he had worked hard to find it. When he was Bernie's age, he could show it to his grandkids and tell them the legend. He could tell them he'd found the doubloons. But he wouldn't tell them where. He wouldn't want them to come looking for the rest of the treasure.

Maybe he would keep it just for himself. Keep it hidden. Not tell anyone. Just get it out sometimes when he wanted to remember that he knew where a treasure was, just in case he needed it sometime. Suddenly he remembered his father hiding a bottle of whiskey. He'd told his son, it was just in case. He'd promised he wouldn't open it. But Lloyd, Sr. had always opened it. His son had scars to help him remember those hidden bottles. Keeping this doubloon was a lot like keeping a bottle of whiskey.

Gritting his teeth, Reed got back up on his hands and knees. Without turning on the light, he threw the doubloon deeper into the cave. As he crawled backwards, he groaned. He couldn't come back here. Somehow he had to forget where this cave was.

When he got to where he could stand up, he shook his

head. He didn't need the doubloons. He didn't need the University of Virginia. He could still make something of himself. By the time he reached the main passage, he was able to smile. He would remember Mina by going to Yavapai and graduating with honors. Every time he looked at his diploma, he would thank her for inspiring him to quit salting those fake doubloons. When he stepped out of the cave under a red and gold sky, he grinned. He was heading home to a loving family and an everything, thick crust pizza.

What more could a guy want?

ACKNOWLEGEMENTS

The Gold Doubloons is the twelfth book I've written (the sixth published). Without question, it was the toughest to write. In the three years I worked on *The Gold Doubloons* I kept going back to a little prayer I heard in a sermon Dr. Luke Powery preached at Duke Chapel: *"Dear God, I can't. You must. I'm yours. Show me the way. Amen."*

At first the writing was fun. I knew the characters, the setting, and the legend that drives the plot. Then the pandemic hit. You remember the disbelief, then the fear, and finally the chaos of that first year. My writing coughed, slowed down, and then stopped. During those crazy months my daughter Jorie (AZ) and my reader Marlene (OR) along with my friends Becky and Jim, Rhonda, and Joanie (AR) helped me grope my way back into the story.

As the first year blended into the second year, I regained a precarious balance, and *The Gold Doubloons* got under way again. Then people in my close circle of family and friends began to die. Four dear ones passed away in twelve months (not from Covid) from cancer, pneumonia, and old age. My daughter Jorie, my stepmother Maggie (NC), my brother Dick and his wife Darlene (VA), my brother Mike and his wife Annaliese (KY), along with my cousins Merry Lynn, Tim, Lew, Steven, Scott, Sherry, and Ros (NC, AK, FLA) wept with me at memorial services we were able to attend for my cousin Priscilla and my father. The next fall, my dear friend Becky (see above) died. Becky's husband Jim and friends Rhonda and Lynda mourned her passing with me. During that season of death *The Gold Doubloons* stayed untouched in my computer.

In October gratitude and joy joined hands with my grief when my first grandchild, Aurora Jane, was born. The first time I held her in my arms, I counted the miles between Arkansas and Arizona (1400+). I knew it was time to move back to Arizona. My friend Vaughn (AZ) helped me find an apartment where I could see the sun come up over Mingus Mountain. Back in Arkansas my house sold quickly, and in December Arkansas friends Rhonda, Jan, and Caron helped me pack. Arizona friends Mary and Jeff Johnson drove the U-Haul truck those 1400 miles. As I flew from Arkansas to Arizona, *The Gold Doubloons* began to stir back to life in my imagination. Mary, Jeff, and Marlene helped me unpack, and a few days later, *The Gold Doubloons* stirred to life in my computer. But life wasn't finished interrupting this book.

My Multiple Sclerosis took a nosedive, bringing *The Gold Doubloons* to another full stop. The February deadline came and went without a complete draft. Linda (AR), my friend and Scrivenings Press publisher, adjusted the schedule and gave me a new deadline. As I groped my way back from the worst of the MS setback, my granddaughter (and her parents, of course) kept a stream of joy coming into my life. Aurora sat up ... crawled ... walked ... danced! When a complete draft of *The Gold Doubloons* finally took shape on my computer, content editor Erin (KY) discovered repetitions, awkward sentences, and story problems.

As I look back over the last two and a half years of writing, I see that God answered my *I can't-You must-I'm yours* prayer. I found the way to *The Gold Doubloons* through a network of family and friends spread across eight states, a network only God could orchestrate. When life threatens to overwhelm me, I still pray, *Show me the way.* But I also pray, *"Dear God, I'm yours. Thank you. Amen."*

I also want to acknowledge three sources I used multiple times because you might find them as fascinating as I did.

Butler, Carolina, and Sigrid Khera, eds. 2012. *Oral History of the Yavapai: Mike Harrison and John William.* Gilbert, Arizona: Acacia Publishing, Inc.

Eswonia, Frieda Ann. 2015. *Survival of the Yavapai.* Sedona, Arizona: Sedona Heritage Publishing, held by the Sedona Historical Society, Inc.

Northern Arizona University. "Arizona Heritage Waters: Montezuma Well." http://www.azheritagewaters.nau.edu/loc_montezumawell.html

AUTHOR'S NOTE

ABOUT THE TRILOGY
Jerome, Arizona
Largest ghost town in America,
Billion-dollar copper camp alive with rags to riches stories, or
Tourist attraction since 1542?
Maybe it's all three ...

I first visited Jerome in the late 1970s. A ghost town of derelict hotels, empty restaurants, and wide-open banks, Jerome was a favorite destination of forty-something motorcycle groups and four-wheel-drive enthusiasts. (My husband and I were part of the second group.) Every empty building we passed whispered a story to me.

Thirty years later, I was still visiting Jerome. By then it had become a thriving tourist town that attracted ghost hunters, mine explorers, and visitors to Native American ruins. One afternoon as I was climbing a dirt road that passed the Catholic church, I noticed an old Victorian house on the hill above my head. A shack with the roof caved in just across the road made a stark contrast. I imagined the occupants of the two houses. Antiques expert Marty Greenlaw had come from Virginia to her grandmother's old Victorian house, and historian Paul Russell was attempting to rebuild the shack. The idea for the mystery of *The Copper Box* began to take shape in my head.

Three years later Kathy Cretsinger (Mantle Rock Press) offered me a contract for *The Copper Box*. A clause at the end requested the first right of refusal for any other books in the series. I don't read series very often, at least not past book three or four, so I'd thought of *The Copper Box* as a standalone story. But that brief sentence was all it took to suggest a trilogy of mysteries themed with the ores mined in Jerome—copper, silver, and gold. *The Copper Box* was followed by *The Silver Lode* and *The Gold Doubloons*.

I could give you more background of these three companion stories, but where's the fun in that? Pick up the books and start reading!

DISCUSSION QUESTIONS

1. How does this story depend on its setting?
2. If you've read *The Copper Box* and *The Silver Lode*, what do you see the author doing with the Jerome setting?
3. Who did you first suspect was the murderer? When? Why?
4. The theme is 1 Corinthians 13:13. How does it apply to Paul?Marty? Scott? Reed?
5. How has this verse applied to you and members of your family?
6. Where does Reed encounter God's desire to help him? Who tells him? (Hint: Reed remembers this when he's in the hospital.)
7. When has God helped you? Where did you learn of God's desire to help you?
8. Which of the characters did you like best? Why?
9. Which of the characters did you least? Why?
10. Does the author do a good job with description? Why or why not?

11. Does this book make you want to visit Jerome, Arizona? Why or why not?

12. Do you think you'll ever read this book again? Why or why not?

13. Would you recommend it to a friend? Why or why not?

14. What would you like to tell the author* about this book?

15. If you've read *The Copper Box* and *The Silver Lode*, which of the three books do you like the most? Why? If you're willing, please share your preference and reasons with the author*.

*Contact her at suzanne@suzannebratcher.com. She'd love to get your comments!

ABOUT SUZANNE J. BRATCHER

A passionate reader since her first encounter with Dick and Jane, Suzanne J. Bratcher wanted to grow up to be a fiction writer. After college, realizing she couldn't support herself on ten cents a word, she became an English teacher, specializing in writing instruction. Over the next thirty years she taught writing to high schoolers, college students, and public school teachers. She continued her own writing: publishing professional articles, two textbooks, short stories, and poetry. Since retiring from Northern Arizona University in Flagstaff, Bratcher has returned to her childhood dream of writing fiction. *The Copper Box*, *The Silver Lode*, and *The Gold*

Doubloons make up the Jerome Mysteries Trilogy. *Kokopelli's Song* (2020) is the first book in the Fantasy Folklore series.

Reviews of Suzanne's books on Amazon and Goodreads help new readers find her work. Please rate the book and add a few lines to share what you liked. These do not have to be recent titles.

Find Suzanne Online:

Visit https://suzannebratcher.com to read her blog and be sure to sign up for her monthly newsletter.

Connect with Suzanne on Facebook: https://facebook.com/authorsuzannebratcher

ALSO BY SUZANNE J. BRATCHER

If you enjoyed *The Gold Doubloons*, please leave a review on Goodreads.com and/or Amazon.com. Thank you.

You may also enjoy these books

by Suzanne J. Bratcher:

The Copper Box

Book One of the Jerome Mysteries Series

Jerome, Arizona: the largest ghost town in America

Antiques expert Marty Greenlaw comes to Jerome to face the horror that haunts her dreams: Did she kill her little sister twenty-two years ago?

Historian Paul Russell is in Jerome to face his own horror: Was the car crash that killed his wife his fault?

Their lives become intertwined when an old lady dies on a long staircase in a vintage Victorian house. As Marty and Paul search the house for a small copper box Marty believes will unlock the mystery, accidents begin to happen.

Someone else wants the copper box—someone willing to commit murder to get it. As Marty and Paul face the shadows in the house and in their lives, they must learn to put the past behind them and run the race God is calling them to.

The Silver Lode

Book Two of the Jerome Mysteries Series

Jerome, Arizona: the largest ghost town in America

Billion-dollar copper camp alive with rags-to-riches stories

Beneath the ghost town that clings to Cleopatra Hill, a maze of abandoned mine tunnels conceals a vein of silver ore mixed with pure gold. Seventy years ago the discovery of that silver lode caused a murder. Are more coming?

Historian Paul Russell is about to lose his job and the woman he loves. He doesn't have time to search for the legendary silver lode. But when a student drops a seventy-year-old cold case on his desk, a murder connected to the silver lode, the mystery offers Paul the perfect opportunity to work with Marty Greenlaw and win her back.

As Paul and Marty search for the silver lode, suspicious deaths begin to happen. When Paul's son disappears, the stakes become personal.

Kokopelli's Song

Book One of the Four Corners Fantasy Series

New Mexico

When seventeen-year-old Amy Adams finds her father's family and a lost twin brother on the Hopi reservation in Arizona, she stumbles into a struggle between shamans and witches that spans a thousand years. After Mahu is attacked and a Conquistador's journal stolen, Amy and her new friend Diego set out on a dangerous quest to find and perform the ceremony that can stop ancient evil from entering our world.

But Amy and Diego are not alone as they race against time measured by a waxing moon. Kokopelli's song, the haunting notes of a red cedar flute, guides them along the migration route sacred to pueblo peoples: West to Old Oraibi, South to El Morro, East to Cochiti Pueblo, North to Chimney Rock, and finally to the Center—and the final confrontation—in Chaco Canyon.

MORE MYSTERIES FROM SCRIVENINGS PRESS

Not a Good Day for Namaste

by Keri Lynn

A Texas-Sized Mystery - Book Two

Witnessing the hit and run of fellow Flamingo Springs resident Ryan wasn't how yoga instructor Misty Van Oepen planned on starting the Thanksgiving holidays.

When Ryan's mysterious brother shows up along with a spree of crime, she decides it's up to her and fellow business owners Lacey and Jeni, to find out what's going on. After an attempt on Misty's life lands her in protective custody at deputy Stetson Owens' ranch, she finds herself in danger of losing her heart to the former bull rider.

With time running out, will Misty succeed in discovering who's behind the attacks? Or will she fail and become the next victim?

The Plot Thickens

by Susan Page Davis

Skirmish Cove Mysteries - Book Two

Jillian only wants to redecorate one room at the Novel Inn—

but first she has to deal with murder.

Murder strikes Skirmish Cove during the coastal town's winter carnival. Jillian Tunney, part owner of the nearby Novel Inn, discovers the body of a clerk at her favorite bookstore. With her sister Kate and brother, Officer Rick Gage, she tries to find out who killed him.

Meanwhile, Jillian is immersed in redecorating one of the themed rooms, but Kate is annoyed when a mysterious guest at the inn doesn't want to leave his room. The innkeepers find they have way too many secrets to solve.

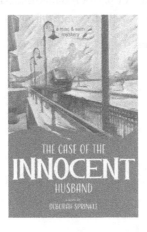

The Case of the Innocent Husband

by Deborah Sprinkle

A Mac & Sam Mystery - Book One

Private Investigator Mackenzie Love needs to do one thing. Find out who shot Eleanor Davis. Or else.

When Eleanor Davis is found shot in her garage, the only suspect, her estranged husband, is found not guilty in a court of law. However, most of the good citizens of Washington, Missouri, remain unconvinced. It doesn't matter that twelve men and women of the jury found him not guilty. What do they know?

And since Private Investigator Mackenzie Love accepted the job for the defense and helped acquit Connor Davis, her friends and neighbors have placed her squarely in the enemy camp. Therefore, her overwhelming goal becomes to find out who killed Eleanor Davis.

Or leave the town she grew up in.

As the investigation progresses, the threats escalate. Someone wants to stop Mackenzie and her partner, Samantha Majors, and is willing to do whatever it takes—including murder.

Can Mac and Sam find the killer before they each end up on the wrong side of a bullet?

CPSIA information can be obtained
at www.ICGtesting.com
Printed in the USA
LVHW071253130623
749647LV00005B/210